Dreaming of a COWBOY CHRISTMAS

ANN EINERSON

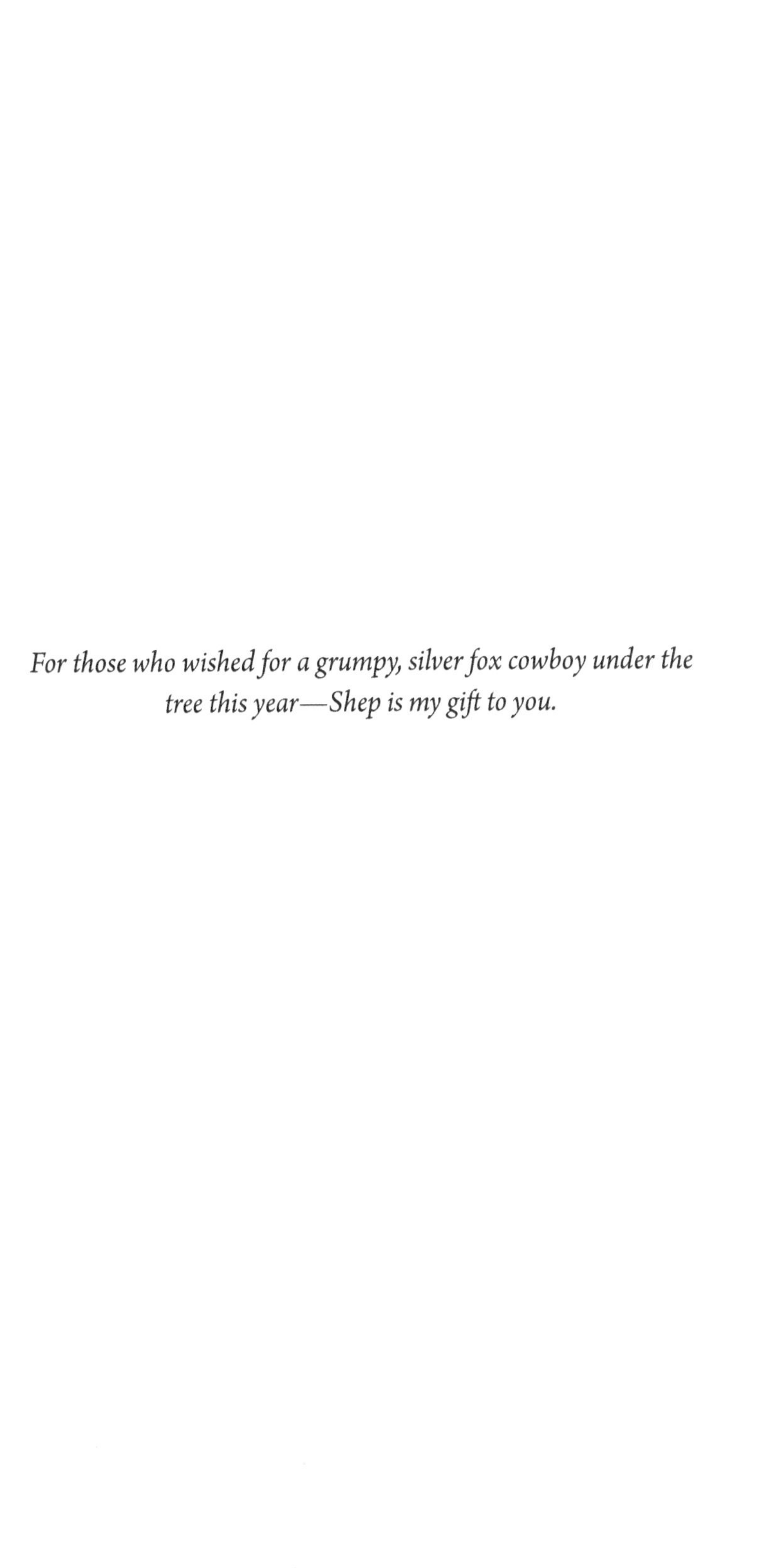

For those who wished for a grumpy, silver fox cowboy under the tree this year—Shep is my gift to you.

PLAYLIST

Butterflies—Kacey Musgraves

Christmas Tree Farm—Taylor Swift

Craving You—Thomas Rhett, Maren Morris

All I Want for Christmas is a Cowboy—Megan Moroney

Tears—Sabrina Carpenter

Santa Tell Me—Ariana Grande

Take Back Home Girl—Chris Lane (feat. Tori Kelly)

Blue Christmas—Willie Nelson

Heaven—Kane Brown

Wood—Taylor Swift

Have the Heart—Post Malone (feat. Dolly Parton)

Have Yourself a Merry Little Christmas—Frank Sinatra

AUTHOR'S NOTE

Hey, Reader!

Thank you for picking up *Dreaming of a Cowboy Christmas*. This romance blends my love for the holidays and being in my cowboy era.

Dreaming of a Cowboy Christmas is a spicy, age gap, holiday novella between a sunshine girl and a grumpy cowboy who uses toys as teammates. This is a fast-paced, light-hearted, and low-drama story meant to get you in the holiday spirit.

Dreaming of a Cowboy Christmas contains explicit sexual content, toy play, profanity, and mentions the death of a parent. Reading is meant to be your happy place—choose yourself, your needs, and your happiness first!

Xoxo,
Ann Einerson

Dreaming of a COWBOY CHRISTMAS

A STANDALONE HOLIDAY ROMANCE

CHAPTER I

Traveling 101: Sex Toys Are Subject to Search

Noelle

"**I**S THERE A REASON YOU HAVE *TWO* TEN-INCH DILDOS IN your carry-on?" the TSA agent asks, holding one up with his gloved hand as if it's evidence of a crime.

My cheeks flush as several travelers whip their heads in my direction, judgment screaming from their expressions. It doesn't help that the agent dumped the bag of toys I meticulously packed into a pile next to my suitcase, adding to my public humiliation.

Two nuns who've just passed the security checkpoint look at me as if they want to douse me in holy water, and a mother shields her toddler from view while she waits for her bag to be checked.

I don't blame them.

My luggage holds the full holiday collection from Twisted Temptations—the biggest online adult shop in the country. With glittery dildos, vibrators, and candy cane-striped butt plugs, one might assume I'm off to an X-rated party at the North Pole instead of a solo Christmas trip in Arizona.

The agent clears his throat when I don't respond. "Well?"

"Uh… they're for work," I say with the most innocent smile I can muster.

Anything to speed this interrogation along before someone decides to livestream and I'm trending on TikTok as #GlitterDildoGirl.

The agent arches a brow. "I see. And what kind of work is that?"

I blush, realizing too late that my answer likely led him to assume I'm a stripper—or a professional for hire. *If only I were that coordinated.*

I clear my throat. Something tells me he's not interested in the full story, so I settle on, "I host a podcast."

"And that explains why you're traveling with all these devices, how?" He gestures to a Christmas-tree-shaped wand that's just started buzzing on the counter.

"Brands sponsor my show, and I like to try the products beforehand. I'd never recommend anything to my subscribers that I wouldn't use myself. Especially not with a sparkly battery-operated device that goes in—" I stop mid-sentence.

I tend to ramble when I'm nervous, even in situations when I'd be better off keeping my mouth shut.

"And you didn't think to check your bag?" the agent asks.

I bite back a laugh as he fumbles to turn off the vibrating wand. I'd offer to help, but knowing my luck, it'd probably land me on a no-fly list.

"No?" I say it as a question.

Note to self: Don't accept sponsorships from adult novelty brands with a tight deadline right before going out of town.

I'm supposed to record the brand's ad spots for the podcast at the start of the year, but I wanted to have firsthand experience with the products first. Unfortunately, shipping was delayed, and the package didn't arrive until this morning. I crammed everything into my suitcase, which made me late to the airport with no time to check my bag. It hadn't crossed my mind that it could be an issue until the TSA agent dumped the collection on the counter.

"Are you asking or telling me?" he questions, exhaling in relief when the wand stops vibrating.

I run a hand through my hair, giving him a sheepish chuckle. "Depends on which option gets me to my gate before I miss my flight. I'm guessing neither comes with complimentary champagne?"

There isn't so much as a twitch at the corner of his mouth. *Someone must be all out of holiday cheer.*

No wonder—it's a week before Christmas, and the airport is packed with travelers who think wrapping paper bans and liquid limits are negotiable. And now he's dealing with a chatty Gen Zer lugging around a suitcase full of adult toys.

"Ma'am, if you don't give me a direct answer, I'll have to escort you to a secondary screening area, and that could take a while." The agent presses his lips into a thin line. "Are you asking or telling me that you purposely didn't check your bag?" His calm delivery is more intimidating than if he had shouted.

"Telling. Definitely telling," I say, tugging my purse strap higher on my shoulder. "I didn't want to chance missing my flight, so I came straight to security."

I fully expect him to tell me to toss the items or go back to the check-in counter. Instead, he studies me with narrowed eyes as he drops the wand and the rest of my toys into the open suitcase and pushes it toward me with a brisk nod.

"Alrighty then. You're all set."

"Um… thanks," I stammer, still shell-shocked from our interaction. "Happy holidays."

He ignores me in favor of changing his gloves before

retrieving the next bag ready for inspection. I heft my suitcase over to the nearest repack station, studiously avoiding glances from the flurry of travelers passing through the checkpoint. That was hands down one of the most embarrassing experiences of my life.

I hate to point fingers, but this is all my ex-boyfriend's fault. If he hadn't cheated which led to our breakup this past summer, I wouldn't be stuck choosing between spending a Christmas alone in New York or hopping on a plane to a sunny destination to drown out my holiday blues.

I usually spend it with my parents, but they booked a Christmas cruise back when Mark and I were still together. They invited us to come along, but he complained about getting seasick, even though he's never set foot on a boat.

After we broke up, my parents offered to cancel their trip since the cruise was sold out, and I couldn't go with them, but I insisted they go without me. The tickets were non-refundable, and after a lifetime of prioritizing me, it was time they treated themselves.

I pushed aside the fact that being alone during my favorite time of year would be unbearable. That's how I ended up scrolling through vacation rentals at the last minute, eager to trade in stockings and mistletoe for tank tops and tan lines. If I had to miss out on the traditions I've cherished since childhood—traditions I won't have this year thanks to Mark's inability to keep it in his pants—I wanted a distraction. And by this time tomorrow, I'll be soaking up the sun in a desert oasis with a margarita in hand, hoping it's enough to fill the void of spending Christmas alone.

On the way to my gate, I text my friend Gemma.

> Noelle: Is it possible to die of humiliation??

> Gemma: Please tell me you didn't send a 'prince' in an obscure country money again?!

Noelle: He was being held prisoner!

Noelle: This is worse. A TSA agent dumped out my luggage, including the giant dildos Twisted Temptations sent me.

Gemma: That's perfect viral material for your next podcast.

Gemma: Episode title idea:
TSA Gone Wild

In addition to being my best friend, Gemma is also my manager and isn't shy about turning my embarrassing moments into content gold. I prefer to keep my personal life private, but sharing certain experiences with my audience is unavoidable. Especially when I think they'll find it relatable or entertaining. Luckily for me, I have an endless supply of them.

Noelle: And let everyone assume I'm single for the holidays and hauling a suitcase of glittery dildos across the country to keep me company? No thanks.

Gemma: Girl, you are single, and your next orgasm is long overdue.

Noelle: You make me sound desperate.

I'm an expert at giving advice, but taking it? Not so much. It's easy to encourage other women not to wait on a man for their next release and to move on when their boyfriend cheats. But I haven't gotten laid in over six months and can't remember when I had my last orgasm. Maybe this trip will be my sexual reawakening and the fresh start I've been hoping for.

Gemma: I did catch you watching those thirst-trap cooking videos on TikTok from @BicepsAndBiscuits69 last week.

Noelle: He's a very skilled chef!

Gemma: Mmhmm. Did security survive looking through your bag?

Noelle: Barely, but they let it through.

Gemma: Thank god your battery-powered boyfriends passed inspection.

Noelle: Just glad I made it past security… I gotta run or I'll miss my flight.

Gemma: Let me know when you get to your rental.

Noelle: Will do!

I tuck my phone in my pocket and speed walk to my gate.

My trip might have gotten off to a rocky start, but I'm confident it will turn into an adventure full of sunshine and unforgettable memories.

CHAPTER 2

Cowboy, It's Cold Outside

Noelle

THANKFULLY, AFTER THE DEBACLE WITH MY BOBs (Battery-Operated Boyfriends), my flight to Arizona went off without a hitch, and I was greeted by blue skies and bright sunshine. I picked up the silver convertible I rented, excited about my solo adventure, but my optimism waned once I got on the road.

The first warning that I'd made a mistake was booking a vacation rental several hours from the airport. With the holiday rush, there were limited listings available at the last minute, and I thought a mini road trip through Arizona could be fun. I figured I'd drive to the nearest town and get day passes at an upscale hotel pool and spa. In hindsight, staying in a hotel would have been the practical choice, but I wanted somewhere I could decorate for the holidays and have my privacy.

Red flag number two came when the desert scrub gave way to

towering pines, and the roadside was covered in snow. I chalked it up to a fluke storm, but as I neared Pine Haven, my supposed destination, permanent road signs warned of ice patches and snowdrifts. I guess I should have paid more attention and assumed the name wasn't a quaint marketing ploy.

When I finally rolled into town, the GPS chirped that I was still fifteen miles from my rental, and that's when it dawned on me that I'd seriously botched things by not checking if parts of Arizona get snow. I never imagined I'd stumble into a snowy wonderland straight out of a Christmas movie, when everything I'd ever seen of the state was cactus and desert.

By the time I hit the mountain switchbacks, sweat beads on my forehead. It's been ages since I last drove, and I'm second-guessing my decision to rent a car as I navigate the winding road. Snow falls in thick sheets as I head further into a frozen landscape I'm woefully unprepared for. As if tackling unpredictable weather in a convertible isn't bad enough, my suitcase is stuffed with shorts, sundresses, and sandals. Not a single long-sleeved shirt or jacket made the trip.

I should've turned back when I had the chance, but there hasn't been a pullout in ages.

Good thing I stopped for groceries outside of Phoenix. Otherwise, I'd be going hungry tonight because there's no way I'm venturing out in this storm once I reach the cabin.

Christmas music plays through the speakers as snow pelts the windshield. Each turn is tighter than the last, and I'm left wishing I had agreed when the car rental attendant suggested I swap out the convertible for an SUV with four-wheel drive after I mentioned I was going to Pine Haven. I'd assumed he recommended it because it cost more, not because he was concerned about my safety.

My spiraling thoughts are interrupted when my phone buzzes from its spot on the console, the screen lighting up with an alert.

DREAMING OF A COWBOY CHRISTMAS

Winter Weather Advisory: Snow and gusty winds expected. Reduced visibility. Drive with caution.

"You couldn't have warned me an hour ago?" I grumble.

My pity party is short-lived when the car fishtails, and I grip the wheel with both hands, doing my best not to overcorrect as the car slides on the icy road.

I let out a shaky breath, nerves stretched thin when the tires finally catch traction and the car straightens out. I'm ready to stop despite the lack of a shoulder when the GPS chimes for me to turn right. Through the flurries, I catch sight of the hidden turnoff, lost behind a snowdrift piled high against the road's edge. There are no signs or markers, but I take the chance, hoping I can turn around if it's a dead end.

I ease onto the narrow lane, the headlights slicing through the swaths of swirling snow. With every bend through dense woods, the road tightens, and I scold myself for the hundredth time for not checking the location before I booked it. Half a mile down the road, the GPS announces my arrival, but there aren't any structures in sight. I worry I missed another turnoff until I spot my destination in the distance.

The cabin is nestled among a cluster of evergreens, its shutters and front door painted cherry red. The porch juts out from the house, supported by rough-cut beams, and the uneven, hand-hewn logs give the place a rustic, storybook charm.

Smoke curls from the chimney, and warm light spills from the windows onto the porch. It's a welcome surprise since the last time I heard from the owners was a week ago, when they confirmed my booking. I've sent multiple messages leading up to my trip, most recently when my plane landed, but they've all gone unanswered. So I'm relieved to find the cabin ready for my arrival.

I text Gemma Gemma to say I've made it to the cabin safely and promise to check in within a couple of days. The service is spotty here, and I don't want her to worry if I don't respond right away. Plus, I'm looking forward to decompressing after a long day of travel and to have some much-needed time to myself. Fingers crossed the cabin has a big bathtub.

The listing only showed exterior shots of the cabin and must have been cropped to hide the forest surrounding the place. There was minimal information about what amenities were included, but I assumed that if the outside was this enchanting, the inside had to be just as lovely.

As soon as I get out of the car, a sharp gust of wind hits me, sending my dress whipping around my legs, and making me wish I'd worn a comfy lounge set instead.

Desperate to escape the cold, I wrestle my carry-on from the back seat. It's heavier than I remember. Teeth chattering, I drag it across the snow-covered gravel, the handle biting into my palms. My wedges slide with every step, but at least I didn't wear my favorite four-inch heels, or I'd already have face-planted by now.

I breathe a sigh of relief when I reach the porch without incident. The respite fades quickly when I notice there's no padlock on the door like the check-in instructions said there would be. I push down the unease rising in my chest and try the knob, only to find it locked. My eyes dart around, searching for a hidden key or lockbox, but there's nothing in sight.

My fingers tremble as I pull my phone from my purse, frowning when I see there's still no response from the owner. I send another message, explaining I've arrived but can't get inside. The apprehension returns, coiling around me in a suffocating grip. It's possible they live nearby and went home to get out of the storm until I got here. I might believe it if I hadn't just driven the last eight miles without seeing another house. The only other structure I passed was a large barn tucked among the trees around a half mile before the turnoff to the cabin.

"What the hell are you doing?" I jump, startled by a gruff voice.

I spin around to find a man approaching the cabin on horseback. With his worn jeans, flannel jacket, and boots planted firmly in the stirrups, I assume he's a cowboy.

"You're trespassing on private property," he grunts, dismounting with practiced movements.

I watch cautiously as he loops the reins around the porch railing. The man is tall and broad-shouldered, and his mustache is flecked with gray. Faint crow's feet frame his chocolate eyes as he aims his scowl at me.

I'm all too aware that I'm alone with this stranger, and he could very well be a serial killer or a sociopath with a fondness for stalking women in the woods. Still, I can't look away as he takes out several pieces of firewood from his saddlebag. Someone this good-looking couldn't possibly be dangerous, right? Then again, serial killers rarely come with warning labels. Just look at Ted Bundy.

"I asked you a question," he demands when I stay silent. "What are you doing peeping through my window? You're trespassing."

His accusation makes me focus, and this time, I answer immediately. "No, I'm not. I booked this cabin for the next week, and even triple-checked the address to make sure I was in the right place," I state proudly.

As someone who's lived in the city since she was ten and relied mainly on public transportation, I've earned a PhD in wrong turns and accidental scenic routes when I drive. So it's a miracle I made it here before dark and only got lost once, given the treacherous weather conditions.

The man shakes his head, letting out a humorless laugh. "Not possible. I'm the owner, and I'd never put the place up for short-term rentals. I live here."

I blink rapidly as I pull up the listing on the rental app and march down the porch steps to where the man's standing with his arms folded across his chest.

I hold my phone in his face. "See? I *am* in the right place."

He studies my phone, his jaw tightening as he reads the listing. "I hate to break it to you, darlin', but you've been scammed."

"What? No. You're wrong," I protest through chattering teeth, clinging to hope.

Determined to prove I'm right, I paste the address into my map app again, only for it to show that I'm twenty feet from my destination. Still in denial, I recheck my messages but only see the one I just sent, joining the others that remain unopened.

"Unless there's some other one-bedroom cabin in this area identical to this one—which I know there isn't—it's obvious you've been conned," the cowboy says, his voice devoid of sympathy.

I roll my eyes. "I heard you the first time."

The truth is a bitter pill to swallow. I got scammed and fell for it hook, line, and sinker. I didn't think twice about sending the full payment outside the app, and when the supposed owners went silent, I assumed they were busy. In hindsight, I realize how foolish I was, and now I'm left paying the price, while standing in a winterscape with a stranger, freezing in a dress that offers no defense against the biting wind.

I'm pulled from my wallowing when our phones go off simultaneously. I glance down at mine to see another weather advisory.

Winter Storm Warning: Blizzard conditions expected in Pine Haven and surrounding areas. Travel is not advised. Seek shelter immediately.

What am I going to do now?

I pride myself on finding the bright side in any situation, no matter how bad things might seem. Like the time I drained my savings to launch my podcast and finished the first season with only fifty followers. I still celebrated each one, confident that small beginnings often lead to big results. And they did when I ended season two with a hundred thousand followers. Or when I upgraded to a nicer apartment with a skyline view after Mark and I broke up.

Still, it's hard to see the silver lining when I'm shivering on a mountain road, miles away from civilization, dealing with a cowboy who probably has the Grinch on speed dial.

His brows tighten as he scrolls on his phone. "A blizzard's rolling in and fast. There's no way you're getting down the mountain in that thing before it hits." He nods at the convertible in his driveway.

"That's just peachy," I mutter, his sour mood rubbing off on me.

"You can stay on my couch tonight," he says, gritting out the words. "But you're out first thing in the morning."

"How thoughtful. I'll be sure to write you a five-star review for your generosity," I deadpan.

"Beggers can't be choosers, sweetheart," he counters. "If my couch isn't up to your standards, you can always bunk with the horses in the barn—perfect if you like frostbite, scratchy bedding, and mice that might mistake your toes for a midnight snack."

I narrow my eyes. "Are you always this welcoming?"

He shrugs. "Most people know better than to show up at my place uninvited. Now, are you staying or not?"

I take a step back, keeping my eyes locked on him. "How can I be sure you're not a killer who's lured me here under false pretenses?"

Maybe his whole spiel about not wanting visitors is a ruse, and he planned this all along, using the unpredictable weather to trap me here. Although he seems more unnerved by my presence than I am by his.

He raises a brow. "Funny that you're accusing me of murder

when you're the one sneaking around like you're casing the place. How do I know you're not here planning to rob me in my sleep?"

I shiver as a breeze passes, drawing my arms to my chest for warmth. I catch a flicker of worry in the stranger's eyes that disappears in an instant.

"If I were stealing, I'd hit a city penthouse, not your remote cabin in the woods during a blizzard without an escape route," I say, trying to keep my teeth from rattling, determined not to show this man any weakness. "Besides, if you're so harmless, how come you haven't told me your name?"

"You didn't ask."

"I'm asking now."

"Shep."

I extend my hand with a smile. "I'm Noelle. And yes, the reason is as cliché as it sounds. My mom loves Christmas and wanted holiday magic year-round. Funny enough, it's my favorite holiday too, so I can't complain." There I go oversharing with a stranger again.

He looks at my hand but doesn't make a move to shake it. "Cute. You always this chatty with people you've just met?"

This man is insufferable. I'm doing my best to be friendly and make our situation less awkward, and all I get in return are clipped answers and a deadpan stare.

I shove my phone into my purse, not sparing Mr. Grumpy Pants another glance, and whirl around to make a dramatic exit. I'll just have to stay in the convertible until the storm passes. It's not my most inspired solution, but that doesn't stop me from marching off like a petulant child with a point to prove.

I'm halfway up the steps to get my luggage from the porch when my heel meets a patch of black ice, sending me sprawling backward like a human domino. I squeeze my eyes shut, bracing for impact, but at the last second, strong arms encircle my waist, lifting me to the safety of solid ground.

"Dammit, woman," Shep growls. "You could have hurt yourself. What were you thinking wearing heels?" I'm momentarily stunned speechless by his concern before I remember he was just scolding me for oversharing.

"They're wedges," I correct him as I burrow deeper into his arms, shamelessly stealing his warmth. "And excuse me for thinking it was hot all year round in Arizona, and that the biggest risk of visiting was tripping into a cactus. Not getting frostbite or nearly breaking my neck from slipping on ice."

He scoffs. "What the hell gave you that idea?"

"Every movie, travel guide, and social media post that conveniently never mentioned the cold weather? Not to mention the photos and description in the listing when I booked this place," I add sheepishly.

Shep shakes his head, muttering something about me being as stubborn as a mule. Yet his arm stays firmly secured around my waist as the scent of leather and musk surrounds me. Despite his stern expression, my pulse skips a beat.

The only plausible explanation is that my stranger danger radar is on the fritz. There's no explanation for why my thoughts drift to labeling Shep the sexiest cowboy I've ever laid eyes on instead of screaming for me to bolt. Granted, I haven't met many in person—Manhattan's Upper West Side isn't exactly cowboy territory—but compared to the fictional ones I've seen on TV, he's far more rugged and... scowl-y.

I meet his gaze, and the way he studies me has my heart racing.

"You can let go now," I whisper, even though my body protests, reluctant to give up its heat source.

"Right." Shep releases my waist, steps around me, and goes down the porch steps. "The blizzard is coming in fast, and I've got more preparations to make. If you're staying, I'll show you inside before I take Blaze to the barn." He gestures to his horse, who's grazing on the last patch of grass not covered in snow under the roof overhang. "If not, good luck getting back to town."

He collects the pieces of firewood he must have dropped in his effort to catch me, leaving me alone on the porch, trembling against the biting wind as I contemplate his offer.

On the one hand, he's a stranger, and no one knows I'm here with him. However, my other options are sleeping in the convertible or trying to get down the mountain before the storm worsens, knowing there's a good chance no car service or tow truck could rescue me if I get stranded.

As much as I hate to admit it, there's only one logical choice, and I'm sure to regret it.

CHAPTER 3

City Girls Are Nothing But Trouble

Shep

A S I COME BACK UP THE PORCH STEPS WITH MY ARMFUL of wood, Noelle holds out her hand. "I accept your offer to stay."

Even in heels, she barely reaches my chest and tips her chin to meet my gaze.

My eyes drop to her hand warily before curling mine around it, noting how small and soft it feels against my calloused palms. I'm also struck by how cold it is, guilt gnawing at me for making her stand outside in a dress doing nothing to shield her from the biting chill.

What I wouldn't give to turn back the clock to this morning, when my biggest concerns were preparing for the blizzard and making sure the animals were safely secured in the barn. Living thirty minutes from town suits me fine, but it means stocking up on supplies and firewood ahead of unpredictable weather that can last for days.

This particular storm better not.

"Cheer up, cowboy. I'm a great roommate," Noelle singsongs. "I make a killer cup of hot cocoa, I don't sing in the shower, and I only hog the bathroom when I'm soaking in bubbles—lucky for you, I forgot to pack my bath bombs."

For someone who accused me of being dangerous, she sure doesn't act scared. Unless she's sharing personal details about herself in an effort to disarm me. Either way, I'd appreciate it if she'd quiet down.

I might live a life of solitude, but I know a city girl when I see one—designer luggage, manicured nails, and zero survival instincts. Her dress and wedges are fit for a beach vacation—not a frozen winterscape. It's obvious she's just another woman with expensive taste who wouldn't last a night alone in a snowstorm. Hell, she's already shivering despite her best efforts to hide it.

Not that I care.

She got herself into this mess. Who doesn't confirm their vacation rental is legit ahead of time or check the weather before packing? *Unbelievable.* I ought to make her fend for herself, but having her stay saves me the trouble of rescuing her later. It has nothing to do with those big blue eyes or that pouty mouth that makes me forget how she derailed my evening.

I shift the firewood into one arm and grab her suitcase with my free hand on my way into the house.

"What are you doing?" Noelle calls out after me. "I can get that."

Not a chance. Her luggage weighs a ton, and I won't have her falling flat on her ass trying to haul it inside. Besides, I'm hoping she'll follow so I can get her out of the harsh winter air.

I wave her off, shaking snow from my boots before going inside. The fire I started earlier fills the space with warmth and the smell of cedar and pine. I set her luggage against the wall and drop the pile of wood into the crate by the hearth.

The footsteps on the floorboards have me glancing up at my unexpected guest. Noelle followed me inside, her cheeks rosy and her eyes wide as she scans the open space—the couch angled toward the fireplace, an old leather armchair in the corner, and the kitchen tucked along the other side of the cabin with a small table and two stools.

I motion to the two doors on the far wall. "Bathroom is on the left. My room is on the right. It's off-limits." Having a stranger in my house is bad enough. I'm not letting her roam my personal space too.

"Copy that. Guess I'll have to resist the urge to go treasure hunting then, huh? Since I'm supposed to be planning a robbery and all," she adds with a wink.

"Unless you want to brave the cold outside, I wouldn't suggest it."

"Don't rob the grumpy cowboy, got it," Noelle mumbles as she moves farther inside, toward the warmth of the fireplace. She brushes her fingers along the couch as she passes. "Your place is so cozy. I'd spend all day curled up by the fireplace if I were you. I bet it looks absolutely magical when your Christmas tree is up. Do you always wait until the week of to decorate, or did the weather make you put it off this year?"

I blink at her. "I don't celebrate the holidays."

Her smile falters. "Oh… I see." She's quick to mask her disappointment. "That's alright. It's still a lovely home."

I clench my jaw in an effort to maintain a neutral expression. Her bubbly disposition is irritating, but worse is how difficult it is to ignore the way she brightens the room.

Against my better judgment, I allow my gaze to roam over her. Her yellow sundress is dotted with white flowers and clings to her hips, and the thin straps show off her sun-kissed shoulders sprinkled with freckles. Her blue eyes are bright and curious, and her lips curve into a soft smile despite her situation.

What was I thinking inviting her to stay?

The last thing I need is to share my space with a stranger for the night. Let alone a pretty little thing with a weakness for designer shoes and not a lick of common sense. I might not know her age, but I'm guessing mid-twenties. Far too young for me.

Needing to quash any lingering desire, I remind myself that the last city girl I brought here broke my heart, and I swore I'd never go down that road again.

The wind howls outside the barn as I finish settling Blaze into his stall. I give him a handful of grain as I straighten the blanket over his back. The storm's only getting worse, and the half mile back to the cabin will be brutal, but I've stalled as long as I can. With any luck, Noelle will be asleep by the time I get there. Even better if the storm clears and she's gone by morning. Might be wishful thinking, but it's what I'm holding on to.

A loud mooing sound echoes from the other side of the barn, repeating every few seconds.

I give Blaze one last scratch behind his ear. "Sorry, buddy, I'd better go. We both know *she* won't stop until she gets some attention. See you tomorrow."

I latch the door behind me and walk down the aisle, past the other horses who are all settled in for the night. At the last stall on the right, Maple's fuzzy nose peeks out of one of the panels of the stall door, sniffing the air. Her tail flicks with excitement as I step inside.

"Hey there, sweet girl," I croon.

When I open the gate, she bumps her head against my pant leg, the small horns beginning to curl above her fuzzy ears just missing me as she roots for a snack.

I chuckle as I take a green apple from my coat pocket. "And

here I thought you were just excited to see me." Maple greedily accepts the treat from my outstretched hand, chewing loudly before letting out a contented snort.

I'm not shocked when my phone rings in my pocket. Only one person would be calling me before a storm.

"Hello," I grunt.

"Oof, somebody's in a mood today," my cousin, Birdie, replies brightly. "I saw a blizzard is headed your way and wanted to check in while I still can."

Reception is hit-and-miss on a good day, and when a storm hits, the mix of heavy snow and distance from the nearest cell tower wipes the signal out completely. I usually lose service for days.

I balance the phone on my shoulder while I give Maple a second apple. "I'm fine."

Birdie laughs. "You always say that."

"Well, it's true."

"I wish you'd reconsider moving to Montana. There's plenty of land for a proper farm, and you'd get to hang out with your favorite cousin every day."

"You're my only cousin," I remind her.

Our moms were sisters. Mine was the oldest, and Birdie's mom came along unexpectedly after my mom graduated from high school. Although Birdie and I didn't grow up together because of our age difference, she still showed up at my mom's funeral a few years back. I think she realized that with both my parents gone, her family was all I had left, so she's made it her mission to look out for me.

For all my griping about her being a nuisance, I'd be lying if I said I didn't secretly appreciate her check-ins. She's like the little sister I never had, always sticking her nose in my business, but she means well.

"Admit it. The only reason you want me there is to pawn off more animals."

She feigns a gasp. "I would never."

I chuckle.

We both know that's a lie.

Birdie's an animal activist, determined to rescue every creature in need and convince everyone in her orbit to adopt them. She should have become a politician or a used car salesperson because when she gives you those puppy-dog eyes, it's impossible to say no.

I was the exception until she called two months ago, begging me to save Maple, a four-month-old miniature Highland cow. She was found neglected in a backyard petting zoo a couple of hours from here. My answer was no, but when Birdie video-chatted, pleading with me on camera, my resolve crumbled.

Maple was only supposed to stay for a week while Birdie arranged transport for her to Montana, but I've since learned she planned for me to keep Maple all along.

"Face it, cousin. You adore Maple," Birdie teases.

"I do not." I yank my hand away from Maple's shaggy coat even though Birdie isn't here to see me petting her.

"If you say so," she hums.

Sure, Maple is cute and even does tricks, but that doesn't mean I want her here. I'm just doing my cousin a favor. As if to call me out on my bullshit, Maple nudges her fuzzy forehead against my arm, refusing to move until I give her a good scratch. She knows this is her forever home, even if I try to deny it.

"You could've at least come to Montana for the holidays. I can't stand the thought of you spending Christmas alone," Birdie adds.

"It's just another day. I'll be fine."

She invites me every year, and every year I turn her down.

She doesn't understand why I'd choose solitude on the mountain over time with family.

When I was with my ex-fiancée Danielle, she went all out, demanding a massive tree and new decorations each year, caring more about gifts and showing off than about the sentiment behind the holiday itself. When she left, I realized that material things could never replace the joy of spending time with family and loved ones.

After that, I spent Christmas with my parents. Even though it was my mom's favorite holiday, she viewed it as an opportunity to serve others and spread kindness. It gave me a new perspective on the kind of partner I wanted. Someone who shared a similar sentiment and valued giving and connection over extravagance and flashy displays.

I never did find that person, and once my parents passed away, Christmas lost its magic—the cheer and traditions lost their meaning without the people I cared about most to celebrate with.

"Besides, my hands are full with an unwelcome guest who showed up at my cabin earlier," I add, not bothering to hide my irritation. "A woman thought she booked it for a week, but she was scammed. Now she's stuck here until the storm passes."

"Is she pretty?" Birdie blurts. "Or better yet, is she single?"

I bark out a humorless laugh. "Pretty sure Noelle's in her twenties. I have no business being concerned about her relationship status." That didn't stop me from checking her out as she stood on my porch, her golden hair dancing in the wind.

"Age is just a number when you find the right person," Birdie retorts.

"All I care about is that she leaves when the storm lets up."

No matter how much I hope that'll be tomorrow, realistically, there's only a slim chance Noelle's convertible will make it down the mountain, even if by some miracle the weather clears up by morning.

"Right," Birdie says, her amusement vibrating through the line. "You ignored my first question, which means she must be pretty. *Really* pretty."

I shake my head. Birdie has a talent for getting under my skin, much like a certain blonde, blue-eyed vixen who's probably taken over my bathroom with her hair and beauty products by now.

"She's not half bad," I answer.

I'm not about to admit that Noelle might be the most beautiful woman I've ever met, or that I can't stop thinking about the way her smile lights up her face. Still doesn't change the fact that I want her gone.

"Careful, cousin, or you might end up keeping her like you did Maple," Birdie teases.

"Alright. That's enough conversation for today." I give Maple a pat on the rump before leaving her stall. "I've got to finish up with the animals before the worst of the storm kicks in."

The cabin is a half a mile away, and the ride back on the snowmobile can be brutal once the wind picks up.

"Be safe out there, and text me once the worst of it is over. And don't go falling for your mystery woman," she says playfully.

"Bye, Birdie." I end the call, shoving my phone in my back pocket.

One of the horses whinnies from a nearby stall, impatient for their nightly carrots. Usually, I'm quick to make the rounds, but it's hard to focus with so much on my mind—mainly the five-foot-nothing, blue-eyed whirlwind who's taken over my cabin.

CHAPTER 4

Caution: A Man in Wranglers Might
Cause Spontaneous Orgasms

Noelle

I ROLL OVER FOR WHAT FEELS LIKE THE HUNDREDTH TIME, burrowing deeper into the couch, but the icy air still nips at my cheeks. The fire went out hours ago, and the thin blanket I found might as well be tissue paper. My satin tank top and shorts aren't doing much to shield me from the draft. What I wouldn't give for a pair of fuzzy socks or a wool cardigan right now.

I should've asked Shep for another blanket while I had the chance, but the scowl he gave me when he came back late kept me from pushing my luck. Before I could work up the courage, he disappeared into his room and shut the door. No way am I disturbing him, no matter how cold it gets. Not when asking for one more favor could convince him I'm not worth the hassle. Far better to endure the cold inside than become an icicle in the convertible. I wouldn't last five minutes out there.

When a gust of wind rattles the windows, I jolt from the couch. It's pitch-black, so I blindly search the coffee table until I find my phone and switch on the flashlight to navigate to the fireplace. I don't turn on the overhead light, afraid it'll wake up Shep.

I crouch by the hearth, staring at the blackened logs and powdery ash. How I wish I'd been a Girl Scout or taken a survival course. Unfortunately, the closest I've come to starting a fire was when I accidentally microwaved a plate wrapped in aluminum foil, which ended with the fire department showing up at my apartment to extinguish the flames.

I sweep the mantel for matches or a lighter but come up empty. At this point, I'd take flint, though let's be real, my *Survivor* skills start and end with the TV show's theme song.

Hoping for guidance, I search "how to start a fire," my fingers stiff as I type. However, I'm let down when seconds later, the dreaded *No Internet Connection* notification pops up.

Fantastic.

I shouldn't be surprised, given everything that's gone wrong since I left for my trip. I can practically feel the universe smirking at me. It's probably payback for forgetting to tip the barista at the coffee shop on the way to the airport yesterday. Still, I refuse to let it get the better of me. I guess I'll have to improvise.

How hard can it be to start a fire anyway?

With a renewed determination, I set my phone down, its glow illuminating the room. My eyes dart around until they settle on Shep's pile of firewood. I look closer and spot a box of matches and a bag of small sticks.

I carry several logs over and toss them in, figuring the placement doesn't matter. I strike a match and drop it on the pile, only to watch it sputter out the second it hits the ashes.

Not willing to give up, I grab the bag of kindling and scatter it over the logs. I light another match and touch it to a piece of wood, watching the flames dance briefly, giving me hope that I've actually done it, until it fizzles out in a puff of smoke.

I run a hand across my face, letting out a humorless laugh. "Okay, so maybe starting a fire is harder than I thought," I mutter.

"Are you *trying* to set the cabin on fire?"

I leap to my feet when the lamp beside the couch flicks on, spinning around to find a frowning Shep standing in the living room.

"I'm sorry. I wanted to—" The rest of my apology catches in my throat when I notice the Wranglers hanging low on his hips.

Correction: He's only wearing Wranglers.

The man is shirtless and barefoot, his frame rugged and his muscles honed. Heat rises to my cheeks as I take in every ripple and curvature of his bare chest, a light dusting of hair trailing over the firm planes of his torso. When my gaze flickers back to his face, he's watching me with an unreadable expression.

"Is there a reason you're rummaging around my living room in the middle of the night?"

"The fire went out, and it was freezing. I didn't want to wake you, so I tried to start it again," I rush to explain.

He moves closer, his eyes narrowed on the haphazard pile of logs as if they've personally insulted him.

"I've never started one before," I admit.

"No kidding," he says dryly. "No wonder you're cold. Why aren't you wearing more clothes?" He gestures at my pajamas.

"I could ask you the same question," I retort.

"I'm not the one shaking like a leaf. Put on a sweater before you turn into an icicle. I'm not spending the night worrying you're going to catch hypothermia because you care more about fashion than basic survival."

Is he serious?

I put my hands on my hips. "I would if I'd brought one. My suitcase is full of shorts and tank tops since I was under the impression I was going somewhere warm." I don't mention what other things I have shoved in my luggage—it's irrelevant. "But I wouldn't expect you to be concerned about my predicament. Maybe if you'd warned me that I'd have to maintain the fire before disappearing into your room, I wouldn't be in this situation."

His brows knit, the stern line of his mouth softening. "Why didn't you wake me up when it went out?"

"You haven't exactly rolled out the welcome mat." He listens, keeping his hands firmly at his side. "I didn't want to chance making you angry and end up booted out into the snow for asking for another blanket."

He purses his lips, shifting his gaze between me and the couch. Without a word, he turns and disappears into his room.

"Right then," I mutter. "Guess I'm on my own."

I'm torn between attempting to start the fire again and retreating to the couch to wait for morning. Before I can decide, the sound of sliding drawers coming from Shep's room catches my ear. I stay put, remembering his warning that his room is off-limits.

It isn't long before he returns, carrying a stack of clothes: gray sweatpants, a fleece-lined flannel shirt, and a pair of socks.

He extends them toward me. "Here."

I nod to the pile. "Um… what's all this for?"

"For you to wear. Since you're cold?"

"Oh. Right. Thank you." I take the clothes and hold them close.

Despite the chill in the air, warmth blooms in my chest. Shep's unexpected kindness leaves me with a mix of gratitude and disbelief. After our first encounter, he made it clear he doesn't want me here, so I didn't think he'd care about my comfort. Yet here he is, proving otherwise.

"Well, aren't you going to change?" he asks.

I nod, hurrying to the bathroom and closing the door behind

me. Once I'm alone, I set the clothes on the counter and look in the mirror.

"Get yourself together, Noelle," I whisper to my reflection.

My cheeks glow crimson, my hair is disheveled, and my lips are tinted blue. I turn on the faucet, letting the warm water run over my hands before splashing some on my face. Next, I slip on Shep's flannel, the scent of his musk and laundry detergent filling my senses. The shirt engulfs me, hitting mid-thigh, making me grateful I have the sweats to wear. I ignore the fact that moments ago, he saw me in barely-there booty shorts.

He probably thought I was trying to seduce him, given how I was openly ogling him. It's not every day a woman comes that close to a shirtless man with abs. That's a view worth appreciating, so it's a good thing I'm only here for one night.

I quickly tug on the sweats and roll up the waistband twice so they don't fall off. When I'm done, I collect my tank and shorts and take a deep breath before opening the door.

Shep is bent over the fireplace, the lamp illuminating his back muscles as they shift with each movement. My pulse speeds up, struck by how distracting he is without even trying. Before he catches me gawking again, I force my attention to where he's rearranged the logs over a small pile of kindling set in the center. He touches it with a match, and the flames take hold quickly, licking the base of the wood as the fire springs to life.

I pad across the room, eager to feel the first hint of heat against my skin. As I draw closer, Shep turns his head in my direction.

His eyes sweep over me, lingering on the oversized flannel hanging loose on my frame. He braces his palms on his thighs and straightens to his feet. Each step he takes is deliberate, and I gulp as he closes the distance between us.

I stay rooted in place, doing my best to look anywhere but at his bare chest. His hair is slightly mussed, and the warm scent of leather and musk grows stronger as he approaches.

He slowly assesses me from head to toe, and my curiosity wins out over caution, wondering what's going through his mind. Could it be that he likes seeing me in his clothes? It's a silly notion, considering we just met, and he's been irritated since the second I stepped foot on his property.

"Are you warmer now?" he asks, standing so close his breath ghosts against my cheek.

I draw the flannel tighter around me. "Yeah, thanks for this and for the fire. You make it look easy."

"It's only because I've had years of practice."

"How long have you lived here?"

"A long time," he answers vaguely.

"How old are you?" I blurt out.

The question's been on my mind since yesterday. He must be at least a decade older, but it's hard to say for sure.

Shep strokes the sides of his mustache. "How old do you think I am?"

I smirk, tapping my chin thoughtfully. "Hmm… that's a tough one. You've got quite a few grays, though I suspect I'm responsible for a few sprouting overnight."

I keep my hands at my side, resisting the temptation to run my fingers along his temple. I have a hunch he wouldn't take too kindly to me touching him without permission.

"I'm forty-five." His deep voice sends a shiver down my spine.

"Oh."

I lean in slightly, without thinking. The silver-fox cowboy is older than I expected—older means experienced. I wonder if he fucks with the same force of his presence: hard, commanding, leaving me breathless and begging.

Bad idea, Noelle.

My stranger danger radar really must be broken if I'm already picturing myself stretched out naked on the bed for Shep.

"How old are you, Noelle?" he asks, studying me.

I send a silent prayer to the poker face gods before clearing my throat. "I'm twenty-five."

Daddy.

The word nearly escapes, but I catch myself just in time. Maybe Gemma's right—I really have gone far too long without an orgasm.

I might sound casual, but the fact that there's a twenty-year age gap between us does nothing but amplify his appeal. In the past, I've mostly dated guys my age, but I've always had this fantasy about being with an older man. Someone confident, assertive—who'd have me begging before he even touched me. But that little daydream of mine certainly does not, under any circumstance, include a broody cowboy who treats me like a thorn in his side. No sir.

My train of thought is derailed when I see the pillows and blankets piled on the couch. Shep must have collected them while I was changing. I'm starting to suspect that behind his surly disposition, he has a thoughtful side. That's the logical explanation for how he's gone from accusing me of trespassing to giving me warm clothes and blankets in the span of a few hours.

"Figured if you had some things to keep you warm, it would stop you from pestering me until morning," he says as if he can read my mind.

"Good thing I'm most irritating after sunrise," I reply cheekily.

He studies me with his lips drawn together. Up this close, I notice the thin ring of gold around his irises, giving his brown eyes a warmth that contrasts with the tension in his expression.

Shep clears his throat as he takes a step back. "It's late. I'd better get back to bed."

"Good idea. Thanks again for the clothes and blankets."

He gives me a curt nod before returning to his bedroom and shutting the door behind him.

By now, the fire is blazing, heating the room nicely. I arrange the pillows on the armrest, layer the blankets over the couch, and eagerly burrow into their cozy embrace.

I roll onto my side, squeezing my eyes shut. As comfortable as I am, sleep eludes me for a very different reason than before. I quickly shove aside the flicker of disappointment that I'll be leaving in a few hours, aware that any lingering fantasies of spending a night in Shep's bed will fade with the sunrise.

CHAPTER 5

Burnt Bacon And Sunshine Smiles

Shep

AFTER BEING WOKEN UP IN THE MIDDLE OF THE NIGHT and the stilted exchanges that followed, I was more certain than ever that Noelle's stay had to be short-lived. However, after hours of restless tossing and turning, the sun rises, the wind still howling outside the cabin, and the snow continues to fall in thick sheets.

Early forecasts promised a short storm, but they were wrong. Which means I'm saddled with my uninvited houseguest until further notice.

Did seeing her huddled by the hearth, shivering with trembling fingers as she tried to coax a fire to life, nag at my guilty conscience? Maybe. Or was it that she only had the thin throw Birdie had sent me last year? A little. The most alarming part? I hit the sack without a second thought for my guest until I heard her moving around the living room and bolted like a dog called to heel.

There's no valid excuse for how I acted. I was irritated by her unexpected arrival, and my only concern was keeping her from freezing in the storm. Not that it helped much, seeing as she nearly became an ice sculpture in my living room, thanks to my indifference.

What made me even more of a jerk was that while she stood there shivering, my eyes kept drifting to her silk top and shorts that left little to the imagination, showing off every curve and the swells of her breasts.

I had hoped that lending her clothes would be a simple solution to ease my conscience, but I was wrong. The sight of her in my flannel and sweats was disarmingly intoxicating. And just when I thought it couldn't get worse, I found out she's twenty years younger than me. God, I'm old enough to be her dad, yet I was painfully aware of how tempting she was—every torturous sway of her hips and each sassy comment from her smart mouth.

I consider sneaking through my window to hide in the woodshop I have behind the cabin to avoid Noelle, when a loud crash echoes from the kitchen, making me bolt upright in bed.

God, what trouble is that city girl getting herself into now?

She may be pretty, but she sure is a handful.

After quickly getting dressed, I leave my room, halting in my tracks when I see the state of the kitchen. Noelle stands at the stove, her cheeks and hair streaked with flour. Bowls and mixing cups litter the counter, and every surface is dusted with sugar. Pans are stacked precariously high in the sink, and the floor is a patchwork of spills.

It looks as if a tornado tore through the place.

I drag my hand across my mouth, taking in the chaos. "God, this place is a disaster."

"Oh good, you're awake." Noelle beams, oblivious to my sour mood. "I just finished your breakfast. You should eat before it gets cold." She pulls a plate from the cupboard and sets it on the only free space on the counter. "I hope you don't mind that I used the kitchen. When I woke up and saw that the snow was still falling, I wanted to do something nice to thank you for putting up with me for a little longer. I promise I'll leave as soon as the storm lets up." She tugs her bottom lip between her teeth.

The biting comments I'd prepared dissipate before I can form the words. I might've told her she could only stay until morning, but is she genuinely worried I'll send her out into the raging storm?

The kitchen's a mess, but she meant well by doing something nice. Another mark on my growing guilty conscience. Reckon I could be less of an ass, given her situation. She expected to spend the holidays alone, enjoying the sun, not being stuck with a cranky man for who knows how long.

"You can stay until the storm passes," I assure her.

Her face visibly relaxes, and she gives me a big smile. "I really appreciate it." She motions to the table in the corner. "Take a seat. I'll bring your food over."

I do as she asks, sitting on one of the barstools, and seconds later, she puts a plate in front of me with several strips of bacon and a stack of pancakes drizzled with syrup. "I hope everything tastes okay." She shoots me a wary gaze as she wrings her hands. "I made my famous homemade hot chocolate and whipped up banana-cinnamon pancakes. I used what you had on hand and a few things I brought, but I didn't have a recipe for those, so I improvised. Oh, and I totally forgot to flip the bacon while mixing the batter, so it might be extra crispy."

Judging by the blackened edges, *crispy* is an understatement. And the pancakes look dense enough to double as hockey pucks. I stab one with my fork and take a bite. The texture is chewy, full of lumps of cinnamon and banana chunks that stick to my teeth, but I swallow it anyway.

Noelle lingers nearby, watching me with a hopeful expression, so I offer a tight smile.

"They're good," I choke out.

She lets out a shaky sigh of relief. "Phew. I'm so glad. I usually eat frozen dinners or order takeout, so I'm not much of a cook."

If anyone else had made these pancakes, I'd have told them they were shit and thrown the things away. But I can't bring myself to do that—not with Noelle looking at me with pride shining in her doe eyes. So I do the only logical thing I can and take another big bite, chasing it down with the steaming cup of hot chocolate she left on the table. Surprisingly, it's delicious, with a touch of vanilla and peppermint. It seems holiday drinks are her specialty—breakfast, not so much.

"Your hot cocoa is really good," I say between sips.

"It's a family recipe," she beams.

I frown when I glance around and notice she hasn't set a place for herself. "Aren't you going to eat?"

"I could only find a small pan, so I made yours first. I was going to make some for myself before I shower, if that's okay." There she goes again, making me feel like an asshole for how short I was with her last night.

"That's fine." I look past her, spotting a banana and the cinnamon jar, sparking an idea. "Why don't you shower now, and I'll make the second batch?"

She rears back, eyes widening. "Oh no, I couldn't ask you to do that."

"It's no problem," I say, waving her off. "You made me breakfast. Flipping a few pancakes is the least I can do."

I'd rather tell her it's nonnegotiable, but I doubt she'd respond well to that approach. She already thinks I'm a jerk, so I'll have to find a more subtle approach if I want my way.

Noelle glances back at me as she moves dirty dishes from the counter to the sink. "Are you sure?"

"I am."

She nods slowly, still hesitant, but doesn't argue. "Okay, but I'll clean this mess when I'm finished," she states.

"Sounds good."

I only say it to placate her. I have every intention of handling the cleanup, but there's no point in arguing.

After I finish my hockey puck pancakes and *crispy* bacon, I go to my room to grab Noelle another pair of sweats and a long-sleeved flannel.

I intercept her as she's walking to the bathroom, toiletries in hand.

"What's this?" She motions to the clothes.

"Reckoned you'd want something clean to wear."

"Oh, thank you." She takes the pile, tucking them under her arm. "I was just going to wear what you gave me last night."

I grunt. "It's nothing."

I'm not doing it to be nice—it's a practical decision. If she stays warm, she won't wear that skimpy sleep set again, and my self-control might stand a fighting chance.

Noelle's eyes twinkle as she smiles. "Regardless, I'm grateful." She ducks her head, darting around me toward the bathroom.

Once the door clicks shut behind her, I go back to the kitchen to start on a fresh batch of pancake batter. I don't want Noelle to taste her cooking and feel bad for serving it. At least one of us deserves a proper breakfast, and it should be her since she's had to put up with me since she got here. It's another practical choice, not a noble gesture.

After tending to the animals in the barn, I retreated to my workshop located behind the cabin. It's a one-room building I use for woodworking with sawdust covering the floor, shelves lined with planes and chisels, and the scent of pine lingering permanently in the air. There's a workbench set up in the middle, cluttered with my current project—a nearly finished rocking chair for my friend Casey and his wife Amy.

Casey's been my friend since high school. He manages High Noon, the honky-tonk I own in town. It used to be a barn for milk cows, but when the local dairy farm went out of business twenty years ago, I bought the place and turned it into Pine Haven's top attraction.

Last month, when I stopped by to do payroll, Casey was looking online for a rocking chair to get Amy for Christmas. They're expecting their first baby, and she wants a handcrafted rocking chair to match the woodland theme of their nursery. The prices were so absurd that I offered to build one. Usually, I sell the furniture I make at the consignment store in town, but I enjoy the occasional special project.

Although this one is bittersweet, a reminder of everything I wanted but don't have. I always dreamed of having a wife and a bunch of kids of my own. I once believed my ex and I would have it all, but lately, I've accepted the possibility of being alone forever, watching friends and acquaintances create the life I wanted while I stand by empty-handed.

I pause my sanding when there's a tentative knock on the door. Glancing out the window, I realize darkness has settled over the sky, and I've spent the whole afternoon out here.

"Come in," I holler.

Noelle pokes her head inside. She's practically swallowed by one of my coats and wearing boots I'd let her borrow earlier, for when she had to go outside since she didn't pack any practical footwear.

"I hope I'm not intruding," she says softly.

She is, but I swallow the retort.

"It's fine. What's up?" I ask.

She holds up a bowl covered with tinfoil. "The timer went off for the chili you had in the crockpot. I had a bowl, and it was delicious. Figured you might be hungry too since you've been in here all afternoon, so I brought you some."

My annoyance at being interrupted eases at the gesture. She didn't have to brave the cold to bring me dinner, but she did it anyway.

Because she's not a jaded asshole with a chip on her shoulder.

"Thanks. You can put it over there." I motion to the rolling cart against the wall.

She nods, placing the chili where I asked, but lingers in the room.

"Did you need something else?"

She sighs, tucking a strand of hair behind her ear. "Honestly, the cabin is too quiet. I don't have service, so I can't work or stream a holiday playlist, and I can only do so much reading before growing restless. I was hoping I could hang out with you while you work." She hesitates, shooting me a sidelong glance before adding, "I'll be quiet, I promise."

I highly doubt that.

Noelle is curious by nature and admitted she doesn't handle silence well. Not to mention, I don't usually let anyone in my workshop. It's where I come when the noise in my head is too loud, and I let my hands do the thinking. There's a peace that comes with transforming raw wood into a tangible object that calms me like nothing else.

I motion to the metal tool chest in the corner closest to me. "Take a seat."

As Noelle passes my workbench, she pauses beside the rocking chair lying on its side. Her fingers trace the headrest where I've carved a fox curled in a bed of leaves.

"Shep, this is beautiful," she says, almost reverently. "Every detail is perfect. Do you make furniture for a living?"

"No, it's a hobby." I set aside my sanding pad and wipe my hands on my jeans.

"Oh? What's your job?"

The silence didn't even last a minute.

"I own High Noon, Pine Haven's only honky-tonk."

Noelle scrunches her nose as she meets my gaze. "Is that some kind of bar?"

"Sort of." I wipe my brow. "We've got alcohol, country dancing, live bands on the weekends, and some of the best damn barbecue in Arizona."

She lets out a soft chuckle. "I don't peg you for a social butterfly who'd willingly host a dancefloor full of strangers."

"I'm not." I shrug. "My friend Casey runs the place. I stop by once a week to order supplies and handle the accounts."

It's been that way for years. I spend my days on the mountain with the animals and in my shop, woodworking. I answer to no one, and solitude is my preferred companion. Yet with Noelle here, chatting constantly, it's not nearly as bothersome as I figured it would be.

She perches on the tool chest, taking off her coat and folding her knees to her chest. My flannel hangs loose on her frame, and the top buttons are undone so one side slips from her shoulder, revealing her freckled skin. Heat coils low in my belly, an animalistic urge to drag my mouth across the exposed flesh and mark her flashing through my mind.

I inhale sharply, forcing my mind on anything but trailing my tongue along her collarbone as she cries out my name—her constant chatter, the mess she made in the kitchen earlier, how she has a habit for showing up where she doesn't belong.

"Please tell me you've got at least one fun hobby like axe-throwing or bowling," she teases.

Grateful for the distraction, I collect my chili bowl and move to stand by the tool chest, deliberately keeping my distance to fend off further intrusive thoughts.

"Right, because being surrounded by amateurs tossing sharp objects and wearing shoes that smell like a locker room is *super* fun," I say.

She laughs. "Alright, Sir Grumps-a-Lot, enlighten me—what counts as fun in your world?"

I shoot her a scowl. "In the summer, I run the local rodeo where Casey and I compete in the team roping event. It might not meet your entertainment standards, but I prefer activities that require strategy and patience."

"Oh, is that a contest to see who can tie a rope the fastest? Or tug-of-war for cowboys?"

I pinch the bridge of my nose, holding back a groan. Noelle couldn't be more city if she tried.

"No, it's a competition where two cowboys chase down a steer—that's a young male cow," I add as she tilts her head, a frown creasing her brow. "One of us catches the steer's head, and the other gets the back legs. The fastest team wins."

"Is that safe?" Her voice goes up an octave.

"Sure. We follow strict rules to ensure the animals aren't harmed," I assure her.

She sits up straight, giving me a nervous smile. "I mean, is it safe for you?"

I wasn't expecting that response. I figured she'd be up in arms about the animals being used for sport, like Birdie is, and my safety would be an afterthought.

"Uh, yeah. The bull riders are the ones who have to worry about getting trampled. My biggest concern is getting my rope tangled." This is where I should cut off the conversation and tell her I have to get back to work, but my curiosity overrides my aversion to small talk. "What do you do for work?"

"I host a podcast. It's a blend of hype-girl energy with honest opinions that empower my audience when life gets messy," she explains, her face flushing with excitement.

What the hell is "hype-girl energy" and why am I not surprised?

From how she describes it, what she does is an extension of her personality. Even after only knowing her for just over a day, I can tell she's happiest when she spreads her sunny outlook on life, regardless of what people think—me included.

"Do you get paid, or is it more of a hobby?" Her smile slips, and only then do I register how rude my question sounded.

She edges closer to where I'm standing, giving me a patronizing pat on the arm. "My episodes pull in millions of views, and I'm consistently in the overall top hundred podcasts, so I'd say I'm doing alright."

I've never listened to one, but that sounds impressive. Now that I think about it, I can see the appeal with Noelle. Her voice is soothing and animated, making even mundane details captivating when she speaks.

"I didn't mean any offense," I admit, spooning chili into my mouth to distract from my obvious misstep.

"None taken." She grins. "Do you make a lot of rocking chairs?"

"Actually, that's my first one." I motion to it, propped up on the workbench. "Casey and his wife are having a baby."

"That's very generous," she gushes. "My grandpa loved woodworking, too. Even though I never met him, I inherited the wooden Christmas village he made for my grandma. Every house is a music box that plays a Christmas song." She pauses, wringing her hands in her lap as sadness laces her tone. "When I moved this past summer, the transport crew dropped the crate holding the three cottages. Luckily, the shops and the church survived, but I was still devastated."

I give her shoulder a squeeze. "I'm sorry you lost them."

She tips her head, giving me a small smile. "I appreciate it.

I'll replace them eventually—they just won't have the same sentimental value as the old ones."

Her story strikes a chord I didn't think still existed. She makes me want to solve every one of her problems, no matter how small, even though I have no business being invested. In less than two days, she's already twisting my head with her relentless optimism and fiery passion.

I don't like how my hand on her shoulder sends a ripple of heat through me. I move it to my side, flexing my fingers to shake off the part of me already disappointed that she'll be gone once the storm passes.

CHAPTER 6

Note to Self: The Cowboy Has A Soft Spot

Noelle

YESTERDAY WAS QUIET, AND I SPENT MOST OF IT READING, except for the hour Shep let me hang out with him in his workshop. I enjoyed watching him work but knew better than to overstay my welcome. It's obvious that it's his sanctuary. I fell asleep on the couch again and only stirred once to see Shep tending the fire. It seems he wasn't willing to risk a repeat of my first night, and I couldn't help but smile at his subtle attentiveness.

This morning, he made delicious sausage, egg, and cheese breakfast sandwiches before disappearing into his bedroom a while ago.

I've attempted to distract myself with another book, this one about a mafia boss forcing his enemy's daughter into an arranged marriage—but I can't seem to get into it. As much as I adore reading, the collection of books I downloaded for this trip can only keep me occupied for so long. That's why I set my e-reader aside when I glance up from the couch and see Shep stepping out of his room in his coat and boots, heading for the front door.

"Where are you going?" I ask.

"To the barn to feed the animals," he says as he slides into his boots.

I spring to my feet. "Can I come with you?"

Yesterday's short trip to the workshop out back was rough in the storm, but now that the snow's eased up, I'm itching to get outside and explore, including the barn.

He stands to his full height, his expression wary. "I don't think that's a good idea."

That's not a no.

"Please? I'm tired of being cooped up in the cabin and would love some fresh air." I tip my chin, giving him the saddest eyes I can muster. "I still don't have service, so I can't work, and I'm not used to having so much downtime."

Shep told me earlier that service here is unreliable on a good day and nonexistent during bad weather, so there's no telling when it'll be back up.

I'm not exaggerating when I say I'm not used to sitting around with nothing to do. I record six podcasts a week—including a Saturday special—while juggling my social media and attending brand events. This trip marks the first time I've taken more than an afternoon off for an appointment or a dinner date in two years.

When I booked my impromptu vacation, I notified my audience and sponsors that I'd be taking a couple of days off from the podcast. I figured that would give me enough time to settle in before editing the videos for the rest of the year. Naturally, my plans changed when I found myself in a winter wonderland without service, making editing or posting impossible for the time being.

It's a sudden change given that until recently, I spent most of my time putting everyone else first both at work and in my relationships, and somewhere along the way, I lost sight of my own needs. I've realized it's time to prioritize my happiness and refuse to settle for less than I deserve. That includes finding a partner who puts me first and stands by me, even when I'm stubborn and set in my ways.

This trip was supposed to be about self-discovery—the first step in learning to love and prioritize myself before letting someone else in. It might not be going as planned, but I'm still determined to make the most of it.

"Fine. You can come as long as you don't get in the way," Shep grunts.

"You won't regret it!"

I could've sworn he tacked on a muttered "I already do," but I can't be sure.

I brush it off, too excited to venture outside. Shep mentioned the mountain roads are still covered in snow and ice, so it might be a while before I can leave. I'm determined to make the most of my time here rather than dwell on things out of my control.

I slip on the boots Shep loaned me—the ones I wore to the workshop yesterday. They're far too big, but he's padded the inside with socks so they fit better.

He eyes the flannel I'm wearing over a long-sleeved thermal. This morning, they were waiting for me in the bathroom, along with a clean pair of sweats. Looks like I'll be borrowing his clothes until the weather cooperates enough for me to head back to Phoenix.

"If you're coming, you're wearing something warmer." Shep takes a coat from the rack near the door and holds it open in front of me. "Put your arms through."

"I can do it." I reach for the coat, but he moves it away.

"Arms in," he repeats firmly.

I shoot him a stubborn glare. "So bossy."

Shep tilts his head, his gaze unwavering. "If you wear a coat the way you prepare for a trip, you'll get frostbite before we reach the barn."

"Fine." I relent, deciding it's better to play along than risk being left behind.

I extend my arms, then remain perfectly still, leaving him to wrestle them into the coat sleeves. Just because I decided to cooperate doesn't mean I'll make it easy on him.

To Shep's credit, he doesn't complain, carefully sliding in each arm and tugging the coat into place as if he's handling something fragile.

This close, I'm enveloped by his scent, earthy and warm, and I lean in a fraction to breathe him in. Thankfully, he doesn't seem to notice as he zips my coat, sliding it up to my neck.

"I feel like I'm in a straitjacket," I complain, pulling the zipper down an inch.

Shep narrows his eyes, moving it back up. "You can thank me later when you're protected from the wind." He shifts his attention to my sleeves, rolling them up until they reach my wrists. "That's better. Make sure you put on these gloves before we leave." He tucks a pair inside my coat pocket, giving it a pat for good measure.

"Yes, *Dad*," I taunt.

Shep's nostrils flare, his chest rising with a deep inhale. The intensity radiating off him is almost palpable. His untamed reaction has heat pooling in my stomach, bringing my reflexive draw to him into sharp focus.

I start toward the door but stop when he snakes an arm around my waist. Another flutter of heat rises in my belly, the contact making it impossible to look away.

"I'm not done with you yet." His voice comes out husky.

He grabs a beanie from the rack and slips it over my head, smoothing my hair over my shoulders. A loose strand falls across my cheek, and I inhale sharply when he pushes it from my face, his fingers grazing my temple.

"There," he rasps, his gaze shifting to my lips.

I feel lightheaded as my pulse hammers in my ears. This attraction to someone I barely know, and who hasn't been receptive to my presence, shouldn't be this powerful. It defies all logic. I should be looking for excuses to keep him at arm's length, not reasons to spend more time with him.

Shep is the first to shake off the daze, his features settling into their usual stoic position as he puts on his own coat and cowboy hat.

"Let's go. The animals are waiting." He brushes past me on his way outside.

"I'm right behind you," I call out after him.

I tug my coat zipper down a few inches in a small act of rebellion. The smoldering attraction is irrefutable, yet I refuse to let him dictate the rules. If anything, I want to push back harder, hoping the gravity of his presence wanes. Rational? Probably not. But still worth a shot.

When I step onto the porch, a soft breeze brushes past. I burrow further into Shep's coat to shield myself, his now familiar scent wrapping around me, as I reluctantly zip it up all the way.

I've seen snow countless times in New York, but it's different here—the sun is shining down on my face, ice crystals cling to every branch, and birds chirp in the distance, celebrating the lull in the storm.

"You coming, woman?"

Shep is in the driveway, leaning against a snowmobile with his arms crossed. It's criminal how handsome he is with his cowboy hat tilted low and his winter jacket stretched across his chest.

As I hurry down the porch steps, his gruff voice cuts through the air. "Slow down and use the damn railing so you don't fall and break your neck."

"Careful, cowboy, or I might think you're starting to care," I holler back.

Shep grunts in reply.

He might act indifferently, but his recent actions have made me more certain than ever that he has a compassionate side.

Case in point—yesterday morning. He thought he was sneaky, but I know what he did with the pancakes. Mine came out lumpy and hard, but the ones he served me were perfectly smooth, fluffy, and delicious. It was thoughtful of him to eat my poor attempt at pancakes. He went the extra mile making me better ones while wanting me to believe it was my batch so I wouldn't be embarrassed. He'd deny it if I called him out, but I can see right through him.

I learned something else about Shep yesterday. The man can cook more than breakfast. The homemade chili he made for dinner was incredible and superior to any takeout I could have ordered or the ready-made meals I pick up at the grocery store.

The path to the snowmobile is dotted with icy patches, and even though it pains me, I take his advice and slow my steps. I'm not about to fall and have him scold me for not listening.

As I near the snowmobile, he steps toward me, sliding a hand under my elbow.

"I should've brought you a helmet," he sighs, exasperation clear in his voice.

"The bright side is I'm probably less talkative after a head injury."

I swear I catch Shep's lips twitching into a smile even his mustache can't hide. He keeps me steady while I swing a leg over the seat, making sure I'm balanced before letting go. He climbs in front, his outer thighs brushing against mine, causing my stomach to do a somersault.

Please don't let him notice how fast my heart is racing.

Once he's settled, he puts the key into the ignition and the engine comes to life with a satisfying hum.

"Hold on tight," he says, guiding my hands around him.

Before I can ask questions, he eases the snowmobile forward, and I instinctively wrap my arms tighter around his waist. When we pick up speed, I cling to him tighter, the wind whipping around us as we glide along. The cabin disappears behind us as we follow the snow-packed road to the barn.

The cold bites at my fingers, but the gloves Shep gave me are tucked into my coat pocket. I forgot to put them on before we left, and I'm too afraid to retrieve them while we're on the move.

I lean forward, resting my head on Shep's back and letting my hands drift up his chest seeking warmth. He stiffens under my touch, and I expect him to pull away—but instead, he shifts in his seat, unzipping his jacket and guiding my hands inside. I let out a soft moan as heat finally reaches my freezing fingers.

The ground is soft underneath the snowmobile's treads, and the trees we pass lean under the weight of the snow, their limbs sparkling like glass. We take the next turnoff, and I spot the barn in the distance, its red silhouette a beacon through the frosty woods.

As we pull up in front, the engine hum fades to silence, and I reluctantly remove my hands from Shep's chest so he can get off the snowmobile. Once he's dismounted, he turns around, cupping my elbow to help me down. The snow crunches beneath our boots, and I shiver despite my layers.

Shep scans my face with concerned eyes. "You alright?"

"Just a little cold," I admit through chattering teeth.

"You should have worn the gloves, like I told you."

"I forgot to put them on," I admit sheepishly.

His features soften as he pulls off his own gloves, tucking them into his back pocket. He takes my hands in his, the warmth from his palms spreading through mine. The teasing brush of his fingers against my skin feels dangerously sinful, and I lean in without thinking.

"Better?" he asks, his voice low.

I look up, his gaze lingering on my lips. "Uh-huh."

I wonder if he kisses with slow and deliberate precision or if he's bold and demanding.

Here I go again, caught in a steamy daydream, imagining him closing the space between us and putting his mouth on mine.

Snap out of it, Noelle.

This isn't a romance novel where the grumpy cowboy gives me a bruising kiss or pins me against a stack of hay bales as he rails into me.

I blink rapidly, reeling in my thoughts before I embarrass myself.

"Should we go in?" I ask.

Something unspoken flickers in his eyes, vanishing as fast as it appeared, and he lets go of my hands.

"Yeah. There's a heater inside, so it'll be warm," he replies.

I nod absentmindedly as he ushers me through the barn door, my jaw dropping at the sight. The space is huge, with high ceilings stretching overhead, twelve large stalls, rows of tack and feed stacked on shelves lining the walls, and an open wash bay near the entrance that smells faintly of hay and saddle soap.

As I approach the stalls, I see the first two on the left have been converted into a chicken coop,

with several hens clucking in their wire-mesh enclosure. In the other stalls, horses stick their heads out, curious about their visitors.

"Shep, this is incredible. Is this all yours?"

He looks up from where he's scooping oats into four large buckets, his eyes soft as he straightens and squares his shoulders.

"Yeah, it is."

I stroll down the barn aisle and stop at the first stall on the right, where the horse Shep was riding the day we met neighs his greeting. His copper mane reminds me of the color of pennies, and he has a white stripe running down his nose. A polished nameplate on the stall door has his name, Blaze, etched in block letters.

"Hello there, handsome." I give him a scratch under his chin.

"Don't let him fool ya." Shep chuckles as he carries over two buckets. "He's got more attitude than manners."

"Don't listen to him," I whisper to Blaze. "You're perfect." He nuzzles my hand, letting out a soft snort. "See? Blaze agrees."

Shep rolls his eyes. "Sorry to disappoint, sweetheart, but he's only after the sugar cubes he knows I'm good for."

I hold out my hand, grinning. "Well? I can't let him down then, can I?"

Shep sighs as he pulls out a handful from his pocket and gives them to me.

"Thanks." I offer a couple to Blaze, who greedily chomps them down. "Can I give some to the other horses, too?"

"Go ahead, but make sure your hand stays flat. Some of them can get overzealous and might mistake your finger for a snack."

"Copy that. I'm off the menu."

A ghost of a smile flickers across his face, the corners of his eyes softening.

As I walk to the next stall, a loud, persistent bleating echoes throughout the barn.

I furrow my brow. "Do you have sheep?"

Shep shakes his head. "Nope. A sheep wouldn't be that demanding for attention."

Eager to investigate, I follow the noise to the last stall on the right, where a shiny black nose pokes through one of the slats, letting out a plaintive bawl as I approach. Without waiting for Shep's permission, I pull open the gate, revealing a fluffy Highland cow with a golden-brown coat.

"You're the most adorable thing I've ever seen," I gush, holding out my hand, letting the cow snuffle my fingers and press her head gently against my palm.

"Blaze might get jealous of all the attention you're giving her," Shep teases as he joins me, with a bucket of oats in hand.

"He'll forgive me as long as I keep giving him sugar cubes," I say, running my fingers through the shaggy tuft of hair hanging over the cow's eyes.

Shep steps around me, tossing the oats into a trough in the corner.

"Sounds about right," he agrees.

I nod to the baby cow who's trying to eat my hair. "What's this darling's name?"

"Maple."

"That's the cutest. Did you name her?"

"My cousin, Birdie, did."

"Oh. Does she live in the area?"

"No. She's in Bluebell, Montana. She rescues animals, and every so often hears about one in trouble in a different state, including this little lady." He pats Maple on her rump before raking around the hay in her stall. "Maple was only four months old when she was found in a backyard petting zoo, jammed into a small enclosure with no roof or grass to graze on. Her coat was matted and caked with dried mud."

"That's awful. You poor thing," I murmur, stroking her neck.

"She was found three hours from here, and Birdie called me asking if I'd take her in," Shep continues.

"It's a good thing you agreed. Who knows what would have happened if you hadn't?" I shudder at the thought.

"Birdie would have picked her up and taken her back to Montana," Shep reassures me. "She'd never leave an animal in a dangerous situation. She has a bad habit of getting into trouble to save them. Good thing her dad's the sheriff in Bluebell, or she'd have landed herself in jail already."

Of course, Shep would downplay his good deed and how much he cares about Maple. But I've learned that how a person treats animals often says a lot about how they treat people. Shep can play the gruff guy all he wants, but driving three hours to rescue a baby cow proves he has a heart of gold.

"Birdie sounds amazing, but Maple seems happy here," I state.

"Only because she gets lots of treats when she does tricks. Wanna see?"

He's dodging the topic of the good deeds he's done, but I let it go, too intrigued to see what Maple can do.

"Is it something they taught her at the petting zoo?"

He rubs the back of his neck. "No. I did."

My eyebrows lift in surprise. "*You* taught Maple tricks? The same man who acts like he doesn't want her staying here? Someone's totally smitten."

"Not you, too," Shep grumbles. "Birdie said the same thing, and it's still untrue."

"Uh-huh." I don't believe him for a second. "Now show me these tricks Maple can do."

Today, it seems I'm discovering a new side of Shep every hour, and I have to admit it only makes him more endearing.

I watch as he takes a bag of sliced apples from his coat pocket and moves to the other side of the stall before holding out the treat.

"Come, Maple," he orders gently.

She sniffs the air, slowly pivoting to face Shep. Her tail flicks as she trots over to him, darting her tongue out to scoop the apple from his hand. She tosses her head proudly as she chews her prize, and Shep gives her a broad smile.

Did I hit my head and tumble into Wonderland, where rabbits wear waistcoats, tea parties never end, and the brooding cowboy's usual scowl has flipped to a smile?

"Such a good girl, Maple," Shep praises. "Want to see her do another trick?"

I draw in a long breath to steady my racing heart. "Yep, I'd love to."

Shep holds an apple slice in one hand, stretching the other out flat in front of him.

"Maple, down."

She flicks her ears at the sound of his voice, shifting her weight as if considering his command. Gradually, she tucks her hind legs beneath her, lowering her broad frame to the ground with unexpected grace. Her large brown eyes remain fixed on the apple slice, but she doesn't move until Shep gives a nod of approval. The second he does, she stretches her neck forward, lips curling around the treat.

"She's so clever," I coo.

Shep gives her another apple slice and grins as he runs his hand over her head. "Atta girl, Maple."

Seeing this side of him makes my heart flutter, and if I'm not careful, I might start hoping the snowstorm never ends.

CHAPTER 7

It's Beginning to Feel A Lot Like Christmas

Shep

BRINGING NOELLE TO THE BARN WAS A BAD IDEA.

I figured letting her tag along would keep her out of trouble or from attempting another experimental recipe that I'd inevitably have to eat.

The problem?

I didn't account for how much I'd enjoy her company or how her sunny disposition would have a way of getting under my skin. No matter how hard I've tried, her presence has found cracks in my walls.

"Am I doing this right?" Noelle calls over her shoulder.

Once I'd shown her all of Maple's tricks, she offered to help with the chores.

I glance up from where I'm changing out Maple's water. Noelle is leaning over the cow, brushing her coat, but her strokes are so light they barely skate over the top coat.

"Try a little more pressure so you're lifting the hair," I suggest.

She gasps. "I'll hurt her."

"You won't," I promise.

She nibbles her bottom lip, her eyes flitting back and forth between Maple and me, still doubtful.

I'm about to lecture her for overanalyzing but think better of it. She's likely never handled farm chores or brushed down a cow before. What's routine for me is probably intimidating to her. It's evident that she has a big heart, and her compassion extends to people and animals alike. If she's worried about hurting Maple, I have to be patient and reassure her by guiding her through how it's done safely.

"Here, I'll show you."

I step behind Noelle, my chest brushing her back as I take her hand. Her breath hitches at the contact, but she stays put. I lean closer, breathing in the sweet smell of vanilla and sugar cookies. It must be the holiday body wash I found in the shower this morning. I take in another deep breath, her scent wrapping around me—sweet, warm and addictive.

It takes me back to the snowmobile ride when her chest was flush against my back, her hands roaming to keep warm.

Christ, get a grip, Shep.

She's barely half my age and will be gone as soon as the storm passes. All the more reason I shouldn't entertain the thought of spinning her around and claiming her mouth.

My hand remains over Noelle's as I guide the brush down Maple's side, pushing firmly enough to get through her thick coat.

"Keep the strokes long and steady." My voice is tight as I repeat the motion.

I can feel Noelle's fingers relax beneath mine as she matches my rhythm. Eventually, I let her take over. I glance at Maple, who's lazily chewing on hay, entirely at ease.

Noelle glances back at me, her eyes shining with pride. "Maple really enjoys having her coat brushed."

Her magnetic joy brightens her expression.

"You're doing so well with her, Sunshine." The nickname leaves my mouth before I can wrangle it back.

Where the hell did that come from?

I'm not the type to hand out nicknames, least of all to blue-eyed city girls blowing through town. Getting attached is the last thing I need. I'm starting to think the old rule about never naming a puppy if you don't plan to keep them applies to people and nicknames, too.

I take a measured breath and step back. "I'm going to bring in another bale of hay from the shed out back."

She turns around to face me. "Is there anything else I can help with once I'm finished brushing Maple?"

"Want to feed the chickens some mealworms? They'll never say no to a snack."

Her lips curve into a smile. "I'd love to."

"Great." I move toward the stall entrance. "There's a bucket with a scoop next to the feedbags on the bottom shelf."

"Perfect. I visited a rescue farm in Upstate New York on a field trip in junior high, and feeding the chickens was my favorite part—though the horse ride was a close second." I glance back to see her smiling fondly at the memory. "The whole experience was so memorable that I spent an entire year begging my parents to move to a farm. I even made a posterboard presentation, complete with a detailed chart of when I'd feed the livestock before and after school."

"Did they go for it?" I ask, curiosity getting the best of me.

She shakes her head. "It was a pipe dream, thinking they would trade city life for a farm full of animals, but I tried anyway. We lived in a small town in Massachusetts until I was ten, and they never stopped longing for the fast-paced city life they'd left behind when I was born. So there was no chance they were giving that up again," she explains with a shrug. "That didn't stop me from begging for a border collie for months even though our Brooklyn Heights apartment didn't have space for a herding dog. They did get me a hamster for Christmas that year."

"That's better than nothing, right?"

"Oh, absolutely. His name was Mr. Peanut, and he was obsessed with lettuce," Noelle says brightly.

Fuck me. The way she looks my direction with her doe eyes, spilling her childhood dreams, makes me want to call Birdie and have her track down a rescue border collie—or hell, buy her a whole farm in Upstate New York. Rational? Not even close. I don't know her well, yet she has me tempted to make promises I have no business making.

"I'd better go get that hay." I don't wait for her reply, high-tailing it out of there.

Once I'm outside, I take a gulp of fresh air. No matter how drawn I am to Noelle, I have to keep my distance. When she showed up at my cabin, it was easier to keep her at arm's length since she reminded me of my ex-fiancée. Both are city girls, have a weakness for high heels, and a habit of traveling on a whim.

However, I quickly learned that's where the similarities end. Where Noelle finds the bright spot in the worst of situations, Danielle always focused on what she thought was missing.

Her family moved to Pine Haven when she was sixteen, and she never stopped comparing our small town to the city. We started dating in our twenties and were together for five years before getting engaged. Shortly after, I bought my property on the mountain and moved into the cabin, with plans to build a larger house.

I'd thought she was happy, but a month before our wedding, she told me she'd secretly been applying for jobs in Chicago and landed an offer she couldn't refuse. She never asked if I'd move with her, having already decided our life together wasn't enough for her.

I'd always wanted a family of my own, but after Danielle left, I resigned myself to solitude on the mountain with the animals, venturing into town only when work demanded it. No one wants to be tied to someone like that, particularly not a woman twenty years younger with her whole future ahead of her.

After I retrieve what I need, I head back to the barn, stomping the snow off my boots before going inside. I come to an abrupt standstill in the doorway when I see Noelle standing on an old milk stool. She's balancing precariously on the death contraption, reaching for a bag of mealworms from a shelf above the feedbags.

"What the hell are you doing?" I ask, keeping my tone low so I don't startle her.

She whips her head in my direction. "I used the last of the mealworms and wanted to refill the bucket so it's ready when the chickens get their next snack."

"I'll take care of that. Get down from there," I grit out, my heart rate climbing.

She rolls her eyes. "It's okay. I've got it."

"Noelle. I'm serious." I drop the hay bale by the barn door to free my hands. "You could fall." I try to remain calm, concealing the alarm in my voice.

She waves me off when I take a step toward her. "I'm perfectly capable of doing this on my own."

Damn her stubbornness.

To make her point, Noelle sweeps her hair from her face and stretches her arm toward the bag of mealworms tucked farther back on the shelf. "Just a little higher," she mutters as she leans forward, the stool wobbling beneath her.

She exhales in relief when her fingers catch the corner of the bag. Her triumphant smile is short-lived when the flimsy stool folds beneath her, and my stomach drops as I watch her fight to regain her balance.

I'm already striding toward her when a startled gasp escapes Noelle's lips. Her eyes squeeze shut, bracing for the inevitable fall. I catch her around the waist before she hits the ground, lifting her into my arms. Her slender fingers cling to my shoulders as she rests her head against my chest. My pulse hammers in my ears as dread coils in my stomach, cursing myself for not acting faster.

I stride to the workbench along the opposite wall and set her down.

"Are you alright?" I question as I scan her from head to toe.

"Is now a good time to admit that I have terrible balance?" she laughs.

"Dammit, woman, you need to be more careful. Would it have killed you to listen to me?"

"Would it hurt for you to be less cranky?" she retorts.

I brace a hand on my hip. "If you weren't so headstrong and constantly challenging me, maybe I'd be in a better mood."

"That's debatable," she mumbles. "I appreciate the rescue, but I'm fine now." She shifts in her seat, wincing when her ankle grazes my leg.

I crouch in front of her, taking hold of her right ankle. Even with the slightest movement, she flinches.

"Sorry, did that hurt?"

She grits her teeth, nodding. "I must have twisted it when I fell. It's tender, but I don't think it's broken."

"At least let me check."

"No, that's okay." Noelle pulls her foot from my hands and attempts to stand, hissing as she sways.

And that's when my patience snaps. "That's enough."

I refuse to let her hurt herself any further. I lift her into my arms and head for the exit.

"Where are we going?"

"I'm taking you back to the cabin so you can rest. Ice and elevation will help with the swelling." I haven't seen her ankle, but her death grip on my shoulder tells me she's in pain.

"Admit it, you're just using me for an impromptu arm workout," she murmurs, her voice strained.

"Woman, I swear I've aged a year since you've been here," I say with a hint of amusement.

I'm hit with a sharp pang of guilt as I carry her out of the barn. She rests her head against my chest, and I breathe in the sweet mix of sugar cookies and vanilla, both quickly becoming two of my favorite scents.

I'd forgotten what it feels like to care for someone else, to put their needs before my own, and seeing Noelle vulnerable in my arms stirs a part of me I thought had long since been lost.

When we reach the snowmobile, I lift her onto it, swinging her uninjured leg across the seat.

I tell myself my reaction to her is normal, simply the concern of a man looking out for a woman in his charge—but the quick thrum of my pulse as she wraps her arms around me suggests otherwise.

CHAPTER 8

First Aid And Foreplay

Noelle

WHEN WE REACH THE CABIN, SHEP CARRIES ME TO the porch, my body flush against his chest. I can't help stealing a glance at his muscular arms and the way they subtly flex as he moves up the steps.

"You can set me down now," I huff out when he gets to the front door. "My ankle doesn't even hurt that much anymore."

That's a lie. A sharp pain shoots up my leg with every movement. But I don't want him thinking I'm even more of a burden now that I'm injured.

Shep doesn't loosen his grip. His brow creases, and he fixes his eyes on me, silently calling me out on my bullshit.

I give him a playful jab in the chest. "I think the real reason you insist on carrying me is so you can feel all heroic."

He gives one of his signature grunts as he swings open the cabin door. "Nice try, Sunshine. You can antagonize me all you want, but you're staying off that foot until it's healed, and that's final."

I blink in surprise when he strides past the living area toward his bedroom.

"Uh… Shep." I still in his arms. "Aren't you going to put me on the couch?"

He shakes his head. "No. You need more room to stretch out so we can elevate your leg."

"I thought your bedroom was off-limits."

"Figured giving up my personal space beats you taking legal action if your ankle gets worse," he grumbles, a hint of amusement in his voice.

I tap my chin thoughtfully. "Come to think of it, there were no hazardous work area signs. Pretty sure that qualifies as negligence." I pause, flashing him a mischievous grin. "If I sued, I could buy a closetful of wedges or finally get that designer handbag I've always wanted. The options are endless."

"Easy there, sweetheart," Shep warns. "Maybe save plotting a shopping spree until you can stand on both feet."

"Ever heard of online shopping?" I counter. "It's this thing where you can order anything you want from your phone and it magically shows up at your doorstep."

"Next, you'll tell me the Earth is round."

I giggle as he lowers me onto the bed, and I take off my coat while he props two pillows against the headboard and eases me back.

"Comfortable?"

I burrow into the pillows with a sigh. "Yes, thanks."

He settles on the edge of the bed, rolling up my pant leg. His fingers drift along my calf, light as a feather, sending electric ripples through my spine.

"Don't worry. Once your ankle's healed, you can go back to

hatching your next scheme to bankrupt me," he says with a ghost of a smile.

If I didn't know better, I'd think this was his attempt at flirting. Butterflies take flight in my stomach, a silent admission that I'd welcome it if he were. Although he's most likely trying to cheer me up the only way he knows how.

I let out an exaggerated sigh. "That's a relief. I was starting to worry you were going soft on me."

A trace of warmth crosses his expression. "Never."

He tugs my boots free, one at a time. I should tell him I can do it myself, but his touch is far too soothing. When he gets to my injured foot, his pace slows, and he eases off the boot inch by inch. After dropping it to the floor, he peels my sock down, revealing the angry swelling at my ankle.

I bite my lip to keep the pain off my face, not wanting Shep to think he's hurting me. On the contrary, his large hands cradling my ankle are a welcome distraction from the throbbing ache.

"You better not use this as blackmail."

Shep glances at me, one brow raised. "What, that you ignored my warning and tumbled off a rickety milk stool?"

"No, that you've seen me without toenail polish." I wiggle my good foot for emphasis. "I always tell my subscribers I never skip painting them because I can't stand seeing my toes bare. But I didn't get a chance the morning I left for the airport. I figured I'd paint them once I got here or splurge for a pedicure, but obviously things didn't go as expected."

He squints at me. "I don't follow."

"Being honest with my audience is part of my brand, and I'd never want them to think I'm misleading them. Although I'm far more concerned about what they'll say when they find out I willingly spent the night at a stranger's house," I add, letting out a dry laugh. "I'm an advocate for putting safety first, whether it's solo travel or dating. In several episodes, I've cautioned against spending the night with someone you've just met, no matter how charming they are."

He smirks. "You thought I was charming?"

I roll my eyes. "More like moody and prickly. Although now that I think about it, a warm welcome would've been far more unsettling, and I might have opted for freezing in the convertible."

"Reckon my crankiness saved you from turning into a popsicle."

"My hero—saving me one scowl at a time." She props a hand on her forehead and mimics a swooning motion. "Though I guarantee I'll still have subscribers who won't care about the circumstances and will go off on me for giving advice about safety that I didn't follow myself."

As my platform has grown, I've struggled to balance transparency and personal boundaries. I want to be fully open with my audience while maintaining my privacy. It's a constant challenge not to feel dishonest when circumstances prevent full disclosure or when my firsthand experiences change my perspective on a topic I've discussed on my podcast.

"Sounds like they need to get a grip and quit fussing over stuff that isn't their damn business."

I shrug my shoulders. "I couldn't agree more. They're almost as bad as the podcast sponsors who forgot there's an actual person behind the mic."

There's one in particular, CoreFuel Labs, that tries to micromanage every episode they're featured in and weren't happy when we informed them that I was taking a couple of days off from posting new episodes. I was supposed to add new videos again starting yesterday and I'm positive I have at least one angry email from them about not holding up my end of the contract. Despite their complaints, it has built-in flexibility, and they don't pay for episodes I don't post.

Shep rubs his mustache, fighting back a laugh.

"What's so funny?"

"You are." He gently repositions my injured foot, propping it up to rest on his knee. "If the worst thing you've lied about is staying with a stranger so you didn't freeze to death or not painting your toes, your audience will understand. Not to mention, your sponsors should want you to take a break so you're more motivated when you get back to work. You shouldn't be trapped by things you've said to strangers on the internet or by executives only concerned about their bottom line. It's your life, and you should be free to change your mind or take a vacation whenever you damn well please."

I'm stunned speechless by his blunt perspective. He's right. My life revolves around my podcast and the advice I share. I'm the type to think about how something will affect my subscribers and sponsors first, long before I stop to consider how it'll affect me personally. Looking back, though, it's silly to assume my opinions would never change, especially when every experience teaches me something that can shift my perspective.

I'm starting to realize there's nothing wrong with putting myself first once in a while—including taking a spontaneous trip that forced me to temporarily step back from the podcast. Spending the holidays away from New York has been exactly what I needed and has turned into an adventure I wouldn't trade for anything.

"You're so right. I suppose it's not the end of the world if my toes aren't painted, but I draw the line at my fingernails. We post my episodes on YouTube, and I can't have people thinking I've let myself go completely." I sigh dramatically as I hold up my hand, showing Shep the nail I chipped when I fell.

He tries to stifle another laugh, but this one escapes as a low, rumbling chuckle. A smile tugs at my lips in response, secretly loving the sound. It sends a flutter through my chest, and I'm honored to catch a glimpse of the side of him that he usually keeps guarded.

"The least I can do is fix you up with a fresh manicure, seeing as you sacrificed your nails for the chickens—they owe you big time," Shep teases.

I clutch my chest, with feigned shock. "Did you just crack a joke? Should I call for help?"

"Don't expect a repeat performance," he warns, though his eyes crinkle at the corners. "I'm going to grab the other pillows from the living room for your foot. I'll be back." He stands, resting my leg on the bed.

"Can you get my phone, please? It's in the front pouch of my carry-on next to my e-reader."

"Sure."

It hasn't been much use with the lack of service, so I left it charging and figured I'd check it later.

When Shep returns he looks flushed. His face is tinged red, and he avoids meeting my eyes when he gives me my phone.

"Thanks," I say, hesitating when I notice the tension in his jaw. "Is… everything okay?"

"Yeah, fine," he mumbles.

It looks like he's back to clipped answers, but I decide not to read too much into it.

I hold my breath as I check my phone. Now that the storm has eased up, I'm hoping I finally have service—squealing when the screen lights up with three bars.

"I'm going to call my friend Gemma. She hasn't heard from me in a couple of days, and I don't want her to worry," I say.

Shep shrugs. "Sounds good."

"I'll start searching for places to stay in Pine Haven, too. The weather app shows another storm coming in tonight, but this one should clear up quickly, so I won't be in your way for much longer."

With only five days until Christmas, I'm anxious to find somewhere to stay through Christmas and get some decorations to make it festive. It doesn't feel like the most magical time of year without a tree and twinkling lights.

A shadow passes over Shep's expression, but it disappears in an instant. "I'll be in the kitchen making lunch while you call your friend." He nods stiffly, and steps back and leaves before I can respond.

What was that all about?

Shep went from playful ribbing to awkward silence, and when I brought up leaving, he shut down completely. Maybe he's not happy that another storm is coming. Not only am I crashing at his place, but I'm now even more of a useless guest with my sprained ankle. It's no wonder he's so tense.

A sharp pang shoots through my ankle. Ready for a distraction, I call Gemma.

She picks up on the second ring. "Finally! I was about to file a missing person's report."

"Sorry for not checking in sooner." I switch the call to speaker so I can rest my head against the pillows. "I got stuck in a blizzard without service."

"Whoa, are you okay?" Gemma's voice sharpens with alarm. "Wait—I thought you were headed to Arizona for endless sunshine?"

"Apparently, if you drive a few hours north of Phoenix, you trade desert heat for icy mountain ranges," I scoff.

Gemma gasps. "You're kidding. I thought the whole state was palm trees and pool weather."

"Me too," I exclaim. "Clearly, we're both overdue for a middle school geography refresher."

She usually handles all my business travel, and when I manage it myself, I send her my itinerary for a quick check. But since this trip was personal and I planned it at the last minute, I didn't want to pull her away from her well-deserved time with family in Vermont. I won't make that mistake again.

"I peaked when I learned the name of every state capital,"

Gemma states proudly. "At least your adventure will make for some great podcast material."

"Believe it or not, that's just the start," I admit, laughing nervously. "The place I rented was a total scam, and the *actual* owner thought I was breaking in when he caught me looking through the window. But then I accused *him* of being a serial killer, so I guess we're even."

"Wow, you're lucky you didn't become a true crime feature. They'd have probably called it 'Snow Way She's Gone,'" Gemma teases.

I pause briefly, twisting my hair into a bun with the tie on my wrist. "You have connections to several true crime podcasters, so at least I'd go out knowing you'd give them my most flattering photos for the episode."

She clicks her tongue. "Obviously. If the world's watching, you're going out in style."

I chuckle, amused by her dedication, and lower my voice slightly. "Shep is definitely a grumpy cowboy, but it turns out he's not serial killer material. In fact, he's actually really sweet. I sprained my ankle this morning, and he insisted on carrying me inside."

Even now, he's in the kitchen making lunch while I'm lounging on his bed chatting with my friend. It's not as if he'd let me hobble around to assist him, but that doesn't stop the pang of guilt cutting through me.

Gemma lets out a sharp gasp, followed by a delighted squeal. "You're snowed in with a single man? Please tell me he's packing."

My jaw drops at her bluntness. The woman has no filter. She's the type who goes to a bar, buys a guy a drink, and lays out exactly what she wants in bed before they step outside. Meanwhile, I've always been cautious, never daring to be that bold, secretly wishing I was brave enough to ask for help exploring my desires without judgment.

"I don't know… not yet. I mean it's not like that," I rush to correct myself, feeling heat rise to my cheeks. "Yes, he's handsome—the hottest cowboy I've ever seen actually—but he thinks I'm a total nuisance. Plus, he's forty-five, so I'm far too inexperienced for him."

A sudden thought crosses my mind that Shep would take it in strides, guiding me with the commanding dominance I've always craved.

"Girl, you've hit the *daddy* lottery. You can't pass this up—opportunities like this don't come around twice. Have you at least tried one of your new dildos yet?" Gemma asks loudly. "The reviews say they hit the G-spot just right and the vibrations match your rhythm."

"Why don't you yell a little louder so Shep can hear you," I deadpan.

"Well?" Gemma whisper-shouts. "*Have* you tried them?"

I shake my head, laughing at her blissful ignorance of volume control.

"Not yet. I haven't had any alone time since I've been here. I can't exactly whip one out in Shep's living room and…" I drift off, an alarm sounding in a far-off place in my mind.

The toys.

My stomach drops when it dawns on me that the pocket where I had my phone charging was on the inside of the front flap of my suitcase. That means Shep had to open it, and there was no way he would've missed the elaborate collection.

Oh. My. God.

I bury my face in my hands, wishing the floor would swallow me whole. No wonder he was acting so strange when he came back to the bedroom. I can only imagine what he must think of me after seeing an entire catalog of sex toys in my suitcase.

"Everything okay?" Gemma asks.

"I just realized there's a good chance Shep found my stash of toys earlier."

She practically screams into the phone. "Maybe he's imagining all the ways to use them on you! Save a horse, ride a toy, *and* a cowboy!"

"Gemma, keep it down," I hiss, scrambling to switch the speaker off and pressing the phone to my ear.

I'm already humiliated as it is. The last thing I need is Shep overhearing my friend trying to drag him into my sexual escapades. I'd also rather not admit that I've rarely used toys in the past, let alone with a man. My past partners weren't exactly enthusiastic about them, treating toys as rivals rather than a way to spice things up.

"All I'm saying is that being trapped on a mountain together is the perfect excuse to have a little fun," Gemma says, and I picture her waggling her eyebrows.

"And I'm telling you, it's not going to happen."

"Why?" she presses. "Because you don't want it to or you're afraid you actually do?"

I only wish she had it wrong.

The reality? I'm battling a fierce attraction unlike anything I've ever experienced. My mind drifts to the barn earlier when Shep was pressed against me as he showed me how to brush Maple. He appeared unfazed. Meanwhile, I was fighting to concentrate with his breath hot against my ear and his hand wrapped around mine.

I clear my throat. "I plead the Fifth."

"Uh-huh. I expect every juicy detail when you give in and let that man fuck you six ways till Sunday."

Oh my god.

Heat rushes to my cheeks, and I'm glad she's not here to call me out on it.

"Can we please talk about something else?"

Seriously, I'd rather discuss literally *anything* other than Shep's cock and having to pretend I haven't thought about sleeping with him.

She lets out an exasperated sigh. "Fine, I'll stop grilling you about your cowboy—for now." Shep's not *my* cowboy, but I don't bother correcting her. "Have you had a chance to do any of your favorite holiday traditions?" Gemma asks.

"Not yet," I admit. "Shep doesn't decorate for the holidays, and I'm not sure when I'll get to visit Pine Haven. But even if there aren't any lights, holiday movie marathons, or cookies baking in the oven, I'll find a way to celebrate."

"Of course you will. You have a gift for bringing holiday magic wherever you go." Through the phone, I hear a door creak, followed by a hushed voice. "Sorry, I gotta go. My mom and I are meeting my sister and the kids at the mall," Gemma tells me.

"Have so much fun and tell Santa I said hi."

"Duh. You're my only hope for staying on the nice list. And remember, don't do anything I wouldn't when it comes to that hunky cowboy of yours," she teases.

"Glad to know I have plenty of wriggle room." I chuckle. "Talk soon."

I put my phone on the nightstand before sinking into the pillows. With my ankle still throbbing, there's not much I can do but wait for Shep to come back. Hopefully, a few hours of rest and some painkillers and ice will ease the swelling, and I'll be walking again in a day or two. Until then, it looks like I'll have to depend on him to get by, which means more time spent together. Here's hoping I can keep my fantasies of him giving me a full-body exam in check.

CHAPTER 9

Pouty Lips And Pillow Walls

Shep

E AVESDROPPING IS WRONG, RIGHT?

I rake a hand through my hair as I stand with my ear pressed to the bedroom door. I was bringing Noelle an ice pack for her ankle but refrained from knocking when I heard voices inside. Normally, I tune people out if they're not speaking to me, but what comes from her friend's end has me hesitating—more out of shock than anything else.

"Maybe he's imagining all the ways to use them on you!"

I kept listening, stunned when I realized they were talking about me. Noelle must have figured out I stumbled across her toy collection earlier. I'd opened her suitcase to grab her phone like she instructed, and was left speechless when I found a pile of holiday-themed glittery dildos, butt plugs, and other devices.

My sunshine guest might not be as innocent as I thought. But as much as my cock disagrees, Noelle is right—nothing will happen between us. Not because I don't want it to. Fuck, the longer she's here, the more tempted I am to cross a line that could destroy the fragile balance that we've established, but my rationality prevails.

When it sounds like she's wrapping up her call, I slowly back away from the door and slip into the kitchen before she notices I was listening in.

I toss the ice pack back in the freezer and start on lunch, grabbing ingredients for grilled cheese sandwiches and a carton of tomato soup I picked up in town before the storm hit. I also swung by High Noon to handle payroll and order supplies. As the busiest tourist spot around, it's always packed before and after a storm. And with Christmas only five days away, Casey wanted to make sure we ordered enough stock for January since many vendors shut down during the last week of December.

I've just put the grilled cheese sandwiches and soup on the stove when my phone buzzes on the counter.

Birdie: Checking in. Text me back when you have service.

Shep: There was a break in the weather. I'm fine.

Birdie: Has Noelle run for the hills yet?

Shep: Told you she was only staying one night.

Birdie: She's still there, isn't she?

Shep: Maybe.

Birdie: Are you being nice?

Shep: Maybe.

Birdie: Do you like her?

Shep: Maybe.

Shit. I hit send before I can edit my response.

Birdie: I knew it!

Shep: Maybe doesn't mean yes.

Birdie: In your world it does.

Damn her for seeing right through me. Doesn't mean I'm going to confirm her suspicion.

Birdie: Don't worry, your secret is safe with me.

Shep: I have to go. I'm making lunch.

Birdie: For Noelle?!

Shep: Bye Birdie.

If she and Noelle ever got together, they'd make sure I had no peace. So it's probably a good thing that'll never happen.

I flip the grilled cheese sandwiches on the skillet and give the tomato soup another stir. It's nothing fancy, but I want to make sure Noelle eats before taking pain meds.

As I gather the tray table I keep on top of the fridge, medicine, bottled water, and a fresh ice pack, I replay the part of Noelle's conversation I overheard about the holidays. She sounded so defeated when she said she wasn't sure if she'd get to celebrate or put up a Christmas tree.

I recall her asking me whether I would decorate, but I brushed it off. I haven't done anything for the holidays in years, and until now, I haven't had a reason.

But maybe now I do.

Two pillows are tucked under my arm as I balance the tray with one hand and tap on the bedroom door with my other.

"Come in," Noelle calls out.

I enter to find her still on the bed, her injured leg stretched out in front of her, the other folded beneath her thigh. Her hair is pulled into a loose bun, and she leans against the headboard, scrolling through her phone. She's stunning with an understated elegance. Two days ago, that was a mark against her, but I've quickly grown to like her confidence and effortless charm.

She glances in my direction as I place the tray on the bedside table.

"You didn't need to knock. This is your room, and you don't need permission to come in," she says, motioning around.

"I wasn't sure if you were done talking with your friend yet." That's partly true—I caught the tail end, but they could have continued after I was out of earshot. Unlikely but possible.

"Gemma is visiting family, so I didn't want to keep her too long."

"That was considerate of you." Noelle watches as I take the pillows from under my arms and slide them under her foot. "Sorry, I forgot these earlier."

Her eyes widen. "Oh, that's okay."

Looks like she's hoping I won't mention what I saw in her bag, and that's fine by me. I'd rather not admit that I haven't stopped thinking about those toys and all the ways I could make her come without even laying a finger on her.

I lift the ice pack for her to see. "I brought this too. It'll help with the swelling." She sighs softly when I put it on her ankle, laying it flat to stay in place.

"Thank you," she whispers, relaxing against the headboard.

"No problem." I take a seat on the edge of the bed. "Mind if I ask why you're not spending the holidays with your family?"

Sadness clouds her features, yet she manages a small smile. "I'm an only child, and my parents are on a month-long European cruise. It's the first year we won't celebrate Christmas together, but they recently retired, and this is the first thing they've done for themselves in a long time. I couldn't ask them to change their plans."

"Why didn't you go with them?" Noelle doesn't strike me as someone who gives up easily on the things she values most.

"They invited me and my ex, but he wanted to stay in New York for the holidays, and after we split this past summer, it was too late for me to get a ticket."

I'm not usually the sentimental type, but I feel for her. I was close to both my parents before they passed, and even when I didn't feel like celebrating after Danielle left, my mom made sure I came over every Christmas. I didn't always show it, but I cherished that time with my parents. Not that I'm about to unload all that on Noelle right now.

"What did he do to make you end things?" I ask.

She tilts her head, smirking. "Why do you assume I was the one who left him?"

I scoff. "Even a fool wouldn't walk away from you willingly."

Noelle is beautiful, yeah, but it's more than that. Her smile lights up a room, and her presence is magnetic. She's selfless, and it's clear that she always puts others first. Plenty of guys would take advantage of that, but no one would give her up unless she walked away.

Her breath catches, a faint flush blooming across her cheeks before she squares her shoulders and says, "He cheated on me with his yoga instructor. I'm not sure if it was the first time, but I made certain it was the last."

On impulse, I cover her hand with mine, giving it a gentle squeeze. "Good on you, Sunshine. If he couldn't see what was right in front of him, then he didn't deserve you." The man is damn lucky he's not around because I wouldn't hesitate to teach him a lesson he'd never forget for hurting her.

Noelle throws her head back and laughs, the melodic sound sending a buzz through my veins.

"You're right. He wasn't worth the trouble, and has freed up space for better things," she says, her tone light but certain.

She deserves to be cherished and the center of someone's world. If she belonged to me, I'd move heaven and earth so she'd never feel second best again. For a moment, I forget I'm supposed to be looking after her because she's injured, not letting my mind wander into foolish daydreams.

She nods at the tray of food. "That smells incredible."

"It tastes even better," I say, glad for the distraction.

I let go of her hand to pick up the steaming bowl of soup and the spoon.

A look of confusion crosses Noelle's face. "What are you doing?"

"Feeding you," I state.

"I can do that myself."

She reaches for the bowl, but I pick it up and hold it just out of reach.

I give her a leveled stare. "You're supposed to be taking it easy, and I'm not willing to risk tomato soup on my comforter."

She rolls her eyes. "Seriously? I hurt my ankle, not my wrist."

Noelle's right. She's perfectly capable of feeding herself, and I couldn't care less if the comforter gets stained. It's a ten-year-old bargain from a local discount store. Still, as long as she's here, I'm going to take care of her. It's been so long since I've had the chance, and I want to do it for her.

Noelle's stomach growls, winning out over any further objections.

With a small chuckle, I bring a spoonful of soup to her lips. "Careful, it's hot," I murmur.

She blows on it before taking a bite. A soft moan escapes her mouth as she savors it, the sound going straight to my cock. Her eyes briefly flutter closed, and I take the opportunity to shift my position to hide that I'm affected by the noise.

When she swallows, I give her another spoonful, topped with a piece of grilled cheese I'd cut up and added to the soup before serving.

"Mmm, that's delicious." She leans in, eager for another bite. "I've never had grilled cheese and tomato soup served in one bowl before. It's so good."

"Glad you like it."

I'm mesmerized as Noelle wraps her lips around the spoon, letting out a satisfied hum. There's something incredibly satisfying about being the one responsible for her reaction.

She eats with fervor, and I proceed to feed her the whole bowl. As she takes the last bite, a drop of soup trickles down her chin. I'm tempted to lick it from her face, but I settle for reaching out and brushing it off with my thumb. She stills under my touch, her eyes locking with mine as I bring my thumb to my mouth and suck it clean.

I put the bowl back on the tray as Noelle holds me captive with her heated gaze. I inch forward, drawn to her like a magnet, and move my hand along the line of her jaw, each touch fueling the electric tension flowing between us. I trace the seam of her lip with my finger, and in turn, her tongue darts out, licking my thumb, her breath coming out in short gasps.

I instinctively lean closer, wishing I was teasing her pouty mouth with mine, or imagine what it might be like to have her on her knees as I feed my cock between those pretty lips.

My runaway fantasy is cut short when Noelle shifts, flinching slightly.

I pull back, frowning. "What's the matter?"

She winces as she tries to wave me off. "I'm okay. My ankle's just acting up."

Goddammit. I can't afford a distraction when she's hurting—not when I'm supposed to be taking care of her.

I turn to grab the two pills and bottle of water from the tray and hand them to her.

"Take these. They'll help with the pain." I nod to her ankle.

"Thank you." She takes the medicine and swallows it down. "Would you mind helping me to the living room? I'm a little tired, and I'd like to take a nap."

"You'll have one here." I take the bottle from her and put it back on the tray. "My bed is far more comfortable. In fact, you sleep here tonight, and I'll take the couch. It'll be much easier to keep your ankle elevated."

I won't lie—I like seeing her here in my bed. Am I playing with fire? Probably.

Despite my decidedly pathetic attempts to keep her at arm's length, I'm quickly becoming attached to Noelle, and it's a scary concept. Hell, I haven't so much as kissed a woman in ten years. At first, it was to avoid opening old wounds, but eventually, shutting myself off became second nature, and I've almost forgotten how to let someone in. Yet, with Noelle, every instinct to stay guarded has splintered, and I wonder if I'm as hardened as I thought.

She vehemently shakes her head. "No way I'm sleeping in your bed. You'd be too cramped on the couch. It's practically a loveseat. Plus, I'd feel guilty kicking you out."

"You're not. I offered," I remind her.

"You're cranky enough as it is," she says, lightly poking my chest. "I can only imagine you after a night spent on lumpy couch cushions."

I playfully swat her hand away. "Well, I draw the line at sleeping in the barn, so what do you propose? You're staying here and that's final."

Noelle twists a lock of hair around her finger, thinking for a beat before saying, "Simple. We'll share."

There's no way I heard her right. "Come again?"

"There's plenty of room for both of us, and enough pillows to make a barrier if you're worried I'll invade your space," she says with a grin.

It's a terrible idea. I should be finding ways to stop thinking about ravishing those pink, pouty lips or how she'd feel beneath my touch as I traced her every curve.

So why haven't I told her no yet?

Because no matter how difficult it is to restrain myself, I can't pass up the chance to be close to her, especially if it's my only chance before she's gone. And like she said, we'll be on opposite sides of the bed with a pillow wall, so it's totally innocent. Right?

"Fine, we'll share the bed." I keep my tone neutral. "But that means you'll stay put and ask me to get anything you need. Your only job is to rest your ankle, got it?"

"I can live with that," she says, smiling brightly.

Fuck, I'm in so much trouble.

CHAPTER 10

Rockin' Around The Kissmas Tree

Noelle

WHEN MY EYES FLUTTER OPEN, THE ROOM IS DARK. Nothing but a sliver of light comes through the gap beneath the door. I check my phone to see it's 7:17 p.m. and can't believe I slept through the afternoon.

I sink deeper into the pillows, breathing in the familiar scent of musk and leather. Maybe I should be mortified that I'm in Shep's bed, but I rather like it. I clench my thighs at the thought of having him beside me later tonight. We're tiptoeing dangerously close to the edge of temptation, but that didn't stop me from making the suggestion.

Somewhere between being cradled in his arms and him feeding me lunch, I concluded that our brewing attraction is mutual and couldn't let the opportunity pass. Maybe it was Gemma teasing me about wanting Shep or knowing that he might have discovered my toys that gave me the courage to act. Regardless, it won't deter me from seeing how this plays out.

However, I've got more pressing matters to address—like my ankle throbbing from rolling over in my sleep, my full bladder, and a warm bath calling my name. I'm tempted to call for Shep like I promised, but I decide against it. I'm already imposing. Besides, he's probably in the barn checking on the animals or in his workshop.

Determined to do this on my own, I switch on the lamp and slowly swing my legs over the edge of the bed, pressing my palms into the mattress for support. I push to stand, a sharp cry escaping my lips as pain shoots through my ankle, and I sink onto the bed, leaning back on my hands with a groan.

Within seconds, hurried footsteps reach the door, and Shep bursts in, panic etched on his face as his eyes find me.

"What's wrong?" He rushes to my side, his gaze sweeping me from head to toe. "Are you hurt?"

I shake my head. "I tried to stand so I could get to the bathroom to take a bath, but it was painful so I'm nervous to try and put pressure on my ankle again."

He folds his arms across his chest, frowning. "You should've called for me."

"I wanted to do it on my own."

"Why do you insist on being so hardheaded?" he mutters under his breath.

I straighten my spine. "Oh, please. If it were the other way around, you'd drag yourself to the bathroom before letting me step in."

Shep scoffs. "I wouldn't be in this situation, because I would've listened when you told me to get off that rickety stool."

I roll my eyes. "Bullshit. You're way more stubborn than I am."

"Dammit, woman, I'm half tempted to bend you over my knee." His face drains of color when he realizes he spoke out loud.

God, the thought of it sends heat racing through me, thinking of being bent over his strong thighs, and the feel of his calloused hands on me… inside me… punishing me.

His eyes lock on mine, all the unspoken words lingering between us. I fidget with my bracelet, noting the blush covering his face, refusing to be the one to break eye contact first.

Shep clears his throat before effortlessly lifting me into his arms. I cling to his neck as he carries me to the bathroom, savoring the warmth of his embrace and his masculine scent. His tight, long-sleeved shirt stretches across his broad chest, emphasizing the curve of his biceps. My eyes shift to the patch of hair peeking out above the open button at his collar, and my fingers itch to trace along his bare chest, trailing down to his V-line in teasing strokes.

When we reach the bathroom, he shifts his hold on me to hit the light switch, gently setting me on the closed toilet lid.

The walls are slate gray, and the space smells faintly of pine and soap. A porcelain sink is set into the countertop with an oval mirror hanging above, and a shower-tub combo positioned next to the toilet.

"Thank you… Aren't you going to leave?" I ask when Shep doesn't move.

"Figured you might need a hand preparing the bath." He nods to the cabinet, likely holding toiletries needed. "Not sure how you'd manage on your own, seeing as you can't stand."

I roll my lip between my teeth, overwhelmed by the flood of emotions crashing over me. I could try it alone, but the faucet is out of reach, and the flimsy towel rack won't support my weight. It'll be much easier with help—especially with a scalding bath calling my name.

My eyes dart to Shep, who patiently waits for my reply. The concern in his expression makes my cheeks flush—not from embarrassment, but from the fact that he cares enough to make this easier for me.

"Help preparing a bath would be nice, thank you," I say quietly.

"How hot do you want the water?" he asks.

"Hot enough to rival a volcanic spring and leave me looking like a lobster," I offer with a cheeky grin.

Shep chuckles under his breath, nodding. "Let's compromise and go with toasty, no lava burns included."

I drum my finger against my chin. "I think that could work."

He moves to the tub and turns on the faucet until steam begins to rise. After testing the water with his hand, he nods in approval and plugs the drain. He reaches for a bottle of three-in-one body wash from the corner shelf and pours in a generous amount. A swirl of cedar and mint fills the air as bubbles rise to the surface.

I make a note to order him some real shampoo, conditioner, and body wash, assuming deliveries exist on the mountain.

Shep shifts around me to the cabinet, retrieves a fresh towel beneath the sink, and places it on the vanity.

He glances back and forth between me and the rising bathwater, concern in his expression. "You need anything else?"

"I'll make do, cowboy, I promise."

He gives me a hesitant nod as he turns off the faucet. "Give me a holler if you need anything."

"I will."

He gives me a simple nod before stepping out and closing the door behind him.

After some careful maneuvering to get my pants and underwear off, I take care of business before slipping my shirt over my head and unfasten my bra. I drop both to the floor and ease myself from the toilet to the tub, wincing when my ankle grazes the porcelain. As I lower myself into the hot water, I sigh with relief, the heat easing the tension in my body.

As I start to relax, it hits me that I never thanked Shep for his help. I'm mortified that he went out of his way, and I didn't even acknowledge it.

Before I can think better of it, I holler, "Hey Shep."

I don't expect a reply, assuming he's gone off to do something else while he waits until I'm done, so I'm surprised when he answers.

"You alright?" His voice drifts from the other side of the closed door. "Once you're finished, I'll bring you some clean clothes to change into."

I grin, knowing he stayed close in case I needed him.

"I'm fine. I just forgot to say thank you. I really appreciate your help."

"Anytime, Sunshine."

I lean back and close my eyes, thinking about everything that's happened today. I can't imagine what I would've done if anyone other than Shep had been here. I feel lucky to have glimpsed a part of him he rarely shows. His patience and thoughtfulness have my heart swelling with gratitude, and it makes me want him more than ever before.

Shep carries me to the living room after I finish in the bathroom, gently putting me in the middle of the couch. Flames dance in the fireplace, filling the space with warmth. A TV has been set up in the corner, angled for me to watch from where I'm sitting.

"What's that for?" I ask, gesturing to it.

"I thought we could watch a Christmas movie," he suggests.

My eyebrows shoot up in surprise. "Really? I thought you didn't celebrate the holidays."

"I haven't for a while, but there's no reason I can't start again now." He turns on the TV and holds a DVD case to show me. "*Elf* okay? It's one of the only seasonal movies I have."

"It's one of my favorites," I say with a grin. "The best way to spread Christmas cheer is singing loud for all to hear."

As a kid, my parents and I watched a holiday movie every night from the start of December until Christmas Day. I tried keeping the tradition going after I moved out, but once my career took off, I'd been lucky to squeeze in one or two each year. That's why I treasure spending Christmastime with my family. Even condensed into a few short days, the holiday magic remains, carrying the nostalgia of the traditions I cherish.

It's a stark reminder that had my solo trip gone as planned, I'd probably be lying on the bed in tears or halfway back to New York by now. Instead, I'm sharing a cabin with a chivalrous cowboy, wondering if this is where I was supposed to be all along.

Shep switches on the TV and scrolls to the main menu. "I put an egg and sausage casserole in the oven while you were taking a bath. It'll be ready in half an hour."

"Smells amazing. I love breakfast for dinner."

He picks up two pillows from the leather chair in the corner, which he must have grabbed while I was in the bathroom. He sets them on the coffee table and then pushes it closer to me, giving me a place to prop my foot.

"Thank you," I murmur.

Shep lays a hand on my knee, giving it a gentle squeeze. "It's nothing."

But it really *is* something.

He saw a way to make me more comfortable and acted without asking—a rare quality. The attention and kindness he's shown me is unlike anything I've seen before. I like to think it comes from his life experience and a deep understanding of how to respect a woman without expecting anything in return. Beneath his gruff exterior lies a genuine decency that only adds to his appeal.

"Hey, Shep?"

"Mm-hmm?"

"Is there a reason you don't celebrate the holidays?"

He's slowly opening up so I have to tread carefully. He's like a wounded wolf, sizing me up to see if I'm a friend or a foe. If I push him too hard, he'll retreat, and I might not get him to let his guard down if that happens.

He takes a seat next to me, leaning against the armrest. "A small part is due to my ex-fiancée turning Christmas into a big production. It was about the extravagant decorations, one-upping the neighbors, and expecting expensive gifts. After she moved to the big city, I realized all that shit was meaningless."

No wonder Shep was apprehensive when I showed up on his doorstep—a city girl who reminded him of the woman who must have stomped on his heart and never looked back. I have so many more questions, but I am once again wary of spooking him.

"After Danielle left, I spent the holidays with my folks," he continues. "Ma loved this time of year, and for her, it was about spreading joy and kindness. She loved donating to the local food pantry and organizing a Secret Santa for the local homeless shelter to make sure everyone experienced a little magic that season." A small smile tugs at the corners of his mouth.

"Your mom's got it figured out. This time of year should be about family and giving back to the community. Some of my favorite traditions are ice skating at Rockefeller Square and picking out gifts for kids who could use a little holiday magic."

"Every Christmas morning, Ma invited the whole block over for her homemade French toast, and we'd go caroling in the surrounding towns with neighbors." The warmth in his tone is unmistakable.

I tilt my head, blinking rapidly. "*You* willingly sang to strangers? I find that hard to believe."

Shep shrugs. "When I was a kid, my dad said Santa might leave me coal if I didn't participate. So I guess you could say I was coerced." The fine lines around his eyes deepen as he laughs, making him look even more handsome. "As an adult, I did it because it brought my mom joy, making it worthwhile, even if my singing probably scared off a few people over the years."

I laugh softly. "Your parents sound like amazing people. Do they live in Pine Haven?"

He lowers his eyes, sadness written across his features. "They passed a few years ago, just six months apart." My heart aches for him, imagining a life without my own parents.

I lean against his shoulder, my hand settling on his chest. It feels right comforting him this way, and the urge to touch him outweighs all logic.

"I'm so sorry, Shep."

He surprises me by resting his head against mine. "Thanks, Sunshine. The holidays were never the same without them, ya know?"

"I can't even begin to imagine," I whisper.

It breaks my heart that he's been hurting for so long. I wish I could somehow restore the magic of Christmas for him, as a reminder of the cherished memories with his parents. No one should be sad during a season meant for joy and happiness.

"I don't talk about them much, but they were good people," Shep says.

"Of course they were. They raised you."

His eyes widen just briefly before he blinks, swallowing hard. "They did their best, but I tested every boundary."

I fake a gasp. "*You* were difficult? I'm shocked."

"Look who's talking, Miss I-argue-about-everything-even-when-it's-for-my-own-good," he counters with a chuckle. "No question you gave your parents hell too."

I peer up at him. "Guess that makes us evenly matched."

He strokes my cheek, warmth shining in his eyes. "I think you might be right."

I reflexively lean into his touch, closing my eyes against the gentle pressure of his hand.

Being with Shep is beginning to feel effortless. There are no expectations to act a particular way or need to steer clear of sensitive topics for fear of offending him. Rather, I'm free to be my talkative, over-enthusiastic, slightly clumsy self, and he matches me in every playful exchange—giving as good as he gets.

Earlier, I started searching for places to stay once the weather clears. My feelings on the matter have shifted since I got here, and though I want to further discuss it with Shep, I'm afraid his reaction will differ from mine and leave me disappointed.

There's only one way to find out.

I open my eyes to find him watching me. "I checked the weather app earlier, and the storm should fully clear in the next couple of days," I remind him as a pit forms in my stomach. "Would you mind giving me a ride into town once it's safe to drive down the mountain? I'll have to arrange for a tow truck to get the convertible."

Shep mentioned that the road to his cabin is one of the last to be plowed after a snowstorm since there are no other houses nearby. He keeps a four-wheel-drive truck equipped with snow tires and chains. It makes me think he knew I couldn't leave after that first night—yet he let me stay anyway.

He visibility stiffens beside me. "Where are you going to stay?"

I straighten in my seat to face him. "I'm not sure. I checked, and every hotel and vacation rental in Pine Haven is booked for the holidays, so I was thinking of heading back to Phoenix or returning to New York early."

Truthfully, neither option feels right, and thinking of spending Christmas alone leaves a hollow ache in my chest. Even if I stayed with Shep and we treated it as a typical day, that would be enough. I hate thinking about him alone on this mountain and would give anything to stay longer.

"Is that what you want?" Shep asks as if he can see straight through me.

"I'm not sure," I confess, scared to voice the truth.

Two days ago, I was counting down the hours until I could leave this cabin. Now, I'm secretly hoping for another storm to keep me here.

"You could stick around and spend Christmas here. Maple's taken a shine to you and would be mighty disappointed if you left without visiting her again." He takes off his hat, holding it to his chest as he rakes a hand through his hair. "But if you're set on leaving, I'll take you wherever you want."

He won't meet my gaze, and his lips are pressed into a thin line. Could he be… *anxious*?

My pulse quickens, and I question whether I'm reading him right, yet his reaction confirms it. It's not Maple who doesn't want me to leave—it's Shep.

I place my hand over his, easing the hat from his grasp, and setting it on the coffee table. I turn back to him, noticing his shallow breathing and shoulders tight with tension, betraying his worry that I might decline his offer to stay.

I graze my knuckle along his cheek as I whisper, "Do you want me to stay for Christmas?"

Please say yes.

He slowly lifts his eyes to meet mine. "I do."

I give him a soft smile, letting my fingers trace along the gray streaks at his temple. "Is that the only thing you want, Shep?"

I move closer until our faces are only inches apart. His muscles tense under my touch, and he grabs hold of the armrest like it's the only thing keeping his self-control in check.

"Noelle, what are you doing?" His voice is hoarse.

I probably shouldn't tease him, but seeing the effect I have, combined with the fact that we're snowed in together, makes me ache to have his hands on me. I won't relent until he surrenders to the sparks igniting between us.

My gaze flicks to his mouth. "Do you want to kiss me, cowboy?"

His chest rises and falls rapidly as he tightens his grip on the armrest.

"It's alright if you do." I lean in, brushing my lips along the edge of his mouth.

The room pulses with the hum of our mingled breaths.

"You're trouble, woman," he growls.

"Only the fun kind," I whisper back.

He cups my chin, letting his fingers glide along my jawline. "Kissing is a bad idea."

"The very worst."

His usually cold expression is replaced with an undeniable simmering hunger that radiates desire.

"Good thing I don't shy away from bad ideas, darlin'."

He closes the remaining distance between us to claim me with a possessive kiss that makes it impossible to think straight. The tip of his tongue glides across my lips, and he lets out a low growl when I open my mouth and welcome him inside. He lifts me into his lap, swinging my legs over the armrest, careful not to further injure my ankle. I weave my fingers through his hair, dragging him closer as our kiss deepens.

"Fuck, I'd have kissed you sooner if I knew you'd taste this sweet," Shep groans.

I couldn't agree more. His mouth on mine is a revelation—euphoric, primal, consuming. I've never experienced anything like it before.

Whatever restraint he had left snaps as his hand roams along the line of my waist. He rocks against me, his hard cock rubbing against my thigh. My nipples grow achy, and my body hums with longing, wishing I could straddle him.

I'm on the verge of begging him to take my clothes off when the timer in the kitchen goes off.

I blink rapidly, awareness sinking in, as I'm met with Shep's heated gaze. His hair is tousled from my grip, and his striking brown eyes study me closely, gauging my reaction. His chest heaves like he's just run a marathon, and his pupils are dilated.

I instinctively brush my fingers against my bee-stung lips.

Oh my god.

I just kissed Shep, and it was better than I could have imagined.

After a few seconds, the timer goes silent and when he speaks, his voice is low and gravelly.

"You better not regret that kiss, Sunshine. It was damn good." He repositions me in his lap, holding me tight as if he's afraid I'll disappear. "Fuck, all I want is to take you to bed, spread you out, and taste you everywhere." My thighs clench, betraying my body's overwhelming longing.

I want that more than anything. But as he speaks, I sense him withdrawing. His shoulders stiffen, his hands falling to his side as he lowers his gaze.

"But?" I ask softly, encouraging him to finish.

With a heavy sigh, he presses his forehead against mine, eyes closed as he breathes me in. "You'll be gone in a few days, and odds are I'll never see you again."

The possibility that this might be the only time our paths will ever cross makes my stomach twist. He'd never visit New York, and I don't have any plans to return to the Southwest anytime soon.

"People have casual hookups all the time…" I say, letting my words trail off.

He leans back to look at me. "Have you ever had one?"

"No," I confess.

I prefer an authentic connection before getting physical with someone. In the past, the path was plagued with uncertainty and second-guessing, and I ultimately walked away after trusting the wrong men. With Shep, things have moved at breakneck speed, but no warning bells go off when I picture a night in his bed where we're doing anything but sleeping. Our bodies a tangle of limbs, unable to be discerned one from the other.

I'm tired of playing it safe and not taking what I want when the opportunity presents itself. Right now, all I want is Shep, even if our time is limited.

"I've never had a one-night stand either." He rubs my back in soothing circles. "Call me old-fashioned, but I'm a commitment kind of guy. And I'm not strong enough to sleep with you only to have to pretend that it doesn't mean anything when you walk away."

"Oh," is all I can manage in response, taken aback at his declaration.

"You're the kind of woman I'd never want to let go of. Just being near you makes me want more," he says, tucking a stray hair behind my ear. "One night and I'd be hooked."

What he doesn't say out loud is that he's afraid of getting hurt. I'm just another city girl leaving him behind in a few short days. I value his honesty, and above all, I want to make the most of the time we have left getting to know each other. With mutual attraction simmering between us and being in such close quarters, keeping things platonic will be a tall order.

"I guess that means we shouldn't kiss again, huh?"

His gaze drops to my mouth. "I wouldn't be able to stop if we did."

"It was a good kiss," I say softly.

"The best damn kiss, Sunshine." He leans forward to kiss the tip of my nose. "Had to sneak in one more before my next dry spell."

"I'm glad you did," I say softly.

Shep gives me a soft smile before lifting me off his lap and setting me on the couch cushion. He leans over to prop my foot on the pillows before putting his hat back on and standing.

"Noelle."

"Yeah?"

"I'm really glad you're staying for Christmas."

I brush my fingers across my mouth, giving him a wistful smile. "Me too, cowboy."

"I'm going to go check to make sure I didn't burn the casserole, and then we're going to watch *Elf* like I said we would," he says, smoothing down his mustache.

"Can't wait." As much as I want to kiss him again, I'm excited to make a holiday memory together.

Shep makes it easy to let my guard down and to be myself, which is why I have a hunch one of us will eventually give in completely. How can our relationship remain strictly platonic while staying under the same roof after that scorching kiss?

CHAPTER 11

Dirty Dreams And A Blue Ball Christmas

Shep

SHARING A BED WITH A GORGEOUS WOMAN, KNOWING what she tastes like, is pure fucking torture. Anyone who says otherwise is already getting laid.

Being this close to Noelle is testing every ounce of my self-control, especially after our mind-melting kiss earlier this evening. I had hoped that giving in to a moment of weakness would quiet my desire for her, but it has only fanned the flames. I'm transfixed by the memory of her fingers tangled in my hair and her soft lips pressed against mine.

A selfish part of me wishes I'd thrown caution to the wind and ignored all the reasons I shouldn't want her. But I have to remember that after Christmas, she'll return to New York, where countless subscribers will hang on every word as she tells the story of being stranded for the holidays. I cringe to think what they might think about her staying with a much older man she just met. Now I sound like Noelle, concerned with what strangers might think when I couldn't give a shit.

The undeniable truth is that I've grown fond of having her in my space, and if I surrender to my growing obsession, I'll only set myself up for a cycle of longing and regret once she leaves.

My cock clearly hasn't gotten the memo, since I woke up consumed by lust. It's pressed against my boxers, pulsing with need for the woman beside me, consequences be damned.

I glance at the clock on the nightstand and groan when I see it's 3:05 a.m. I rarely wake up with a hard-on in the middle of the night, but I'm only human. It's impossible to control my reaction to Noelle curled against me in nothing but her tank top and skimpy shorts. She claimed it was too hot for sweats and a T-shirt, but I swear she knew the effect they'd have on me. I didn't miss her staring while we were getting ready for bed, her gaze drifting to my mouth as she bit her lower lip. She seems intent on teasing me, unaffected by the same battle to keep her guard up that I'm losing.

The moon's silver light shines through the curtains, casting a soft glow in the darkened room. Noelle's leg is draped over my hip, and her head rests on my bare chest. Shortly after she fell asleep, she migrated to my side of the bed, and I wasn't strong enough to move her away. The pillows I'd put between us didn't stand a chance and are now scattered across the floor.

The responsible choice would've been to sleep on the couch, but I allowed myself this one indulgence, soaking in her warmth before she's gone. I checked the forecast last night, and it should be clear enough for a trip into town within the next couple of days. Noelle may have agreed to stay through Christmas, but I worry she'll rethink it once she's back in civilization and no longer stuck with a cranky recluse. So I'm holding on to this moment before it slips away.

I circle my arm around her waist, and my hand rests on her skin where her tank top has lifted, fighting the urge to move it past her waistband. Since I've been awake, she's been restless, twitching every so often.

When she shifts again, her thigh brushes against my dick. She mumbles incoherently, and I take in a sharp breath as she grinds against my leg, her breasts rubbing against my bare chest as she moves against me in a steady rhythm.

My cock jerks when her moans fill the room as she rides my leg. It seems I'm not the only one who woke up sexually frustrated. I stifle a groan when Noelle picks up her pace, heat from her body radiating through the fabric between us.

From this angle, I can't see her face. I assume she's teasing me again, and it's fucking working.

She digs her nails into my arm. "Shep," she whimpers.

"Noelle," I rasp against her neck.

The last ounce of my strength breaks when she clenches around my leg. I push my thigh against her core, giving her the pressure she's searching for. My fingers wander to the waistband of her shorts when she tips her head back with a low moan, giving me an unobstructed view of her face in the dim light.

Her lips are parted, and frustration consumes me when I see that her eyes are shut.

Fuck. She's not teasing, I think she's dreaming.

I reluctantly move my hand. I'd like nothing more than to make Noelle come, but not like this.

Though I can't claim her the way I want to, I'm not going to stop her from finding the release she's aching for. After all, I'm a man who believes a woman should experience pleasure on her own terms, even in her dreams.

Noelle shifts beside me as she searches for more friction. She arches her neck, peppering kisses along my neck, her breath skating across my skin. I grit my teeth, finding the will to keep one hand at my side and the other above her head in a clenched fist.

It's been over a decade since I last slept with a woman, and just the thought of sinking into Noelle's wet pussy has me hard as granite.

Moonlight filters through the window, illuminating her hand slipping between her parted thighs. The crude sound of her fingers entering her pussy echoes throughout the room as she pushes in and out in steady strokes.

Noelle's breathing comes out in shallow bursts, the faint light catching the thin sheen of sweat at her collarbone. She's fucking stunning with her hair fanned around her like a halo, her lashes flickering as she mutters something unintelligible in her sleep.

I watch mesmerized as a raspy moan passes her lips as she drives her fingers in with fast, urgent surges. Her face is scrunched up with frustration as she struggles to climax, flipping on her back to find a better angle.

It's apparent that whatever she's dreaming about isn't enough to push her over the edge. At this rate, it'll take a miracle for her to find her release, and I wish more than anything I could intervene.

She lets out a sharp huff of breath, and before I can move, Noelle goes rigid, her eyes snapping open. She blinks rapidly, adjusting to the dim glow, hesitantly glancing between me and her hand still pressed between her thighs. Her eyes widen as she scrambles to sit up, leaning over to turn on the bedside lamp.

Her cheeks are flushed crimson. "Please tell me you just woke up too."

I prop myself up on one elbow, grimacing. "It's hard to sleep with you pressed against me, crying out my name."

"Oh god." She tips her head, watching me as she processes. "Did I hump you too?"

"You did."

She groans into her hands. "I was hoping that part was a dream."

I sit up and move to her side of the bed, drawing her into

my lap. "There's nothing to be ashamed of. It's a natural reaction when you're sexually frustrated."

It might be better if I gave her space, but not comforting her feels wrong. I tell myself it's all for her, though deep down it's for me too. I can't deny that I want her here in my arms.

She frowns. "Why would you assume I'm sexually frustrated?"

"Because maybe I am too," I confess, trailing my thumb along her jaw. "Not to mention, our kiss left you wanting more. Unless of course you snuck one of your toys into bed while I was in the shower before we turned in for the night, and that's why you were having a hard time getting off just now."

Her mouth falls open, and she jabs a finger into my chest. "I was right. You *did* find them in my luggage."

"Sunshine, anyone with eyes would have. You've got a collection that'd make even a dominatrix blush."

"They're not mine," she blurts.

I arch a brow. "And who exactly is packing dildos and butt plugs in your suitcase without your permission?"

She nibbles on her bottom lip, looking at me through hooded eyes. "They're from a PR company that's going to advertise on my podcast next month. I wanted to test their products beforehand."

Even knowing this was supposed to be her solo trip, relief washes over me, confirming that she hadn't planned to use them with another man. I'm not sure what my reaction would have been if she had. Sharing a bed with her must be going to my head. I don't have the right to dictate her choices, even if my territorial instincts disagree.

"Have you… tried them out yet?" I'm only torturing myself for asking, but I have to know.

She casts me a sidelong glance while pretending to pluck lint off my flannel. "Not yet. I haven't exactly had a chance."

"Do you use toys often?" I force my voice to remain casual.

She shakes her head. "Let's just say the guys I've dated weren't enthusiastic about adding toys into our sex life, and I didn't use them much when I was single."

I trail my fingers down her thigh in slow circles. "A real man would be confident enough in himself to explore his partner's sexuality along with her."

"Is that so?" Noelle shifts in my lap so she's straddling me, moving slowly to protect her injured ankle. She leans in, looping her arms around my neck. "Would you play with me, cowboy? If we were having that fling you said we couldn't have, would you teach me how to use a vibrator together?"

Fuck. Me.

I slip my fingers in her hair at the base of her neck. "I'd use your toys to fill every. Fucking. Hole."

"Which ones?" she pants.

"I'd start with a plug to get you nice and primed for me."

Nolle moans, her pupils dilated. "No one's ever taken me there before."

I nearly come undone, knowing I'd be the first to claim her ass. I'd make it so damn good and ruin her for every city boy who comes after me.

"The things I could teach you, baby girl," I say like a promise.

I brush my lips against hers in slow strokes, and another soft moan slips from her mouth. I'm careful to not kiss her fully, only giving her a taste.

"We can't kiss again, remember," she whispers.

"Definitely not," I choke out.

Noelle glances down where my cock strains against my sweatpants. I inhale sharply when she moves her hand between us, tracing the outline of my dick. A guttural groan passes my lips when she moves her fingers in a circular motion, teasing me. Even with the material between her hand and me, I'm struggling to keep from coming. It's been so damn long, and controlling my physical reaction is a losing battle the longer she taunts me.

"You're so big," she murmurs.

The last of my restraint evaporates, and I put my hand over hers, pushing our joined fingers firmly against my hard-on. "Feel what you do to me, baby."

Noelle gazes up at me with a mischievous glint in her eye. "Are you sure you don't want to have a one-night stand?" she asks with doe eyes, nipping at my bottom lip, her hand still on my cock. "I've never been with an older man, or someone so big. I'm not even sure it would fit."

Holy shit.

My mind short-circuits, her words striking like lightning and I want nothing more than to give in and show her what she's been missing.

Just as my mouth parts, ready to give in and welcome Noelle in for a taste, she pulls back.

"On second thought, you're right. I think hooking up is a terrible idea." A groan escapes me as she withdraws her hand from my cock, and climbs off me. She moves back to her side of the bed, propping up her ankle, before shutting off the light. "Good night, cowboy."

I'm left staring into the dark, half convinced I must have imagined that. The woman just made me almost whimper like a damn dog begging for its favorite bone.

That's when it hits me, sitting in the silence, how close I came to giving in. There's no denying that Noelle has occupied my every waking thought since she got here. Fuck, she's plagued my dreams too. Trouble is, she's given no indication she plans to stay beyond the day after Christmas. To her, this is just a vacation, an escape from her usual routine. I'm merely a novelty she doesn't have in the city, and within a few days she's prepared to pack her suitcase and leave without a second glance.

She's unforgettable, and giving in would mean losing myself

to her completely. It would cost me someone else who's important to me, but this time, I'm not sure I'd survive it.

It should be as simple as restraining myself. The problem is Noelle is addictive as hell, and I'm running out of willpower to resist claiming every inch of her when she begs for every dirty thing I want to teach her.

CHAPTER 12

A Little Jealousy Might Do Him Good

Noelle

TWO DAYS LATER

SHEP HAS BEEN AN ATTENTIVE CAREGIVER FOR THE PAST couple of days. He's made sure I take painkillers at regular intervals, kept my leg elevated, and cooked all of our meals. Luckily, my ankle has healed quickly, and as of this morning I was able to walk on it without hurting.

The downside of being holed up for two extra days is that Shep's kept his word about not kissing me—let alone doing anything else. It wouldn't be so challenging if we weren't together practically all day and night. He's let me tag along to visit the animals and hang out in his woodshop.

The only time we've been apart was this afternoon when he was putting the last touches on the rocking chair while I responded to a flood of emails. I decided to tackle as many as I could so Gemma wouldn't be overwhelmed when she returns from vacation after the holidays. Not to my surprise there were multiple emails from CoreFuel Labs, the health and wellness advertiser that's been giving us grief about taking time off from posting new podcast episodes.

Between the bad weather and my ankle, I haven't had a chance to edit the prerecorded episodes I planned to post through the end of the year. I explained the situation and let them know my next video will go up a couple of days after Christmas. It was a difficult decision to make considering I'm a chronic people pleaser and don't like letting anyone down, especially where business is concerned. But in this instance, I had to prioritize myself, and that meant making the most of my time with Shep.

The mountain road was finally plowed this morning, and with the weather cleared up, he surprised me by taking me into town.

"What do you think of Pine Haven?" Shep asks from the driver's seat.

It's dark as we drive, Main Street glowing under strings of twinkling white lights draped from the lampposts. Every shop window is dressed for the season with holiday murals, and each door has a wreath with red velvet bows. In the middle of the town square, a towering pine tree is decorated with rope garland, hand-painted wooden horseshoes, cowboy boots, and deer, and topped with a matching star. It's nearly the size of the one in Rockefeller Center—an impressive feat for a small town in Arizona.

I press my nose against the glass to get a better look. "It's so pretty. The Western theme for the tree is so fitting, and those ornaments are stunning."

"The city council picked the theme, but I made them," Shep tells me.

I spin to face him, my mouth falling open in surprise. It's no secret he's a master woodworker, but I didn't anticipate him investing his talent into a project for a holiday he's not fond of.

"You made *all* those?" I motion to the tree now in the rear-view mirror. "There has to be at least fifty."

His eyes remain fixed on the road ahead. "Actually, there's a hundred and twenty. The mayor wanted forty of each for some reason."

"Wow." I let out a low whistle. "You must keep busy with your woodworking business."

He shakes his head. "Nah, I mostly make things for folks in town, free of charge."

Shep owns the local honky-tonk, but I assume the margins are low in such a small town. I'm sure he could make more selling his furniture, so why skip out on a big payday?

"My parents were close with the mayor and the city council, so it's a good way to give back to the community in their honor," he explains, running his fingers along his mustache. "For me, woodworking isn't about the money—it's about doing work I love, and it's even better when it's for someone who appreciates it."

I'm floored by his generosity. He keeps to himself on the mountain, hiding behind an indifferent front, yet underneath, he's a man who serves others unconditionally. I think back over the past few days. Not once has he hinted that I owe him for letting me stay. If anything, he's gone out of his way to look after me because he genuinely cares. Even at his grumpiest, he's never been outright cruel or criticized me for the mistakes that led me to his cabin.

At the edge of town, we pull into a full parking lot next to a large barn. Cedar hitching posts line the porch, and neon cactus and boots hang above a metal sign that says *High Noon*. There's even a Christmas tree at the entrance strung with colorful lights, silver tinsel, and the same wooden ornaments as the tree in town, but on a smaller scale.

"You make those too?" I tease.

"I was strong-armed into that project," Shep mutters. "Casey's wife was set on having a tree out front even though I reminded her that people come for the drinks and live music, not holiday displays."

"Hate to break it to you, but she's right, cowboy." I lean over, giving his arm a nudge. "It's nice to see it, especially for those far from home and yearning for Christmas cheer."

I was hoping we'd get to town before the shops closed so I could find a few decorations for the cabin, but Shep was busy in his workshop finishing Casey's rocking chair.

We also had to stop by the barn and feed the animals before going down the mountain. There's no chance the convertible would have made it. Even with the roads cleared, they're still slick with patches of ice along the switchbacks. It's a miracle I made it up during the storm as it is.

On the ride into town, I had time to reflect. I see now that my fixation on the tangible trappings of Christmas has made me forget the real reason I feel so much loss—being without my family. Yet, here with Shep, I've found a peace I wouldn't have if I were alone, and I've come to accept that even without a Christmas tree or decorations, there's still joy to be found in the season.

The low rumble of the engine stops when Shep pulls into a parking spot at the back of the lot.

"Stay put," he orders as he climbs out.

He circles the front of the truck and opens my door, offering his hand to help me down.

"Aww, you're my knight in rugged denim," I say with a playful smile.

"Someone's gotta keep an eye on you. You're begging to catch a cold in that outfit." He throws his arm around my shoulder, shielding me from the wind.

If it were up to Shep, I'd be wearing his sweats and flannel sweater. Instead, I chose a red knee-length dress with puffed sleeves that I packed for my trip. It's more fitting for a warm summer afternoon than a frigid winter night, but I refuse to meet his friends like I just rolled out of bed—even with the chilly air nipping at my ankles. It's a good thing we'll be indoors for the rest of the evening.

Shep draws me closer as he ushers us toward the entrance. I melt into his touch, resting my head against his chest. My nipples tighten under my dress at the memory of waking up pressed against him two nights ago while I touched myself. I'd been lost in a dream about our kiss, except it didn't end there. He'd turned me to face the TV, my back to his front, telling me not to make a sound as he slipped his hand inside my pants, fucking me with his fingers while he peppered my neck with kisses. Just as I was on the verge of coming, I woke up, hit with the reality that it was nothing more than a dream, and the ache between my legs was all too real.

An ache blooms in my core, and I wish I would have had a chance to use one of my toys before we left the cabin. Worse, I can't shake the idea of Shep using one with me—a vibrator in my pussy as he fucks me in the ass.

I'm relieved when we reach the building. The doors swing open, and the warmth washes over me, banishing the cold and my dirty thoughts.

We enter a foyer where we're surrounded by people and the low hum of conversation. A hostess stands behind a small podium, checking tickets. Dozens of posters promoting upcoming bands cover the wall behind her. I recognize several as famous country groups, and almost every poster is marked "Sold Out" with red stickers. It has me doubting my earlier assumptions about Shep's success.

He places his hand on my lower back, guiding me along the edge of the entrance. The hostess starts to scold him for cutting in line but freezes when she recognizes Shep.

"S-sorry, boss. Go right in," she stammers.

Even his employee is intimidated by his presence. It's

probably a good thing he has someone else managing his business because his interpersonal skills could use some work.

Shep lets out a disgruntled huff before ushering me through a set of oak doors leading into the main area. It's just past seven, but the place is swarming with people. There's a big dance hall with a raised stage in front where a band plays country music as couples spin across the polished floor. Tables line the back half of the converted barn, packed with patrons watching the show from a distance. Servers thread through the crowd with trays of food and drinks, while the bar along the left-hand side is lined with people who couldn't get a seat.

The room is a sea of cowboy hats, boots, and full country attire. I frown, glancing down at my dress and sneakers, instantly feeling out of place. Shep vetoed my wedges despite my ankle being better, and the only other option I had was the sneakers I packed.

Shep leans in to whisper, "You okay?"

Goose bumps ripple across the nape of my neck as the tickle of his mustache brushes against the shell of my ear.

"I'm the only one here not wearing boots or a hat," I note.

His eyes roam over me, slow and deliberate. "Not much I can do about the boots. You'd be tripping over in mine, and I'm not letting you twist another ankle. But I do have a solution to your other problem." He takes off his hat and puts it on my head, adjusting the brim so it stays in place. "There. Now you fit right in." Shep fixes me with the same look he gets when I'm wearing his clothes—possessive with a touch of ownership.

I rise on my toes, pressing a kiss to his cheek. "Mighty kind of you, cowboy."

I wish he'd throw caution to the wind and give in to this thing between us already.

We both know it's inevitable.

Shep's gaze holds mine as his thumb grazes my bottom lip. "You're so damn beautiful," he murmurs.

My heart hammers against my ribs as he leans in closer, cupping my cheeks. His darkened gaze flicks to my mouth, and I sense he's teetering on the brink of letting go of the restraint he's been clinging to—when suddenly, a loud voice from behind him startles me.

"Look who finally decided to show up. I was beginning to think you might not come off that mountain until after Christmas."

"Dammit, Casey," Shep mumbles low enough so only I can hear.

The man in question comes into view behind Shep. Loose curls of sandy-blond hair spill out from beneath his wide-brimmed hat. His cream-colored shirt and leather vest are paired with dark jeans, and a faded red bandanna is tied loosely around his neck.

He stops short when he spots me standing so close to Shep, his gaze darting between us with an amused curve of his mouth.

"How come you didn't tell me you were dating again?" Casey asks, grinning.

Shep takes a step back, a faint blush creeping over his cheeks. "I'm not. This is my friend Noelle." He refuses to meet my eyes as he introduces me.

His friend?

My stomach drops, stung by his offhanded delivery. What just happened felt beyond friendly. If we'd had a few more seconds, he would have had his tongue buried in my mouth again.

I extend my hand toward Casey, plastering a smile on my face. "It's a pleasure to meet you."

He accepts my handshake. "Not from around these parts, huh?"

"What gave me away?"

"Local folks aren't so polite, and only tourists show up to the honky-tonk in fancy dresses."

Shep grunts, shooting daggers at where my hand still rests in Casey's. First he friend-zones me, then gets his feathers ruffled when his *married* friend is nothing but courteous?

A man approaches Casey, handing him a beer. "One cold IPA, nice and chilled." He has on a leather vest and a bolo tie, the same uniform I've seen the servers wear.

"Thanks, Jake." Casey takes a swig, letting out a satisfied sigh. "Just what I needed to get through tonight."

Shep folds his arms across his broad chest with a raised brow. "Drinking on the clock again, are we?"

"It's the price of leaving me in charge. Call it compensation for handling all the heavy lifting for the past decade," Casey says, unapologetically.

"That's what your salary is for," Shep replies.

Casey rocks back on his boots, swirling the drink in his hand.

"You want a cold one, boss?" Jake asks Shep. "Or what about your girl? The specialty drink tonight is the Bootylicious Blitzen. It's a mix of bourbon, peppermint schnapps, and a splash of cream."

"Sounds delicious," I say, resisting the urge to bite my lip.

"Sure is, sugar." He grins. "But I'm gonna need to see some ID. Surprised the boss is stepping out with someone so young. He's easy on the eyes, but these days he creaks when he stands and has more silver than black on top."

I tip my head back, laughing. Shep, meanwhile, stands there with a scowl set like stone.

"You're fired," he grits out.

Jake smirks, completely unfazed. "Relax, boss. I'm only messing with you. Besides, you can't cut me loose. Casey wouldn't last a day without me. I'm his right-hand man and the one keeping morale up around here."

Casey shrugs, tipping his beer to Jake. "Can't argue with that. Gotta hand it to the kid for saying out loud what we're all thinking.

You're basically our resident senior citizen. You do love a good early-bird special."

"You're only two years younger than me," Shep grumbles, and we all erupt into another round of laughter.

"Guess I'm aging like fine wine. We can't all be that lucky," Casey taunts, playfully slugging Shep's arm.

Watching someone else rib him is oddly satisfying. He may appear indifferent, but it's all bark and no bite. If he really had a problem, he'd be far grumpier. I like that his employees are his friends and not afraid to roast him while still having his back.

"What's the verdict on ordering that Bootylicious Blitzen?" Jake asks me, wiggling his brow.

"How about a soda instead?" Shep suggests. "She's still healing from a twisted ankle, and I'd rather not risk her falling again. We don't need any setbacks."

"We're at a bar, not an obstacle course. What's she gonna trip over, a beer bottle?" Jake snickers, earning a sharp glare from Shep.

"Don't you have work to do?" he snaps.

"Aye aye, boss," Jake says, giving an exaggerated salute before strolling to the bar.

I put a hand on my hip, giving Shep a mock-serious look. "Playing doctor now, are you Shep? Good to see your talents extend past scowling and grunting, although your bedside manners could use some improvement." It's too much fun riling him up when he makes it so easy.

He rubs the back of his neck and shrugs. "You're accident-prone enough without adding alcohol to the mix, but if you still want a drink, I'll make it for you myself."

My traitorous heart races. I'm such a sucker for his nurturing side and brand of protection. It's impossible not to swoon when the rugged cowboy is zeroed in on my safety, even if it's over the top. I'm not much of a drinker anyway, so I'm not bothered by missing out.

I pretend to examine my nails, feigning indifference. "I'll skip the drinks tonight, but only because I'm confident you don't know how to make a Bootylicious Blitzen."

Casey snorts.

"Did I miss the memo that tonight's 'Roast the Boss' night?" Shep complains.

"That's every night you show up." Casey's mouth twitches in amusement as he holds up a hand to signal he's got more to say. "Before you threaten to fire me, too, did you bring the rocking chair? I'd better get it in my possession before I'm sacked."

Shep shoots him an exasperated eye roll. "It's in my truck bed."

I saw the finished product while he was loading it, and it's exquisite. His engraving skills are remarkable. The piece looks like something you'd find in a SoHo showroom.

"Thanks, man," Casey says enthusiastically. "It's all Amy's been talking about for weeks, and I can't wait to see her reaction when I give it to her."

"It's nothing." There Shep goes being modest again. "I'll grab it from the truck and stash it in my office. I've got some paperwork to tackle, including termination forms." He shoots Casey a subtle smirk before glancing at me. "Want to stay out here or come with me?"

As much as I want to see his workspace, I'd rather people watch. After days away from civilization, I want to take it all in. Besides, if we're in a cramped space alone, I'd be tempted to distract him, and he probably wouldn't get anything done.

"I can stay," I say.

Shep points at Casey. "Don't let her out of your sight."

I roll my eyes. "I've got this, no need to fuss."

"Never said you didn't, but Casey's still keeping an eye out for you," he states curtly.

Unable to resist teasing him one last time before he goes, I rest my palm on his chest, rising to my toes to whisper in his ear. "Yes, *Daddy.*"

His breath catches, gaze dark and stormy, and I can't resist watching him struggle to rein in his emotions.

Casey clears his throat, causing Shep to retreat a step, his jaw tight.

"I'll be back," he rasps before walking away.

As he heads toward the exit, I catch the subtle flex of his left hand. A smirk crosses my lips, pleased that he isn't immune to me after all.

I glance at Casey, who's dragging a hand down his beard as he studies me.

"You're staring," I remark.

He shrugs unapologetically. "Just trying to wrap my head around Shep strolling into High Noon with a woman on his arm, and letting you wear his hat no less. Is hell freezing over?"

I tip my head, laughter bubbling up. "Now you're being dramatic."

"No, ma'am, I'm not." He rests against the wall, taking a sip of his beer. "Shep *never* flirts with anyone when he's here. It's not from a lack of trying on the women's part, either. The man's got plenty of admirers. He's a bona fide rugged cowboy, and the ladies are constantly vying for his attention," he says with a wink.

Jealousy coils in my stomach as I scan the room, wondering if anyone here has tried their luck with Shep in the past. I wouldn't blame them if they had. His muscular frame, mustache flecked with gray, and brooding gaze make him dangerously striking without even trying.

"He's not exactly the most approachable person," I agree.

Casey arches a brow. "You think? One time, a woman asked if she could try on his hat, and he threw her out for even asking. He'd wrestle a bull before he let anyone touch the thing. It belonged to his dad, so it's sentimental." He tips his head in my direction. "Yet here you are with the thing perched on your head, and he didn't so much as complain. Shit, he actually looked pleased you had it on."

I trace my fingers over the brim, each crease and indent a piece of Shep's story, and I'm humbled he's trusted me with his family heirloom.

It's another reason I'm frustrated by his hesitation. He wants me, and everyone can see that, yet he's convinced that restraining his desire is the "right" choice. Naturally, I disagree, desperate to make him abandon his self-imposed restraint and give in to what we both want.

"Shep probably feels bad because I got scammed and thought I was renting his cabin for the holidays." The crowd cheers when the band finishes a song, and I shift closer to Casey so he can hear me. "He was kind enough to let me crash there when the storm hit."

Casey scratches his forehead. "You're staying at his cabin?"

"Shep didn't have much of a choice unless he wanted to explain to the sheriff why a human popsicle ended up in his driveway." I shudder to think what might have happened if he'd turned me away.

"Damn. He never lets anyone stay the night. On the rare occasion I come by, he won't let me drink, afraid I'll have to crash on his couch. The man guards his privacy like a fortress."

"Because of Danielle?"

Casey's eyes go round. "He's told you about her?"

I nod. "He did."

"That woman was a nightmare who only looked out for herself." He drains the last of his beer with a frown. "She did a number on Shep when she left. He's always been reserved, but he used to be more easygoing and relaxed. After Danielle walked out, he withdrew completely."

I've only just met Casey, but I appreciate his genuine affection for Shep. He wants the best for him, and watching Shep suffer has taken its toll.

I respect Shep's practical side but treasure the glimpses of the carefree man he used to be. It infuriates me that Danielle exploited his generosity, making him jaded. From what I understand, he gave her the world, and in exchange, she walked away thinking she deserved more. The stark truth is that someday, if she hasn't already, she'll learn that what she left behind was better than anything waiting for her elsewhere.

"Shep deserves better," I say.

"Sure does. I'll tell you, though, I haven't seen him as happy as he's been tonight in ages," Casey adds, nudging my arm with a grin.

I snort. "Right. Nothing says *happy* like threatening to fire people and glaring at anyone who passes."

"Oh, that's because he didn't like how Jake and the other guys were looking at you." He glances at Jake, who's walking toward us, sweat dotting his forehead. "Speak of the devil." Casey shifts to manager mode, straightening his posture as Jake approaches. "Everything okay?"

Jake runs a hand through his hair. "The bar is slammed and orders for Bootylicious Blitzens are multiplying faster than we can pour 'em. Can you help mix drinks while I run to the storage room for more bourbon and peppermint schnapps?"

I giggle. The name is as hilarious as the first time I heard it. Still hard to believe Shep owns a place that serves drinks with silly names and a bustling dance floor.

"You bet. I live for the chance to show folks my expert mixing skills." He turns to me. "You alright on your own for a bit? Or do you want to sit at the bar while I work?"

I look over at the stage as the musicians resume playing after a short break. "I'm going to take a closer listen to the band."

"Go ahead, but stay out of trouble, or I'll be the one in hot water with the boss." He winks.

"As if he could be any grumpier," I call back over my shoulder.

I drift along the edge of the room, listening as the band's lead singer belts out a twangy two-step. Patrons at the tables sing along while couples near the front spin across the floor in time with the music.

Who'd have thought a small town like Pine Haven would be home to a honky-tonk famous enough to draw crowds from across the country? As I listen to conversations around me, I overhear several people say they planned their trip a year in advance to make sure they could stop here for a night of music and dancing. Shep might not care about prestige or status, but transforming this place into a tourist hotspot is impressive.

After several songs, a man I hadn't noticed before comes to stand beside me.

"Hey there, sweet thing," he drawls.

The stranger is tall and lanky with messy brown hair and a crooked grin. He's got that boy-next-door charm, and if I'd met him a week ago, I might have asked him to join me for a drink. But now, the only man who holds my interest is a grumpy silver fox who enjoys a verbal sparring match.

"Hello," I say politely.

He extends his hand. "Care to dance?"

I offer him a kind smile. "Thanks, but I'm good listening to the band from here."

He leans in, brushing my arm with his fingers. "Just one dance? I promise I won't step on your toes."

I chuckle, admiring his persistence, though still set on declining his offer.

I open my mouth to say so, but my gaze lands on Casey, who is juggling drinks for a group of giggling women in short skirts and heeled boots. He stops mid-pour when he sees me with my new friend, shaking his head as if warning me how Shep will react when he returns.

He shouldn't be concerned. Shep's made it clear that our kiss and the dry-humping incident were both one-offs. So it shouldn't matter if I dance with another man, right?

Even I know that's bullshit. He might restrain himself, but he'd still get possessive if another man made a move, especially if I encouraged it. A playful smirk spreads across my face as the thought sets my gears spinning, plotting to finally break his resolve.

I turn to the guy still waiting. "On second thought, I think I will take you up on that dance."

What's the harm in making my grumpy cowboy jealous?

I thought he would have given in to the undeniable chemistry between us after that first night we shared a bed—but he hasn't. I'm not sure if it's because of our age difference, my impending departure or our opposite personalities. He's stubborn as a mule, and it'll take nothing short of a shove in the right direction to make him stop denying the fire burning between us.

Casey frantically signals for me to join him at the bar, but I wave him off. I'm not about to let him derail my mission. Maybe if he gets flustered enough, he'll fetch Shep for me.

"Good choice, sweet thing," the stranger says.

It's really not, but I couldn't be more ecstatic about it.

As he puts his hand on my lower waist and guides me to the dance floor, I catch a glimpse of Casey rushing toward the hallway leading to what I assume is Shep's office.

It won't be long now.

CHAPTER 13

All I Want For Christmas Is His Two Front Teeth

Shep

'M REVIEWING A NEW WHISKEY SUPPLIER PROPOSAL WHEN my door flies open and Casey barrels in.

"Boss, you might want to co—"

"I put the rocking chair in your office," I say without looking up. "Once the baby arrives, I'll stop by and engrave the name on the headrest." I pause, flipping to the next page of the document I'm reviewing. "Let Noelle know I'll be right out. I'm just finishing up."

I don't plan on stopping by High Noon again until after the new year. I've got far more pressing matters demanding my attention. Christmas is only three days away, and Noelle's flight back to New York is soon after, leaving little time for a holiday miracle. She's been a good sport about staying in a cabin without decorations or twinkling lights, but I'll be damned if she doesn't get the Christmas she's been wishing for. I push aside the thought that by this time next week, she'll be gone for good. All I can do is give her fond memories to take with her.

I blow out an exasperated sigh when I notice Casey is still standing in the doorway.

"What is it?" I glance up to find him staring at me with wide eyes.

"You might want to get back out on the floor to check on your *friend*," he suggests with a smug smile.

I shove my chair back and stand, tension coiling in my shoulders. "What's wrong? Is Noelle hurt?" I curse myself for not making her come back here with me.

Casey rubs the back of his neck, giving his head a small shake. "It's nothing like that, man."

I narrow my eyes. "Then what the hell is going on? Where is she?"

"On the dance floor," he says nonchalantly.

I grit my teeth, unable to hide the suspicion creeping in. "With who?"

"A handsome fella from town asked her to dance."

Of course, someone asked her. The woman's a fucking vision.

"And you didn't step in?" My tone edges toward panic as I move across the room. "What happened to keeping an eye on her?"

"We got busy, and I was helping the bar staff while Noelle watched the band from the side near the stage. But y'all are just friends, so her dancing with another man ain't a big deal, right?" He hooks his thumbs in his belt loops and rocks back on his heels, shooting me a smirk.

When he asked me who Noelle was earlier, it caught me off guard. I didn't miss the hurt flicker in her eyes when I said she was a friend. What I feel for her is far more complicated, and I wasn't sure how to explain it to someone else when I can't even put it into words myself. I've spent all my energy resisting the magnetic draw toward her and haven't confronted the reality of how much I want her.

One thing is certain: What I want to do with Noelle goes far beyond friendship.

"It's none of your business," I grunt, pushing past Casey.

"Don't expect me to babysit your livestock if you get your ass hauled off to jail," he calls out after me.

Goddammit.

Noelle is going to be the death of me. She knows exactly how to push my buttons, and I swear every decision she makes is designed to torment me. She's all sunshine and laughter, but hell hath no fury when she's riled up, and it seems I bring out that side of her often.

I'm both terrified and exhilarated by how easily she can bend me to her will with a single glance or smile. Even now, the thought of someone else touching her makes my blood run hot.

I stride into the main hall, brushing past bodies as I scan the crowd for Noelle. Being a head taller than most folks should make it easier to spot her, especially with her blonde hair and that red dress. The band plays a slow country ballad as dozens of couples dance near the stage.

There she is.

Noelle is at the edge of the dance floor, and my pulse spikes when I see she's with Thatcher Hall, a local ranch hand. He's a regular at the honky-tonk, notorious for his flings with women passing through. He's holding Noelle's hand while his other one rests on her back. I clench my fists at my sides, fighting to stay calm. But when his hand dips a few inches lower, I snap.

I move in their direction with determination, aware of the wide berth the crowd gives me as I pass.

As I approach, I step beside Thatcher and firmly tap his shoulder. He jerks his head around, panic flashing when he sees me. Good. My reputation precedes me.

I ignore his uneasy stare, turning to Noelle. "We're all finished here. Let's head home now."

Thatcher frowns, giving her a puzzled look. "Please tell me Shep isn't your uncle or something. God, I knew I should have asked who you were visiting."

Noelle covers her mouth to stifle a laugh. "I can see why you might think that with the silver streaks at his hairline." Clearly, testing my patience is her new favorite pastime.

"We're not related," I grit out.

Thatcher raises a brow. "Are you two dating?"

"Nope. We're just *friends*," Noelle interjects, batting her lashes. "Isn't that right, cowboy?" She turns, giving me a patronizing pat on the chest.

If we were alone, that heart-shaped ass would be mine.

I scowl at Thatcher, whose arm is still draped around her. My first warning must have gone over his head, making a more direct message fitting.

"If you don't take your hands off her, I'll kick you out myself," I rumble.

My words might be for him, but my gaze is fixed on Noelle, who's wearing a cheeky grin. The little minx is enjoying every second of this.

Thatcher yanks his hand to his side, stumbling back. "I didn't know she was off-limits."

"Now you do," I bite out. "Find someone else to warm your bed tonight or consider yourself banned from High Noon."

He scurries away, disappearing into the crowd. A quick look around shows everyone averting their eyes, pretending they weren't just watching our exchange like it was a damn soap opera.

"Must you always be so grumpy? You're going to end up with permanent wrinkles," Noelle teases, reaching on her toes to trace the lines on my forehead. "No wonder Thatcher assumed you were my uncle."

"Woman, now isn't the time to test me," I say, my tone clipped.

She drapes her arms around my neck. "What are you going to do about it?" Her eyes sparkle, daring me to act.

Not one to disappoint, I bend low and hoist her over my shoulder in a fireman's hold, tuning out the gasps rippling through the crowd.

"Better hold on to your hat, Sunshine," I warn.

"Shep, be reasonable." Noelle grips my waist to steady herself with her free hand. "I'm wearing a dress, for crying out loud. Everyone is going to see my backside."

"Nobody will see a damn thing," I grumble, tugging down the hem of her dress and adjusting my hold to keep it in place. "Now, behave." I give her a playful swat on the ass.

She blows out an exasperated huff. "The least you can do is buy me a Bootylicious Blitzen for putting up with your mood swings."

"You're enough trouble sober," I mutter.

"Funny, I thought it was because I'm accident-prone," she retorts.

I pinch the bridge of my nose. Noelle is dismantling my last frayed nerve. Goddammit, why does she have this power over me? One look at another man's hands on her, and I've lost my damn mind. Our age gap, her fleeting stay, and her city roots mean nothing in the blur of my envy.

I don't slow my pace as I stride out of the main room. It's no surprise to find Casey waiting in the hallway, hands stuffed in his pockets, and a cheeky grin plastered on his face.

"Thatcher Hall is banned," I bark.

Casey tips his hat. "Got it, boss."

"You said he'd only be banned if he didn't walk away," Noelle chimes in unhelpfully.

"I changed my mind."

"Sounds like a reasonable response for him dancing with your *friend*." Casey smirks.

I grunt, stalking past him to my office, glancing in the mirrors lining the wall as Noelle pushes off my back to look at him. "Thanks for ratting me out. You're a lifesaver," she exclaims, blowing him a kiss.

Casey chuckles at her enthusiasm. "Sure thing, sugar. Don't push the old man too hard. He doesn't handle stress well."

"You're really fired this time," I growl as I enter my office.

"I'll clear out my things before I leave tonight," he deadpans, then adds, "Have fun, you two," as I shut the door behind me.

I lower Noelle to her feet, and her mouth presses into a thin line as she studies me with an unrelenting gaze.

She's so damn beautiful it hits me like a punch, stealing my breath. In the span of a few days, she's torn down the last of my walls, leaving me defenseless and wanting. I was stupid thinking I could rein in her effect on me by holding back. Instead, it's intensified the longing and fueled the fire of jealousy raging through me.

"Why are you looking at me like that?" she whispers.

I take a step toward her. "Like what?"

"Like I belong to you."

I walk us backward until she's pinned against the door. "Let's get one thing straight, sweetheart. As long as you're in *my* bed, wearing *my* clothes, you're mine."

She shakes her head with a dry laugh. "Hate to break it to you, cowboy, but I'm not doing either of those things right now."

I put my hands on either side of her head. "Are you forgetting whose hat you've got on?"

Noelle grips the collar of my shirt, then runs her hand down my chest.

"Yours." She exhales softly. "Does this mean you're done pretending you don't want me?"

"I've wanted you since the moment I saw you on my porch, peeking through my window."

Her breath hitches, pupils blown. "Then why fight what we both want? Or am I imagining how strong this connection is?" She rests a hand over my racing heart. "Maybe I'm better off tracking down Thatcher before he's booted from the premises. I'm sure he'd have no problem giving me what I want."

I let out a low growl. The woman has another thing coming if she thinks I'd allow that. She's off-limits to every other man as long as she's here with me.

I'm down to two choices: I can play the coward, hiding behind my fears, or I can make the most of being the lucky bastard Noelle wants and not waste a single minute I've got with her. The decision is made for me when her stormy blue eyes catch mine, holding me captive.

"Fuck it." I frame her cheeks with my palms. "The only man who can give you what you need is me."

"You sure about that, cowboy?" she murmurs.

"You. Are. Mine," I growl.

All the need I've buried crashes through me like a storm tide rising, fierce and relentless, dragging me under without mercy. My hat falls off her head, toppling to the ground as I angle her face and slip my tongue past her parted lips, the sweet taste of her flooding my senses. She lets out a soft sigh, tightening her grip on my collar.

Noelle wanted me to cave, and she's about to get what she wished for, along with every possessive, jealous, and overbearing tendency I have. It's all hers, and there's no undoing what she's unleashed. Even if it's temporary, she belongs to me, and it's damn time she knew it.

I shove the fabric of her dress past her hip and hike her leg around my waist. When she tugs me closer, I shove her panties aside, running my fingers through her wetness.

Teasing her pussy, I find her skin bare beneath my hand.

"You're fucking soaked."

"It's all for y-you," she moans.

Holy. Fuck.

It makes me feral knowing that I'm the reason she's dripping all over my fingers.

Noelle arches against me as I sink a finger inside her tight pussy, her warmth drawing me deeper. I run my tongue along the column of her neck, grazing my teeth along her collarbone.

"More. Please give me more," she begs.

"I've got you, baby. Hold on tight like a good girl."

She wraps her arms around my neck, threading her fingers through the hair at the nape of my neck.

I thrust a second finger inside, her strained cry colliding with the ragged tempo of our intermingled breaths. My cock is painfully hard, but it's a reminder of the pleasure I've denied us both these last couple of days.

With my free hand, I slide along the neckline of Noelle's dress and pull one of her bra cups down to reveal her breast. I run my finger along her nipple, the pink bud puckering at the slightest contact, before I lean down and run my teeth along it.

"Shep," she cries out.

"Easy, Sunshine, keep that up and the whole honky-tonk will hear what I'm doing to you."

The flush on her cheeks deepens and she lets out another needy sound when my thumb moves to her clit. I catch her mouth with mine, muffling the noise.

Her reaction to the thought of being overheard is hot as hell, but even her broken moans belong to me alone. Even if Casey's probably blocking off the hallway to make sure we're not interrupted, I'm not risking anyone else hearing a single note of her pleasure.

I grind against her, my boxers sticky with precum as I wind her tighter with every plunge of my fingers.

"Don't stop. I need this. I need *you*," Noelle begs loudly.

"Not until you come for me."

Wanting to give her the push over the edge she desperately wants, I apply pressure to her clit, sending her shattering around my hand. She lets out a strangled cry that I swallow with another kiss.

She's stunning, closing her eyes as she surrenders to the fading waves of ecstasy. I've imagined her like this countless times, with my hand wrapped around my cock while I'm in the shower, but no fantasy compares to seeing it in person.

As she drifts down from her high, she goes slack in my grasp. I hold her up with one arm as I slowly pull my fingers from her. A sated smile crosses her face as she clings to me. I can't help but smile back, her contentment contagious.

Her lips curve up when she shifts her gaze to the patch on the front of my jeans—evidence of my own release. Fuck, it's like I'm a teenager again instead of a forty-five-year-old man who's supposed to have discipline. Good thing I keep a spare change of clothes in my office for the rare times I meet a band manager or supplier in person and want to ditch my shirt and tie afterward.

"That's so hot," Noelle whispers.

"I've got no control around you," I groan against her mouth.

"Does that mean we're doing this again?" There's a hint of excitement in her voice.

"This Christmas, you're mine," I promise.

Now that I've seen her fall apart in my arms, I'm hooked. We only have a few more days together, and I want to memorize her body and learn all the ways to make her come.

"So definitely not my uncle then," she sasses.

"You're going to pay for that later," I vow.

CHAPTER 14

Oh, Holy Toys

Noelle

WE DON'T TALK MUCH ON THE DRIVE TO THE CABIN as Christmas music drifts from the radio. Shep is focused on the winding road ahead, and I'm distracted by the earlier events.

The moment we shared in his office was the most erotic experience of my life—his finger stroking deep inside me, his breath hot against my neck, and his hard cock pressed against my thigh. I didn't care that only a wall separated us from a room full of people—truthfully, the risk of being overheard only added to the thrill.

Part of me worries Shep might close off again, but I hope not because I'm ready for him to properly claim me tonight. An hour ago, he gave me an orgasm that left me reeling, yet my body still thrums with want. It's been ages since I've experienced this kind of satisfaction, and now I'm so wound up and desperate for more, I can barely think about anything else.

As we round another bend, the cabin comes into view, and I gasp at the unexpected festive display before me. Strings of multicolored lights run along the roofline and frame each window. A fresh wreath with a bright red bow hangs on the door, and a herd of metal reindeer twinkles with white lights on the front lawn, each wearing a Santa hat.

I clasp my hands together and squeal. "This is incredible. Who did all this?" None of these Christmas decorations were here when we left earlier, and Shep was with me all night.

He puts the truck into park, casting a soft smile my way. "Stewart, the owner of the hardware store, and his assistant set it up while we were gone."

"It's like a postcard come to life. I love it," I exclaim.

"I'm glad, because it's all for you," Shep says.

My heart nearly leaps out of my chest. The man doesn't celebrate Christmas, much less decorate, but he went out of his way to transform the house and yard into a winter wonderland simply because he knew it was important to me. The most touching part is that, despite knowing the display would only be up for a few days, he still went through all the trouble for no other reason than to make me happy —and that means everything.

Without thinking, I launch myself across the bench seat and into his lap, throwing my arms around his neck. "Thank you, Shep. This is the best surprise ever."

He emits a soft grunt as I collide with him but quickly recovers, drawing me into his chest.

"You're welcome, Sunshine."

"How did they manage to get it done so fast, and in the dark no less?"

He runs his knuckle along my cheekbone. "I would've had it done sooner, but I had to wait for the storm to pass."

That means he's been planning this for days. Even before I

agreed to stay, he was plotting how to turn the yard into a scene straight out of a Christmas movie, all because of me.

"It's perfect timing," I beam.

"There's another surprise waiting for you inside," he says softly.

I pull back to search his eyes, resting my hand on his chest. "What is it?"

"If I told you, it wouldn't be a surprise." He presses a kiss to my temple. "Why don't you go in and find out?"

I furrow my brow. "You're not coming with?"

"Gotta tend to the animals, but I'll be back soon." He captures my mouth in a kiss that steals my breath. "You'd better wait for me, because I've got big plans for you."

"What plans?" I murmur against his lips.

"Ones that involve you moaning my name till the sun comes up."

My hand drifts higher along his thigh. "What if we started those plans now?"

"If I start now, I won't be able to stop." He brings my fingers to his mouth, grazing the tips with his teeth. "I'll be back within an hour, and I promise I'll make it worth your while."

I meet his gaze, my heart skipping a beat. "Then you'd better hurry."

His mouth curves into a smile. "Behave while I'm gone."

"The clock's ticking, cowboy," I say, tapping my wrist for emphasis.

I give him one more kiss before sliding off his lap and climbing out of the truck. The cold bites at my cheeks as I move across the yard and up the porch steps, stealing a glance back at Shep's truck as it rolls down the driveway and rounds the bend out of view.

I'm not surprised to find the cabin's front door unlocked, and I slip my shoes off once I step inside. I'm greeted by the scent of pine, awestruck when I see the living room has been transformed into a cozy holiday dream. It's bathed in a soft glow from the twinkling lights on a fresh Christmas tree in the corner, and from the garland draped above the fireplace. Strands of popcorn drape across the branches of the tree, nestled among wooden ornaments similar to those on the town square tree, only smaller.

I'm reminded of the holidays at my parents' house. My mom let me decorate the tree since I was a kid, never correcting the crooked and uneven ornaments. Once I got older, my placement improved, and it was one less thing she had to worry about doing herself. This was the first year they didn't put up a tree since they won't be back from their cruise until January, and it's been one of the things I've missed most. Sure, I always decorate my apartment too, but it doesn't compare.

As I get closer, I notice three ornaments that are different from the others—a miniature Highland cow with a tuft of hair on its head, a three-legged stool resembling the one I stumbled off in the barn, and a cup of hot cocoa with marshmallows.

I smile fondly as I trail a hand over each one. Shep must have made them earlier while he was in his shop. I'm learning that he doesn't miss a thing, filing away every little detail and shaping them into memories we can hold on to.

I curl up on the couch, knees tucked to my chest, the fire's warmth wrapping around me. As much as I'm grateful I had a moment to take this in, I'm eager for Shep to return so I can thank him properly. The anticipation burns hotter than the flames as I wait for him to make good on his promise of us naked in his bed, and him leaving no part of me untouched.

I only last twenty minutes. The ache between my thighs is maddening, and my skin is flushed with heat from the fireplace, only fueling the lust gathering low in my belly.

A brief look out the front window confirms Shep isn't back yet. I'd hoped he'd be as restless as I am and return early. He told me to wait for him, but how does he expect me to do that when I'm on the verge of combustion? One release while I wait is harmless, right? After all, he seemed supportive of me using toys, and it's the perfect opportunity to start testing them out.

With my mind made up, I go to Shep's bedroom and make a beeline to the chair in the corner where he moved my suitcase.

I open it, digging through the toys and pulling out a candy-cane-striped rabbit vibrator. I have one like it at home, but this festive version is perfect for the occasion—and guaranteed to get the job done quickly. I skip the peppermint flavored lube since I'm already wet and ready.

My gaze shifts to the door, and I decide to leave it ajar in case Shep gets back sooner than expected. He was aware of what state he left me in, and I won't feel guilty about taking full advantage. Maybe next time he'll think twice about leaving me alone like this.

Eager to get out of my clothes, I peel off my dress and toss it over the chair. Next, I slide off my lace panties, kicking them aside, and unhook my bra, sighing as my breasts are finally liberated from their confines.

Vibrator in hand, I crawl to the middle of the bed and lie on my back. I'm not normally this brazen, but when I think about the way Shep looked at me earlier as I rode his hand, I'm filled with a newfound sense of confidence. A shiver runs down my spine as I push the tip inside myself to get it nice and wet, groaning as pleasure blooms at the intrusion, pretending it's Shep's thick cock. It's the one part of him I haven't seen yet, but judging by the bulge in his Wranglers earlier, it's obvious he would be the biggest man I've been with.

A soft hum buzzes through the air when I turn the device on. The pulse courses through me, and I moan softly as the vibrations tease my entrance. Wanting more friction, I move the device in a steady motion, my mind wandering to an image of Shep between my legs, using his skilled tongue, licking me as he coaxes pleasure from my body. His fingers pressed into the tender flesh of my thighs, nearing the perfect balance of pain and pleasure.

I pick up my pace, desperate for more friction as a groan passes my lips.

"Oh god, Shep," I groan, remembering how his fingers stroked me as I tumbled into a blissful orgasm.

I angle the toy so the small arm finds my clit, still sensitive from earlier, sending a rush through me that knocks the air from my lungs. My free hand fists the comforter while my hips roll in circles, and I drag the tip over the nub until I'm lightheaded. I press the main shaft in deeper, a moan tearing from my throat as my climax looms—only to snap out of my haze by the unmistakable shuffle of boots on the floor.

My pulse quickens as I raise my head, my gaze darting to the open doorway where Shep stands. He's leaning against the frame, his eyes blazing with lust as he shamelessly peruses my naked body.

"You were supposed to wait for me," he says, voice like gravel.

I nibble my lip, lifting a shoulder. "You left me waiting too long."

"Seems one orgasm earlier wasn't enough, or maybe you're just a greedy little thing." He folds his arms across his chest, the corner of his mouth lifting. "I'm wagering the latter."

The vibrator continues to pulsate inside me, my vision swimming as I struggle to focus long enough to form a coherent sentence.

"Maybe if you'd been here sooner, I wouldn't be so needy," I manage to pant out.

"What if that's exactly how I wanted you?" he asks, his ghost of a smile deepening to a smirk.

I groan softly as I shift on the bed, the main shaft brushing against a sensitive spot by accident. I start to pull the device out, but Shep clears his throat to get my attention.

"Did I say you could take the vibrator out?"

"I want you," I rasp.

"You'll get my cock when I'm ready. Right now, you're in my bed, and I'm in control of when and *if* you come." His tone leaves no room for argument. "First, I want to see if you can be a good girl and listen to my instructions."

That's when it clicks—he left me alone at the cabin deliberately, wanting me simmering in sexual frustration. It confirms the theory that he's not threatened by my toys. If anything, the sight of me building to climax only makes him harder.

He runs a thumb along his mustache as he patiently waits for me to comply.

I prop myself up on my elbow, stealing a better look at him. His short-sleeved shirt clings to his biceps, flexing with every movement. The way he tracks me with those piercing eyes makes every nerve buzz with awareness. His body is a feast for my eyes, and I take advantage of the view as I ease the vibrator back inside.

Shep watches, unmoving, when I push the device even further, his muscles tense with every moan that falls from my mouth. I roll my hips, guiding the vibrator to my G-spot, unable to pull my gaze from the outline in Shep's jeans that swells against the fabric.

"You're so fucking beautiful putting on a show for me," he growls, shifting to grip himself firmly.

Witnessing his unfiltered reaction only fuels my own hunger, and I bite my lip as my free hand moves to my left breast, cupping it firmly as I flick the nipple. The extra stimulation sends a ripple straight to my core, and my eyes shutter closed as I'm lost in a wave of bliss.

"Eyes on me." The authority in Shep's voice demands obedience. "When you come, you'll look at the man who made you lose control."

I obey, snapping them open, wanting him to witness every

tremor that claims me as I chase my release. It's all because of him, and my body's surrender is a silent confession.

My eyes are trained on his hand adjusting his cock through his jeans.

"I want to see you," I plead.

Wordlessly, he unbuckles his belt and unzips his jeans, dragging them past his hips at an agonizingly slow pace. He tugs his boxers down next and pulls out his cock. It's huge, stone-hard, and I'm unsure how it's going to fit inside me.

"Don't worry, baby, it'll fit." He smirks, as if he can read my mind. "But let's make sure you're nice and ready for me." He nods toward the device in my hand, encouraging me to continue.

My breath hitches when I turn up the speed of the vibrator, eyes locked on his cock as he spits into his hand and pumps up and down along his shaft.

"Use the little arm of the vibrator to put more pressure on your clit," he roughs out. "The sooner you push yourself over the edge, the faster I can be inside you."

I lick my lips and follow his directions and push down on my nub. With my other hand, I pinch my nipple hard, my back bowing off the bed as I fall apart, Shep's name escaping in a trembling gasp. My body is burning with a lustful haze, and I feel like I'm floating, suspended on a cloud of bliss.

My head collapses on the pillow as I catch my breath. "I need you, Shep."

His hand is still wrapped around his cock, but he hasn't come. "If I get on that bed, you're mine as long as you're here, Sunshine."

I'm flooded with conflicting emotions. I want to be worshipped and wrapped up with him for as long as I can, but the idea of leaving him behind knots my stomach. A fleeting thought whispers in the back of my mind that I could extend my stay. My team is out through the new year, and I don't have any pressing matters waiting for me in New York. Then again, would prolonging the inevitable be fair to either of us?

I push aside worries about what comes next, letting myself get lost in the heat of the silver fox who's looking at me like I'm his favorite vice.

I beckon Shep over with a crook of my finger. "I need you, *Daddy.*"

He pushes off the doorframe, stalking toward me with a determined glint in his eye, and I know I'm not leaving this room until I've been well and truly fucked.

CHAPTER 15

A Not So Silent Night

Shep

YANK MY SHIRT OVER MY HEAD, TOSSING IT TO THE FLOOR before stepping out of my pants and boxers.

It's a miracle I didn't come in my pants again. It's been ages since I've been with a woman, and the memory of my fingers inside Noelle only hours ago, paired with the sight of her sprawled out and naked with a vibrator humming inside her, nearly shattered my control all over again.

I should be more concerned with how much younger she is than me and the implications of wanting her so damn much. Hell, even my friends couldn't stop teasing me about our age difference. The contrast is amplified by her optimism and warmth against my jaded, hardened self—but I'm still helplessly drawn to her brightness, like a moth to a flame.

All I can think about is how she makes me feel alive,

awakening impulses I'd long since buried—reminding me of what I've denied myself for so long.

That ends tonight.

Whether she's only here with me for one night or a few days, I plan to treasure every second because having her in any measure is better than not having her at all.

I crawl onto the bed, the mattress creaking beneath me as I settle over Noelle.

"Finally," she murmurs.

Her eagerness fuels me as I bend down, trailing a finger over her nipple in gentle strokes. The rosy bud hardens at the tip, its base dotted with small, sensitive bumps. She whimpers when I roll it between my fingers, my free hand anchoring her smooth, perfect skin at the hip.

"Shep." My name falls from her lips like a prayer.

"Yes, ma'am." I plant a soft kiss on her jaw. "I'm going to give you everything you've been begging for."

I wrap my mouth around her nipple, gliding my tongue across the swollen tip. Her hips buck, seeking more friction. She inhales sharply as I alternate between flicking her nipple with my tongue and tugging it taut with my teeth.

She's a fucking goddess, my every wet dream come to life and all mine to please—and I'll be damned if this isn't a night neither of us will forget.

"Why did you stop?" Noelle whines in protest when I release her nipple.

"Patience, woman." I give her breast a light squeeze. "Don't forget who's in charge."

She squirms beneath me, drawing her lower lip between her teeth.

I drag my thumb across her bottom lip. "Say it, Noelle. Who's in control?"

She nips at my skin, enough to sting, a wicked glint sparking in her eyes. "You are, *Daddy*."

My breath catches as all the blood rushes to my cock. Damn, she's deliberately tormenting me, knowing exactly which buttons to push to make me lose control. I'm a sick man for getting off on her games, but she's impossible to resist.

I pepper kisses down her stomach, running my tongue along her navel. My hands wander along her curves, leaving a trail of goose bumps behind. My touch is light and teasing as she writhes beneath me, weaving her fingers through my hair. It's a silent plea to move farther south.

My cock throbs, a reminder that I'm not immune to the burning agony I'm inflicting. I continue running my tongue along her skin, her moans growing louder by the second.

I lift my head to find her molten gaze staring back.

"Remind me, one more time darlin.'"

"You're in control," Noelle mewls, her voice strained.

I can sense it's on the tip of her tongue to beg for more, but she thinks better of it.

"You've been such a good girl," I croon. "Reckon you deserve a reward."

She hisses as my stubble rubs against her, and she arches into me, her legs quaking when I reach the apex of her thighs. I inhale the sweet scent of her musk, and it burns through me like fire. Fuck, my control is slipping through my fingers, the overriding need to taste her taking over.

I run my tongue along the seam of her pussy. Her body moves on instinct, lifting her legs over my shoulders to draw me deeper between her thighs, overtaken by the taut wire of desire stretching between us. I eagerly explore her, alternating between licking and sucking. I dig my thumbs into her waist as she draws her ankles together, her hips rolling as she grinds against my face.

"You ride my stache so good," I groan into her pussy.

My dick twitches when she cries out as I move my mouth to her clit, skating my teeth across it. Each whimper fuels me, and I flick my tongue over her nub in rapid strokes.

I push two fingers inside her, the warmth enveloping me. Small tremors rack her body as I move faster, driving her toward climax. Her nails dig into my shoulders, but the sharp sting only heightens my focus. I'm overcome with the need to feel her fall apart.

I lift my eyes to meet hers, fierce and untamed. "Come for me."

I softly bite down on her clit, my fingers still pumping inside her. She cries out as she chases euphoria, and I greedily lap up her essence, groaning as her sweetness floods my senses.

Noelle's eyes are hooded, still glazed with pleasure, as she runs her fingers through her hair.

"You've got a little something there." She giggles, motioning to my top lip.

I catch her hand before she can wipe it off, moving up so I'm hovering over her, and dip my head for a kiss. Her tongue flicks along my top lip, grazing my mustache. Our mouths move together in a slow, sensual rhythm.

When Noelle meets my gaze, the sheen on her lips makes my cock pulse, and I let out a ragged breath as she licks them.

"That's my girl," I rasp.

She trails a red nail along my chest. "I want you inside me, right now. Please don't make me wait, Shep."

How could I? She's sprawled out like a temptress, every curve and smooth inch of her body an open invitation as she tracks my movements. Fuck, I might have come once tonight, but my cock's already ramrod straight again, all the teasing and foreplay leaving me straining with impatience to finally be inside her warm, wet pussy. Just the thought sends another jolt straight to my dick, a low rumble escaping my chest.

I'm drawn from my haze long enough to realize that I've been so caught up in my head that I let a critical detail slip my mind. One that could derail our entire night.

"Slight problem," I mutter, pushing a hand through my hair. "I don't think I have any condoms, and if I do, they're ancient."

Fuck, why didn't I plan ahead? In my defense, we've been snowed in for days, and until a few hours ago, I was battling the overwhelming urge to fuck Noelle.

"It's okay, you have been a little distracted." Noelle grins sweetly. "Don't worry, I've got you covered. The Twisted Temptations PR box came with condoms. I only packed them because they came with the lube."

Relief floods through me as I kiss her temple. "I like a woman who comes prepared."

I push off the mattress, striding to Noelle's suitcase. Sure enough, beneath the pile of toys, I spot a box of condoms. I grab a ribbed Santa-themed one labeled "All I Want for Christmas is Sex."

I hold it up for Noelle to see. "Looks like we got ourselves a Christmas miracle."

She tosses her head back and laughs as I tear the thing open with my teeth. I quickly roll the condom on, climb onto the bed, and position myself back over Noelle.

"You ready, baby girl?"

She rolls her eyes. "Been ready forever."

"Give me that mouth." I slide my hand in her hair, tipping her head back to claim her lips.

Her body arches into me as our kiss deepens. My dick brushes against her stomach as I take hold of my cock, sliding it along her slit to coat myself in her arousal. She's fucking soaked again. I move my dick lower, and it makes me feral knowing that I could be the first one to claim her ass. When I nudge at her tight entrance, she moans, looking up at me with wide eyes.

"Before you leave, I plan on claiming every one of your holes, baby."

Color blooms across Noelle's cheeks. "No one has ever…I've never tried that," she admits in a whisper. "I want to but I'm scared it'll hurt."

I slide my cock over her clit, rubbing back and forth. "I'd make it feel good for you, darlin', I promise."

"I know you would."

Unable to wait a second longer to be inside her, I line up with her entrance, pushing in to the hilt in one stroke.

"Oh god," she cries out.

Her slick walls grip me, my balls tightening as her inner muscles flex around me. I breathe through my nose, fighting every instinct to pound into her.

I push her hair from her face, pressing my mouth to the hollow of her throat. "You're taking me so damn well," I praise, holding still to give her time to adjust.

"You're so big," she moans, rolling her hips to meet mine. "Please move."

That's all I have to hear before rocking into her in steady strokes. Her silky flesh stretches around me, every gasp falling from her mouth tearing at my control. The pressure winds tight inside me until it finally snaps, urgency taking the reins as I quicken my pace. I'm driven by the obsession to make her addicted to the way I fill her up, unable to think of anything but being stuffed full of my cock.

"Shep. You feel so good," she cries out.

"You're perfect for me," I growl.

She digs her nails into my shoulder blades, gasping for air as I slam into her—harder, faster—with each thrust pulling us closer together, until I can't tell where she ends and I begin. I was a damn fool for fighting so hard to resist her. There's no denying that I'm powerless against this woman, and I'm basking in the satisfaction of claiming what's mine.

She lets out a low, desperate whimper, her back arching violently, telling me I've hit her most sensitive spot. The sound of flesh slapping against flesh resonates in the air, and I drop my head to her shoulder, my brow damp from the exertion. Each stroke is more desperate than the last until we're nothing but sweat, need, and tangled limbs.

"Scream my name when you come," I grunt out.

I reach down and roll her clit with my thumb and forefinger, and soon, we're both barreling toward release. She shatters with a force so fierce that another cry tears free and my name falls from her lips. My own pleasure hits me, and I tense above her, my throat raw and vision blurry.

Fuck, nothing has ever felt so right.

I nuzzle my nose into her neck as I ease out, not wanting to hurt her.

"I needed this. Needed you," I say reverently.

She releases a contented sigh in response, smiling dreamily.

I push off the bed and remove the condom, tossing it in the trash bin. I move to Noelle's side, and draw her close as I pull the covers over us.

She hikes her leg over mine stroking my hair as she speaks. "Thank you for the Christmas tree. I meant to tell you sooner, but I was a little preoccupied." She giggles. "It was another wonderful surprise."

I lean in and kiss her temple. "Anything for you, Sunshine."

I can finally admit that my feelings for Noelle are growing faster than I can control, and there's no containing them. Watching her enthusiasm for holiday lights and decorations has me wanting to make the last two days before Christmas unforgettable. I'm prepared to do whatever it takes to hear those adorable giggles and be the recipient of her megawatt smile.

And who knows—maybe I'll rediscover my own holiday magic.

"Rest up while you still can, sweetheart." I trail a finger over her bare shoulder, giving her a rueful glance. "Because I intend to keep you up all night."

Noelle tips her chin, a grin spreading across her face. "Looking forward to it, cowboy."

CHAPTER 16

Santa Claus Is *Coming* To Town

Noelle

CAN A PERSON DIE FROM TOO MANY ORGASMS?

Shep made good on his promise, keeping me going until dawn. I cried out his name until my voice broke, losing track of how many times he pushed me over the edge after my sixth release. The man has the stamina of a wild mustang, and I could barely keep up. After letting me sleep in, I woke up to him peppering kisses along my collarbone as he pushed inside me. He must have gone outside beforehand, judging by his cold hands and the faint scent of pine and winter air. Regardless, it was a pleasant way to start the day—one that I'd take any morning.

God, being with him has allowed me to explore a part of myself I didn't know existed. It's not just the mind-blowing sex—he's considerate, kind, and even tender when the situation calls for it. Saying yes to staying after the storm passed was easily the best decision I've made in ages.

Lying in his sheets with his fingerprints etched on my skin, I'm second-guessing my decision to leave the day after Christmas. There's no way two days is long enough to satisfy my desire for him.

After our last round of escapades, Shep showered and then disappeared to the kitchen, and the sweet aroma of cinnamon and vanilla tells me he must have made breakfast. My stomach rumbles, reminding me I haven't eaten since we left for the honky-tonk last night.

I climb out of bed and grab one of his flannels hanging from the closet door and put it on.

As I pass the living room, a silly grin spreads across my face at the sight of the tree by the fireplace. Its twinkling lights fill the room with a warm, cozy glow. Atop the tree is a wooden star that wasn't there before, so I'm guessing Shep placed it there this morning.

Just as I suspected, he's at the kitchen counter whisking batter. What I didn't expect is him humming along to "Santa Claus is Coming to Town" playing from the radio on top of the microwave. His hair is damp, and he's wearing nothing but his Wranglers, riding low on his hips. His bare chest is all broad planes and hard muscle, and my tongue darts out to wet my lips. Tired or not, I wouldn't object if he carried me back to bed right now.

His face lights up when he notices me, and I slip behind him, wrapping my arms around his waist.

"Hey there, cowboy. So you decorating for the holidays wasn't a dream," I murmur, running my hands along his stomach.

He might have done it for me, but I can't shake the feeling that it's just as much for him. A way to honor his mom and to remember the joy of celebrating this season.

"Nope, it's real." Shep sets aside the batter and turns around to kiss me. "There's plenty more where that came from. With Christmas only two days away, we've got to squeeze in all the traditions you've missed this year and sprinkle in a few from my family too." I blink, stunned, wondering if this is real life.

God, I hope so.

"You mean it?" I exclaim.

He nods. "I know it's hard being away from your parents, but I'll be damned if you don't get the Christmas you deserve. First up, eggnog waffles." He gestures to the vintage waffle maker on the counter. "When I was a kid, my dad woke up early on Fridays to make breakfast so Mom could sleep in. Every month, he'd try a new waffle flavor, and in December, it was always eggnog."

"A girl could get used to mornings like this," I say with a sated smile.

"Good, because if cooking makes you smile like that, I'll be in the kitchen every morning."

I roll my eyes, playfully swatting his chest. "Please don't tell me sleeping together has made you go all Hallmark on me. I rather like your grumpy side."

"Don't worry, sweetheart. I'll be cursing at the waffle iron in no time and we'll be right back to normal."

I wipe my brow with exaggerated flair. "Thank god. I'd have to stage an intervention if you started smiling all the time or, heaven forbid, traded in your flannel for matching holiday pajamas."

He leans back, eyes wide in mock shock. "Whoa there. Too far."

"Maybe there's hope for you yet." I laugh, draping my hands around his neck. "So what's on the agenda after breakfast?"

I'm already giddy thinking about what he could have planned, especially since whatever it is will be Christmas-themed. When he smiles, his eyes shining with mischief and warmth, my stomach does a little flip. There's nothing better than seeing him happy, and I'm lucky to get a front-row seat.

In Christmases past, I thought the key to a perfect holiday was family traditions, giving to those in need, and finding meaningful gifts for everyone I loved. Staying with Shep, surrounded by nature and living simply, has taught me that it's much less complicated than that.

The heart of the season lies in finding joy in the small, beautiful moments. It doesn't require grand gestures or flawless planning—just sharing it with someone special. And Shep has quickly become the one to teach me the beauty in slowing down and creating holiday memories I'll treasure forever.

He kisses my forehead. "After breakfast, we'll check on the animals, then head out. Our stop is close to the edge of my property."

"Sounds ominous," I tease. "You sure you can't tell me what we're doing?"

My mind races with possibilities—building snowmen, taking a sleigh ride, or making snow angels… The options are endless, and I can't wait to see what's in store.

"You'll see soon enough," Shep says, chuckling when my stomach rumbles. "But first, let's get some food in you."

I rise on my toes to kiss him. "Deal. I'll whip up some hot chocolate to go with the waffles."

"Sounds like a mighty fine plan," he replies as he kisses me back.

"You've got this, Maple," I coax with a gentle tug on her lead rope.

She plants her back hooves into the snow as though my pep talk personally offends her.

I huff, brushing my hair from my face. "Ten feet. That's all I'm asking for. After those two apples I gave you, I'd say that's more than reasonable, don't you think?"

She tosses her head from side to side with a soft grunt. Great. I'm being rejected by a baby cow.

Unbelievable.

It's no wonder she and Shep get along so well. They're equally obstinate and resistant to change. Yet they're both also irresistibly endearing, outweighing their stubborn nature.

After Shep whipped up a delicious batch of eggnog waffles this morning, he brought me to the barn so I could hang out with Maple while he chopped wood.

I was brushing her down when a wild idea popped into my head: What if I took her to the cabin? Sure, she's the size of a Saint Bernard, but she deserves a cozy playdate. We could snuggle on the floor by the fire while we watch a Christmas movie, and I'd make us popcorn. I mean, I don't know for sure if cows can even eat that, but I'll check online. The last thing I want is her getting sick, and turning Shep's living room into a buttery, slobbery disaster zone won't win me any favors with the man.

The first step of my genius plan is getting her to the cabin, and the truck isn't exactly cow-friendly. That's why I've been trying to teach her to walk on a lead. Keyword: *trying*.

The problem is that when she's told to come, she only takes a few steps, and at this rate, covering the half mile to our destination will take ages—not to mention the mountain of apples needed to bribe her.

I switch hands holding the rope and pull out another apple slice, dangling it under Maple's twitching nose. "Come, Maple. Please?"

She eyes the treat with suspicion, acting as if she's never obeyed the command in her life.

"Don't you want to come to the cabin? It's warm, and I'll put together a yummy veggie-and-fruit tray for you. We can watch *How the Grinch Stole Christmas*. Shep got the animated version, which is hands down the best."

Not only did Shep task Stewart with decorating the cabin, but he also had him pick up a stash of holiday movies on VHS from the local rental store. It's likely one of the last of its kind, but it's fitting since Shep is old-school and still owns a tape player. I want to get him a DVD player for Christmas so he can catch up on the modern classics that never came out on VHS. I'll have to ask Casey where to find one in town if I see him again.

Maple flops in the snow with a plaintive moo, acting like she's totally wiped out even though she's barely gone a few yards from the barn. She's clearly unimpressed with my attempt at bribing her with snacks and a movie.

"You're totally messing with me, aren't you, girl?"

I drop the lead rope, prepared to admit defeat, when my ringtone slices through the stillness. I peel off a glove and swipe to answer the video chat, Gemma's face filling the screen.

She's sitting cross-legged on a bed, painting her nails. Her black hair is pulled into a braid that hangs over her shoulder, and her oversized sweatshirt swallows her slight frame.

"Morning, Gem."

"Oh, good, you're standing. That means your ankle's better, right?" She purses her lips, giving me a slow, suspicious once-over. "On second thought, that's kind of a bummer. I had my heart set on a dramatic mountain rescue so I could be there to check out the medics. Figured one of them would be hot."

"Glad my prolonged suffering wouldn't have been wasted and might have scored you some eye candy," I deadpan.

She lifts her left hand, blowing on her freshly painted nails. "Can you blame me? Vermont isn't exactly overflowing with good-looking men who have stable jobs."

"What about Crew?" I ask smugly.

She's been keeping me up on all her holiday drama over text, while I've been dodging questions about Shep.

Her family's close friends who live across the street had plumbing problems, so they're crashing at her parents' place. She's been forced to bunk with their adult son—their rich and handsome son, might I add. They've been rivals since childhood, and with their next-level holiday prank war that's gone on for years, he's far from boyfriend material in her eyes. Although I secretly think they could make a good pair if they ever managed to stop tormenting each other long enough to actually talk.

"That man should be counting his days," she mumbles under her breath.

I pace through the crunchy snow as we chat, an old habit I've never managed to shake.

"What did he do now?"

"Yesterday he covered all my clothes in wrapping paper and spent breakfast grinning at me from across the table." She glances across her room like she's making sure he's not around before leaning in and whispering, "But he won't be so smug when he logs into his laptop and sees a warning about a catastrophic North Pole Virus. Extremely serious stuff that can take days if not weeks to repair."

I give an exaggerated shiver. "Note to self: Never cross you if I want my computer intact."

"Don't worry, if you did, my revenge options would be limited since you're my boss. Someone's gotta pay for my Hermès addiction." Gemma winks before her expression shifts into one of shock. "Is that a Highland cow behind you?" she squeals.

I frown, glancing down to see Maple rooting at my coat pocket, the rope dragging behind her. I take a few steps back, and sure enough, she trots after me. It seems walking away is what gets her moving.

"This is Maple," I tell Gemma, crouching to angle the camera so she can see her better. "I've been trying to leash train this one so I can take her back to the cabin, but apparently the trick is to ignore her."

"She totally has to join a podcast episode," Gemma exclaims as she blows on the nails on her right hand.

I bite back a laugh. "Sure. She can dish on all the barnyard drama. I've heard it puts reality TV to shame."

Honestly, it's not even close to Gemma's wildest ideas. There was the time she suggested I interview a professional clown to share confidence tips, or when she pitched having an influencer to come on the show who matched women with prisoners.

"Haven't you seen the guy on social media who films videos at home with his pet cow? Chaos always ensues, and he goes viral every time. That's just a dairy cow—Maple's even more adorable with that fluffy little head. No one watching your live stream would survive the cuteness overload."

I playfully cover Maple's ears. "Don't listen to her, girl. I'd never use you for fame and fortune."

"You've gone full Snow White, except the woodland creatures have been replaced with farm animals." Gemma caps the nail polish bottle and puts it on her nightstand. "Did that silver fox cowboy finally have his way with you?" She waggles her brows. "It would explain why you're strolling through the woods wearing his clothes and that goofy grin."

I duck my head, pretending to adjust my sleeve.

Gemma lets out a delighted gasp. "Oh my god. You totally got laid, didn't you? You're practically glowing."

"I might have," I say, laughing softly.

She bounces on the bed, waving her hands in the air. "This is the greatest news ever. My best friend was finally fucked by a real man. Hallelujah."

My cheeks flush, and I quickly look around to make sure Shep isn't nearby to overhear.

I shake my head, giving an amused snort. "I'll never get over how proud you are of my sexcapades."

"Only when it means you're probably going to move to the middle of nowhere, exclusively wear Carhartt, and have adorable cowboy babies," she explains cheerfully, reclining on the pillows propped up against her headboard.

My brows draw together. "Whoa, slow your roll. In case you forgot, I'm heading back to New York after Christmas. Shep and I both knew this was temporary."

The same uneasy feeling churns in my gut whenever I think about leaving.

Gemma waves me off. "Plans can change. The odds of finding another grumpy mountain man who's a sex god *and* has a miniature Highland who's just as obsessed with you? Slim. In New York? Zip."

I look over at Maple, who nudges her nose against my coat to beg for more apples. I pull a few slices from my pocket and let her eat them straight from my hand.

"What would you ever do without me if I left New York?" I tease Gemma.

"Easy. Find a new best friend who will never leave me," she replies, her serious act undermined by the playful pout tugging at her lips. "Honestly, I'd probably entertain my mom's endless pleas and move back to Vermont. I don't hate the idea as much as I've led her to believe. Our team's remote, so why can't we be too? As long as you've got a spot to record the podcast, we're golden. Plus, we'd save a fortune ditching that overpriced studio."

"Why didn't you mention thinking about moving back before now?"

We tell each other almost everything, and I don't like the idea that she might have withheld this from me because she's worried about how I'd react.

She shrugs. "I hadn't genuinely considered it until this trip, and nothing's been decided. I'm just saying if you ever consider moving yourself, even temporarily, I'll fully support you." She fluffs her pillows and lies back on the bed. "But if it comes to that, we'll have to get all the episodes scheduled beforehand, or we could end up with disgruntled sponsors and subscribers for taking another hiatus to change studios."

I furrow my brow. "What makes you say that?"

"I skimmed your emails this morning and saw a reply from CoreFuel Labs. They're still upset about the extra time you took off for the holidays."

I blink at Gemma, stunned. I've gone above and beyond for them, including tossing in free additional ad reads on the rare occasion they didn't hit their sales goals for a specific episode. And that's not a part of our contract.

"Guess they weren't impressed with my last reply." I sigh.

"Girl, don't sweat it. We'll figure it out. Advertisers come and go, and with how popular the podcast is, there's no shortage of companies that want to work with you," she assures me. "Everyone will survive waiting for a new episode until after Christmas. I'm just glad you finally took some much-needed time off."

"Thanks, Gem."

"Always, babe."

I know she's right, but this business with the sponsor has me worried—I can't help it. I hate upsetting people, and normally I'd stew about it for days. But I can't let it ruin the limited time I have left with Shep. Work will wait until after Christmas, and I'll dive back in once I return to the city. The unease that creeps in whenever I think about leaving comes back, giving me no choice but to stay in denial and focus on making the holidays with Shep the best I possibly can.

Reality can wait a little longer.

CHAPTER 17

Baby It's Cold Outside

Shep

"**I**S THIS THE PART WHERE YOU CONFESS YOU'VE BEEN A serial killer the whole time, and tell everyone I went back to New York when I go missing?" Noelle asks, her breath visible in the cold air.

"You caught me. I lured you into the forest in the freezing cold for that very reason," I say, tossing her a wink.

After swinging by the barn to check on the animals—and coax Maple back to her stall following Noelle's attempt to walk her like an oversized puppy—we stopped by the cabin so Noelle could change. My sweats and flannel weren't going to cut it for this adventure, so I'd picked her up some proper clothes and boots in town that actually fit. Once she finished getting dressed, we drove to the edge of my property.

"You could always sneak me into the local morgue's

incinerator. You'll just have to make sure there are no cameras around," Noelle informs me cheerfully.

I shake my head, running a gloved hand across my face. "Sounds like someone's watched too many murder mysteries."

"True crime podcasts, actually," she corrects me with a grin. "That and bingeing romance novels are my favorite pastimes."

I slow my pace as we climb another crest, our boots crunching over the frosted trail. Thankfully, I came out early this morning to pack down the snow to make the walk easier.

"That's an unusual combo."

"What can I say, I'm unpredictable." Noelle pauses as I lift a low-hanging branch for her to duck under before I follow. "One day I'm hooked on true crime, the next I'm lost in a smutty mafia romance with a morally gray antihero who doesn't hesitate to cut another man's dick off for daring to look at his woman."

I wince, instinctively shielding my crotch. "That's a reasonable reaction," I say flatly.

Noelle tilts her head with a sly grin. "Coming from the guy who kicked someone out of his honky-tonk just for dancing with me."

"Booting Thatcher is one thing. But maiming him? Too messy."

"What a relief that you're the type to exile, not dismember," she replies with a dramatic swipe across her brow.

I don't mention that if anyone tried to hurt her, all bets would be off, and I'd gladly steal a tactic or two from a fictional mafia boss.

I'm saved from replying when Noelle gasps, her hand flying to her mouth as she takes in the view when we reach the top of the ridge.

Below is a small valley with a frozen pond surrounded by pine trees. Icicles hang heavy from the lower branches, catching the light and turning the grove into a cathedral of glass. The pond is smooth and glossy, a solid sheet of ice gleaming like polished marble.

"Shep, this place is amazing," she says in awe.

"I knew you'd like it." I tuck her hand in mine, guiding her along the trail I've already packed down to the pond. "What do you say we go ice-skating?"

While planning out the two days leading up to Christmas, I recalled her telling me that ice skating at Rockefeller Center was one of her favorite traditions. That's when I knew I had to bring her here.

Her eyes widen with a mixture of delight and disbelief. "Seriously? Is it safe?"

"Of course, darlin.'"

I came out early this morning to test the ice thickness and cleared off one of the wooden benches I built ages ago. The pond had been a selling point when I bought the mountain property, but I haven't been here in a long time.

Noelle rests her hand on my shoulder, and I glance around to see we've reached the bottom of the trail and have come to a spot near the pond.

"You alright?" she asks softly.

For a moment, I'm tempted to dismiss her concern, but I rethink it. She draws out a side of me that wants to be honest and share what I tend to keep under lock and key.

"It's been years since I was here. Growing up as an only kid, I pictured having a big family and wanted to turn this place into a retreat with a gazebo, a fishing dock, and a firepit for summer nights. When I realized that I'd probably never have kids of my own, I stopped working on it… and eventually stopped visiting this spot."

"There's still plenty of time to have everything you've always wanted," Noelle says with a soft smile.

I scoff. "I'm forty-five, not exactly in my prime. I've accepted that finding someone who would want to live on a mountain and start a family may not be in the cards for me."

It's not lost on me that my long stretch of isolation hasn't done me any favors. Casey constantly needles me to hang out at High Noon or grab a meal at the diner in town—the one I've avoided since my parents died because it was their favorite place—but I've grown so used to being alone that socializing feels… foreign. It's ironic that the woman who finally gave me a reason to come out of my shell showed up on my doorstep.

Noelle steps closer, her fingertips tracing the coarse line of my mustache, waiting for me to meet her gaze before she speaks. "Don't say that, Shep. You'll make an amazing father someday."

Her conviction makes it hard to argue.

"There's no guarantee of that," I whisper.

"Life has a way of surprising us," she says, letting her hand drift to the nape of my neck, threading her fingers through my hair. "As long as we stay open to the possibilities it brings along."

I want to believe that more than anything, but the longer I spend with her, the more I doubt anyone will ever compare. And I'm starting to wonder if it was fate that led her to my cabin.

Noelle leans in, capturing my mouth in a tender kiss. "I'll believe for the both of us until you're ready to believe it too."

Fuck, this woman is perfect. What I wouldn't give to have her stay longer.

I trace a finger along her jaw. "Thanks for giving me a reason to hope again."

She doesn't have to know that I mean it in more ways than one.

"Always, cowboy." She presses one more chaste kiss to my lips. "Now, didn't you say we were going skating?"

I nod, grateful for a lighter shift in the mood and can't wait to make a new memory in a place that's long been shadowed by what might have been.

Noelle giggles when I scoop her into my arms and carry her to the bench I'd cleared of snow and covered with a blanket. At one end are the two pairs of skates and a thermos of hot chocolate I brought out earlier when I was prepping the area.

I set her down and crouch in front of her, resting her foot on my knee. I hum in approval, pleased she wore the thick socks I told her to. The sun might be out, but the cold is still biting, and I want to make sure she stays warm.

I ease her foot into the skate, the blade still sheathed in its guard. The leather's stiff from the cold, so I go slowly, looping each lace until the boot molds snug around her ankle. After tying a double knot, I reach for the other skate and repeat the process. The only other sound is Noelle's breath, rising in visible puffs against the chill. Once I'm satisfied both skates are secure, I take off the guards and put them on the bench.

"You'll tell me if your ankle starts acting up," I state.

She nods. "I will. But it's better now. I promise."

"And we're going to make sure it stays that way." I give the laces an extra tug before helping her to her feet and leading her to the ice. "I'm going to put on my skates, and I'll meet you out there. Don't go too fast, okay?"

"Yes, *Daddy*," she says, her eyes twinkling with amusement.

She damn well knows what that name does to me, and all I can do is stand there, jaw slack, as she plants a kiss on my cheek before skating away.

After lacing up my skates as quickly as possible, I clumsily make my way to the pond. Once I'm on the ice, I concentrate on putting one foot in front of the other, wobbling with every step. I spread out my arms like a windmill, in an attempt to keep myself upright.

I glance over at the other side of the pond, where Noelle glides across the ice with effortless grace. She's a damn vision with her hair spilling in golden waves beneath a black beanie and her eyes shining with pure joy. For a second, I pause to take in the view. This woman preoccupies my every thought, and after last night, my need to lose myself in her light is unrelenting, making me wish I could freeze this moment to make it last forever.

She circles back to where I'm inching along the edge of the pond. Funny how I worried she might fall, but here I am, the real rookie. I guess being out of my element overrules any misplaced confidence I might have had.

I'm expecting a teasing remark, but instead, Noelle moves to my side and threads her gloved fingers through mine.

"Wanna play a game?" she chirps as she leads me across the frozen surface.

"Like what?"

"'Would you rather.'"

"Never heard of it," I grunt.

"It's easy—I give you two options, and you have to pick one." Her hand tightens around mine as we follow the curve of the pond, keeping me upright. "For example, would you rather wake up early or stay up late?"

I scoff. "Wake up early. There's too much to do to waste daylight."

Although I wouldn't mind sleeping in if I woke up to Noelle in my arms every morning.

"Now it's your turn," she encourages.

"Uh… would you rather have coffee or hot chocolate?"

"You already know the answer to that one, but I'll cut you some slack since this is your first time playing."

She rests her free hand on my arm, the subtle pressure serving as an anchor.

"You might love hot cocoa during the holidays, but how do I know you're not the type who needs a strong cup of coffee to survive a busy Monday morning?"

"Hate to burst your bubble, but I'm definitely not in the early bird club. My creative energy doesn't even clock in until noon, and I record my podcasts in the evening." She gradually picks up our pace, but I hardly notice, absorbed in this little game of learning more about her. "When I do have to be up early, I survive off caramel macchiatos with oat milk and two extra shots of vanilla."

I give her shoulder a playful nudge. "There is one perk to you sleeping in."

"What's that?"

"It means I get to join you back in bed."

After prepping the path to the pond this morning, I went back to the cabin to find Noelle still fast asleep, stretched out on my side of the bed, the blankets pooling around her bare hips.

"I do like sleepy sex with you," Noelle murmurs with a sultry smile. "Now it's my turn. Would you rather fight one horse-sized duck or a hundred duck-sized horses?"

I arch a brow. "What kind of question is that?"

"A smart one. It could save your life someday," she states matter-of-factly.

"Right… because giant duck apocalypses are normal around here."

"There's a first time for everything, and I'd hate for you to be unprepared."

"Wouldn't want that." I chuckle. "I'll take the herd of tiny horses. Toss a handful of diced apples into a stall and they'll be corralled in no time."

"Excellent choice."

She lifts our joined hands as she glides out in front of me and spins in a slow circle. Her skates cut smooth arcs across the ice as her laughter rings through the air. I'm struck by her effortless ability to find joy in the ordinary.

"Would you rather live in the city or the country?" I ask.

It's another question she'll probably accuse me of already knowing the answer to, but I'm a glutton for punishment and can't help but wonder if a small part of her secretly longs for a quieter life away from the hustle and bustle of the city.

Noelle slowly comes to a stop in front of me, prompting me to do the same.

She turns to face me as she lets out a thoughtful hum, considering. "I've lived in New York City my whole adult life. The food scene's fantastic, and there's an endless stream of boutiques, music venues, and pop-ups to check out." My stomach tightens as I brace for what I assume is the inevitable answer. "Still, it has its downsides. It's really loud, people aren't very friendly, and everything costs a fortune. Most of my team works remotely, but we still rent a studio to record my podcast, and the monthly cost could easily pay for a luxury getaway somewhere tropical."

"Maybe if it hadn't cut into your travel budget, you could've taken a trip out of the country instead of roughing it in Arizona for the holidays," I joke, though I'm genuinely intrigued to know what her response will be.

Noelle shakes her head, her expression soft and reflective. "I'm glad I didn't. This trip has been full of surprises, but I wouldn't trade it for anything. It was about time—I was due for a little adventure."

I release a breath I didn't realize I was holding.

"So which one would it be, Sunshine—the city or the country?"

Time seems to stretch on while I wait.

Noelle lifts her eyes to meet mine, reaching up to take off my hat and perch it on her head.

"The country. Definitely the country."

Her answer is straightforward, yet significant. There's something powerful in knowing the simplicity of a small town doesn't put her off, and it sparks a flicker of hope I have no business holding on to.

As flurries begin to fall around us, I'm struck by the realization I'm falling for Noelle—and fast.

If given the choice, she's the person I want to experience the small joys and big milestones with. We haven't known each other long, yet it feels like I've been waiting for her my whole life. I'm faced with the reality that this could all be over soon, and I might be a footnote in her story. But for me, she'll forever be a bright spot.

"Would you rather have a Pause button or a Rewind button in a video game version of your life?" she asks.

"Pause button," I state with zero hesitation.

Noelle lifts her hand to rest it against my cheek.

"Me too, cowboy," she whispers. "Me too."

CHAPTER 18

Making Spirits Bright

Noelle

YESTERDAY COULDN'T HAVE BEEN BETTER. FROM breakfast to skating, snuggling by the fire and watching the original *Miracle on 34th Street* to hanging stockings—Shep has outdone himself in the holiday tradition department, and I couldn't be more grateful that I get to share it all with him.

This morning, he greeted me with plans for another day full of surprises—made even sweeter because it's Christmas Eve. With every thoughtful gesture, both big and small, he has me convinced "acts of service" is a cowboy's universal love language. Either way, I'm definitely not complaining.

Even our early start this morning couldn't dampen my excitement.

Shep wouldn't say exactly where we were headed first, only hinting that we'd be going into town, so it's no surprise when we end up on Main Street.

A bell jingles as he pulls open the door to the Cactus Bloom Café, the local diner.

"After you, Sunshine," he drawls, tipping his hat.

"Why, thank you."

The place is packed, humming with the din of chatter, clinking silverware, and the soft crackle of Willie Nelson's version of "Blue Christmas" playing from the jukebox in the back corner. Locals occupy the red vinyl stools along the counter, bathed in the amber glow of festive lights strung from above. The booths are upholstered in worn leather, and black-and-white rodeo photos add to the diner's decor. The scent of cinnamon, coffee, and melted butter fills the air.

The second we walk in, the conversation dips, and every head in the place turns in our direction. A few jaws even drop at our arrival as if it's groundbreaking.

"Is there a reason everyone's staring?" I whisper to Shep with a tight smile.

I might be the only one not in a flannel or a cowboy hat, but surely, tourists frequent the place too.

"If there's one thing folks around here love more than breakfast, it's other people's business," Shep grumbles.

That doesn't exactly answer my question, but a quick look around confirms everyone is watching him, not me. Before I can dwell on the reason why, a woman who appears to be in her late sixties walks our way, adjusting the ties on her denim apron.

She comes to a standstill next to the hostess booth, resting a hand on her hip, and lets out a long whistle. "Well, butter my biscuit! Look who the wind blew in."

Her silver hair is tied in a loose braid down her back, and she's wearing a red sweater with a light-up reindeer on the front.

"Mornin', Marge," Shep says sheepishly.

"Don't you 'Mornin Marge me, young man." She glares,

leaning over to swat his arm, then mutters something that sounds like "strolls back in here like it's any ole' day."

I stifle a giggle at her calling Shep a young man, though I suppose in her eyes, he is.

Shep scratches the back of his head. "I've been busy."

"Hogwash. You've been holed up on that mountain for years, and you haven't so much as stepped through those doors since your ma passed. Now, suddenly you show up on Christmas Eve like you used to with your folks?" Marge shoots me a curious look, the Santa hat perched on her head tilting precariously. "Does your sudden return to civilization have anything to do with this pretty young thing?"

Shep used to come here with his parents? Being brought to a place that must hold so many memories makes my heart skip a beat.

"I'm Noelle," I say, holding out my hand to Marge.

She disregards my outstretched hand and pulls me in for a bear hug instead. I'm momentarily caught off guard, but quickly reciprocate, figuring it's the small-town version of saying hello. Honestly, it's refreshing compared to the stiff greetings I get in the city—even from people I'm familiar with.

"It's a pleasure, sugar. Shep treatin' you right?" Marge asks, stepping back to get a better look at me, her eyes twinkling. "I was his mama's best friend, so if he gives you any grief, you come find me, and I'll set him straight."

"He's a sweetheart once you get past the tough exterior. Though he acted like I was trespassing on top-secret government property when I accidentally showed up at his doorstep." I nudge Shep's arm with my elbow, grinning when he cuts me a half-hearted scowl. "I'd recommend keeping him off any welcoming committees or he might scare off newcomers before they even unpack."

Marge lets out a hearty laugh. "Well, aren't you a firecracker?"

She shoots Shep a pointed look. "You hold tight to this one, she's a keeper."

"Told him the same thing." The familiar voice has me looking up to spot Casey weaving through tables, stopping beside Shep, and giving him a mock salute. "Out in the wild twice in one week? Careful, Shep. At this rate, we're gonna have to revoke your hermit status."

"We having a town meeting this morning I didn't know about?" Shep grunts.

As a group of customers leave the diner, calling their thanks to Marge, we move to the space next to the hostess stand where people usually wait to be seated, staying out of the way of foot traffic as we chat.

"Reckon if that's the case, we gotta wait for Amy to get back from the restroom or she'll have my hide for missing all the gossip." Casey stuffs his hands in his pockets and turns to Shep. "And don't act surprised to see me. We've been coming here for Christmas Eve breakfast the past fifteen years. You damn well know that, since we used to come with you and your folks."

Shep takes off his hat, running a hand through his hair. "I figured you'd be at home since Amy's family is in town."

It dawns on me that, as much as he's started coming out of his shell, being back at this particular place after so long can't be easy. I'm sure he didn't want to make a big production out of it. Although whether he'll admit it or not, I think it's a good thing Casey's here to offer emotional support, even if it's in the form of teasing.

"When I caught Amy's mama alphabetizing our spices before 7:00 a.m., I told her it was time for just the two of us to escape to the diner for breakfast. With the baby due any day and her folks planning to stick around, this might be our last reprieve for a few months."

Marge wags a finger at him. "Y'all will be thanking your lucky stars when they're around to help with midnight feedings and diaper duty."

"I have no doubt, but a man's got his limits—like her mama folding my underwear and strolling into our room unannounced asking how to use the TV remote."

I can't help but giggle at that.

Marge leans forward and playfully smacks Casey upside the head. "If it bothers you, do your own laundry, and be grateful her mama is pitching in. Men, bless 'em, always complaining about something," she adds with a sigh.

"Don't drag me into it," Shep cuts in. "Just 'cause Casey's grumbling about getting help doesn't mean we'd all look a gift horse in the mouth."

Marge rolls her eyes. "You're no better. Remember that winter you were sick, and your mama did your laundry? She accidentally tossed your only white collared shirt in with a red towel, and you carried on about it for days like it was the end of the world."

Shep huffs out an exasperated sigh, but I don't miss the faint flush creeping up his cheeks. "I had a meeting with the manager of a world-famous country band about having them play at the honky-tonk and didn't notice the damn thing was pink until it was too late to find something else to wear."

"It was priceless. He looked like a strawberry milkshake," Casey snickers.

I bite my lip, trying not to laugh as I picture Shep muttering under his breath and adjusting his pink collar. "I don't know, Shep. Salmon might be your color."

He strokes his mustache, doing a poor job of hiding his amusement.

Suddenly someone yells Marge's name from across the room, and we all turn to see an elderly man waving his empty mug in midair.

"I'll be there in a minute, George," she shouts, then turns her attention back to us. "Best get back to it soon or folks will start fussin'. Owner's duties, I suppose. Shep, you and the pretty lady know what you want? Same as usual for you?"

His eyes light up, a small smile forming on his lips, clearly touched that she remembered. "Yes, ma'am, and a cup of coffee. I reckon Noelle might need a minute with the menu."

"What's the usual?" I ask, glancing back and forth between them.

"The rancher's special—two eggs over easy, four strips of bacon, hashbrowns, and biscuits smothered in gravy, made from Shep's mama's secret recipe." Marge rattles it off like it's second nature. "She helped me get the menu together when I opened this place. Folks loved her additions, but I never could get her to go into business with me."

That's when it hits me—Shep must've learned his exceptional cooking skills from his mom, which makes it even sweeter that he's been using them to make me feel at home during my stay.

"That's because the hours were long, and she liked being home evenings and weekends," Shep says, his tone warm. "Still, she sure loved coming by to lend a hand when the diner got busy."

"She was a treasure, and she sure adored you and your pa," Marge replies with a wistful smile.

I step closer to Shep and slide my hand into his, giving it a squeeze. A silent reminder that I'm here for him and thankful to share this moment.

The same man calls for Marge again, and she hollers back, "Don't get your britches in a twist. I'm comin'." She leans in, speaking to me. "These folks have no manners. Want to take a look at the menu, sugar?"

I shake my head. "I'll have the biscuits and gravy, a side of fruit, and hot chocolate if you have it."

There's no chance I'm missing out on trying a recipe created by Shep's mom.

Marge flips open a small notepad and jots down our order. "Sure thing. I'll have that out in a jiffy. Take a seat at the bar till a booth opens up."

"Bring their food to our table when it's ready," Casey pipes up. "Can't let Shep skip out on this year's Christmas Eve tradition. Besides, Amy will want the inside scoop on him and his woman."

I rather like the sound of being called Shep's woman.

"You got it," Marge says as she slips away to handle her disgruntled customer.

Shep and I follow Casey through the diner, weaving between tables. When we reach a booth in the back, Casey slides in, motioning for us to sit across from him. Judging by the half-empty cup of coffee and orange juice on the table, they're still waiting for their breakfast order.

I scoot in first with Shep right behind me, his hand settling possessively on my thigh under the table.

A woman steps out of the nearby hallway, who I assume is Amy. She's wearing a red sweater that stretches across her round belly, with brown hair piled into a messy bun. Her hazel eyes brighten when she spots us.

She's practically glowing, and it makes me wonder what it will be like to be pregnant someday. As an only child, I've always wanted siblings, so having a big family of my own has been a lifelong dream. A series of images flashes through my mind—Shep and I finding out we're expecting, our baby nestled in my arms in a rocking chair by the fire, and the three of us visiting Maple and Blaze at the barn.

I mentally scold myself for letting my imagination run wild when things between us are still so uncertain.

"What a pleasant surprise," Amy exclaims when she joins us at the table, tucking a rogue chestnut strand into the bun atop her head. "You must be Noelle. Casey told me Shep brought someone special to the honky-tonk the other night, and I was hoping to get the chance to meet you."

Casey helps her into the booth beside him, then drapes an arm around her as she settles into the crook of his shoulder.

"It's nice to meet you," I say with a smile. "Shep said you were behind the Christmas tree outside High Noon. It was the perfect touch."

"I'm glad *someone* appreciates it." She glances at Shep and Casey, giving them both a pointed look. "Those specialty drinks with festive names were all me too."

"The Bootylicious Blitzen *is* an iconic name." I grin.

"That was one of my better ideas, if I do say so myself," Amy states proudly before taking a sip of orange juice.

"Since you're the brains behind this operation, I'm thinking I should hire you and let this husband of yours learn from the sidelines," Shep says, tipping his head toward Casey.

"Just 'cause I handle all the boring stuff like scheduling and inventory instead of naming drinks after famous reindeer doesn't mean I'm not pulling my weight," Casey mutters.

Amy pats his chest with a teasing laugh. "Relax, babe, your job's safe from me. I rather like you earning the money while I find ways to spend it." She cuts a mock glare at Shep. "You wouldn't dare fire him, not when we're about to have another mouth to feed." She rubs her belly for emphasis.

Shep grunts, but there's a softness in his gaze.

I appreciate that his friends can playfully challenge him while offering unwavering support. He may have believed he was alone for all these years, but he had plenty of people ready and waiting to embrace him with open arms.

"On a brighter note," Amy chimes, "Casey gave me my Christmas present early, and I love it. Thank you, Shep. The rocking chair is perfect."

Shep waves her off. "It's no trouble. Once the baby's here and has a name, I'll engrave it."

"That'll be really special." Amy beams. "Bring Noelle along and we'll make a proper evening of it. I'm sure I'll be craving some adult company beyond my hovering mother or my worrywart husband." She leans over and pecks Casey on the cheek.

Shep gives my thigh a squeeze as our eyes meet, heavy with unspoken sadness. The reality that I'll be gone soon hurts more than I could've ever anticipated.

Just then, Marge arrives carrying a tray loaded with drinks and our breakfast. My biscuits and gravy are piping hot and look downright delicious.

"Enjoy your meal, y'all. If there's anything else I can get you, just holler," she says before moving on to take another table's order.

A chorus of *thank-yous* fills the air before we dig in.

I cut into a steaming biscuit, stab a forkful, and blow on it before taking a bite. The sausage gravy is creamy and peppery, while the biscuits are light, fluffy, and buttery.

"This might be the best breakfast I've ever had," I say between bites.

Shep chuckles. "Glad you like it."

I lean in close, letting my lips brush his ear. "Thanks for bringing me here and sharing this tradition with me. I wouldn't trade being here with you on Christmas Eve for anything."

"Glad you're here too, Sunshine. More than you know."

I'm outside the diner, glancing at Shep through the window, while he handles the bill. He's still at the cash register where Marge is talking his ear off. Her warm smile makes it obvious she's happy he stopped by. From this angle, I can't see Shep's face, but his posture is relaxed, and he seems completely at ease with her.

Another reason I love small towns: The connections people form never fade, no matter how long someone's been away. I can't help but feel a pang of envy, longing for a community that is close and unshakable. I have Gemma and my parents, but there's something special about having an entire town embrace you like family, even if you aren't related by blood.

It's one of the things I've missed about small-town life. I was young when we moved to the city, but I still remember the neighbors who stopped by with treats, the backyard birthday parties, and the small acts of kindness that made ordinary days unforgettable.

Just then, Casey and Amy step outside, with him fussing with her coat zipper as if it's the most important job he has. Seems I'm not the only one whose man is obsessed with safety and comfort.

"Noelle, there you are," Amy says in a sing-song voice. "Shep should be out soon."

Casey snorts. "Sure, as soon as Marge lets him get a word in edgewise. Serves him right for insisting on paying for our meal. I tried slipping Marge some cash, but Shep threatened to withhold his ma's lemon meringue recipe that she's been after for years."

I giggle. "What did Marge do?"

"Told me my money was no good at the diner," he says, clutching his chest dramatically. "Shep's never been one to play fair. When he wants something, he doesn't quit until he gets it." He tucks a few twenties back into his wallet. "It's really good seeing him act like his old self again. He hasn't been this happy in ages, and it's all thanks to you."

"He makes me happy, too," I say with a smile.

More than I can say.

"How long are you going to be in town?" Amy asks tentatively, her expression apologetic.

"As of now, the day after Christmas?" The statement comes out more like a question, but it's all I can manage.

Casey cocks his head. "You say it like you're not sure."

I shrug. "Guess I'm still figuring out what comes next."

Amy puts her hand on Casey's arm. "Alright, let's leave the poor girl alone. We'd better head out so we can finish our last-minute shopping."

I sigh in relief. If I had the answers, I'd gladly share them, but as it stands, it's unclear what the future holds for us.

"It was so nice to meet you," I say to Amy. "And it was good to see you again, too, Casey."

"Same here. Take it from me. Shep is crazy about you. If the feeling's mutual, I think it's going to work out just fine."

His confidence softens the uncertainty I can't shake.

"Thanks. I appreciate it."

"Anytime," Casey says, tipping his hat.

They wave goodbye, and as they disappear around the corner toward the bustling town center, my phone buzzes with a new notification. I must have forgotten to turn on Do Not Disturb before we left the cabin this morning. I've made a point of avoiding distractions so I can soak up every minute with Shep.

My stomach drops when I see it's a new email from CoreFuel Labs. They're ending our partnership once the contract expires at the end of the year, citing my "failure to meet obligations." I scroll furiously, reading about how they appreciate the working relationship we've shared over the past few years, but want to put their marketing dollars into "more reliable, performance-driven partnerships." They expressed disappointment over the last-minute notice that I'd be taking more time off from posting podcast videos than my team originally indicated, even though I explained it was due to circumstances beyond my control.

I shouldn't be surprised—they've been our most demanding sponsor from the start, always pushing me to do more than is reasonable. Even though I know taking some much-needed time off was the right choice, I can't shake the disappointment.

I'm pacing back and forth, fidgeting with my hands, when Shep steps out of the diner. He furrows his brow, immediately picking up on my unease.

"Noelle, what's wrong?" He nestles me into his side, guiding us away from the window and toward an outdoor heater by the diner's entrance.

I'm grateful no one else is out here, not wanting an audience as I process this news.

"Remember the podcast sponsor I was telling you about who was unhappy with my recent posting schedule?"

I filled Shep in on the situation earlier when he sensed I was stressed. It's incredible how attuned he is, picking up on the smallest shifts in my mood.

He steps in front of me, pulling me into a hug. "Yeah."

"They've decided to discontinue our partnership," I say into his chest, his coat brushing against my cheek.

He grunts his disapproval as he rubs soothing circles on my back. "That's pretty shitty to do on Christmas Eve."

I take a deep breath as I sink further into his embrace. "That's corporations for you—no loyalty or leeway if they think it could hurt their bottom line."

I'm guessing they didn't hit their Q4 projections, so management scrambled to find places to cut the budget. I was likely an easy target, since they're apparently unsatisfied with our partnership even though it was profitable for them.

"Do sponsors normally try to run the show? You're the boss. They have no business controlling how you run things or when you take time off, particularly around the holidays," Shep grumbles.

"Most are easy to work with. I could use a third-party agency, but Gemma and I like handling them ourselves to preserve creative vision."

He tips my chin to meet his gaze. "How big of an impact will losing this sponsorship have on your revenue?"

"It should be minimal. Companies contact us every day, many offering higher rates as our audience grows." Warmth creeps up my neck, suddenly feeling a little sheepish about my initial reaction. "But I've worked with this sponsor since my podcast took off, and it feels like I've let a friend down. I just wish I could make it right, even though I know it's not in my best interest."

My need to please everyone is in overdrive, and it's difficult to admit that it's an impossible feat.

"They don't deserve a second thought after how they've treated you," Shep states, tracing a line along my jaw. "In my opinion, you shouldn't partner with a company that ignores your limits. You have every right to set boundaries, even if it means taking time off on short notice. If they can't respect that, you'll find others who will."

"Thanks for standing up for me. It's not my strong suit," I admit.

"Always, sweetheart. You've got a heart of gold, and some people will try to take advantage of that. The key is to be willing to put yourself first every now and then and not feel guilty for saying no when it's necessary."

God, I had no idea how much I needed to hear that. I'm still a little flustered, and the sting of rejection won't disappear overnight, but Shep has shown me how to process it without letting it take over. I've faced criticism in the past and have let other people's opinions make me feel like a failure and that I was letting people down. I'm quickly learning that my mental and emotional peace have to come first. At the end of the day, my priority has to be making the best decisions for myself and letting everything else fall into place after that.

In the future, I'll definitely be taking more time off while making sure I use my team and resources to keep everything running smoothly. The business is successful now, and I don't have to carry all the responsibilities like I did when I first started.

I place my hands on his shoulders, rising on my toes to kiss him. "Okay, no more doom and gloom. What's next on the agenda? Are we going back to the cabin?"

He's kept our plans under wraps like a scavenger hunt for adults but without the clues, and each surprise so far has topped the last.

"Not yet. There are a couple more stops. The next one's just down the block," he says cryptically.

"Lead the way, cowboy."

He takes my hand, guiding me down the street until we reach a toy shop.

"Here we are," he says, smiling as he gestures to the sign above. The Wooden Wagon is scrawled in black cursive, and the chains holding it against the archway look ready to give way.

"What are we doing at a toy store?" I ask.

He's shared how painful the thought of never becoming a father is and for years has stayed away from the pond on his land since it reminded him of what might never be. So it's a little bewildering to see him now, about to walk into a toy store like it's the most natural thing in the world.

Shep takes off his hat, running a hand through his hair. "After Ma passed, someone else in town took over organizing Secret Santa for the homeless shelter, but I still wanted to find a way to contribute in her honor. So I built a big toy chest for the staff at the shelter to keep in the storage room and every couple of months I stock it with presents they can give out for birthdays, holidays, and other special occasions. I always fill it on Christmas Eve, just in case any children were missed by Secret Santa." A faint blush colors his cheeks, as he glances at the ground. "You mentioned one of your favorite traditions is picking out gifts for children who could use a little holiday magic, so I figured we could get some toys to drop off at the shelter."

Shep might hide behind a mask of indifference, but his actions speak louder than his words.

I give him a broad smile. "I'd like that very much."

He opens the door, ushering me inside. The place is bustling with people navigating crowded aisles, grabbing last-minute gifts for Santa's big day tomorrow.

"Welcome in, Shep. Figured I'd be seeing you today," the clerk calls out with a grin. "I even cleared out some room for your things on the counter." He waves to an empty space behind him with a little flourish.

Shep gives him a curt nod. "Thanks, Jonny."

He grabs two carts, pushing one toward me, letting me lead the way down the first aisle filled with stuffed animals and plushies.

"Fair warning, I don't believe in shopping on a budget," I say over my shoulder as I toss a floppy-eared bunny into my cart. "I sure hope you brought your big spender energy." I add two unicorn plushies to my load for good measure.

I spin around to find Shep watching me, amusement flickering in his eyes. "You drive a hard bargain. I might have to reconsider my early retirement plan."

"*Early* retirement? You're practically there," I tease.

He playfully glares at me. "I'm gonna let that one slide for the kids' sake. We've got lots of shopping to do and not much time." He drops an armful of dinosaur plushies into his cart. "And don't worry, there is no budget."

It's as if time stands still and the noise of the shop fades away. *I'm falling for this man.*

His grumpy disposition, the playful banter, and the unspoken acts of kindness are responsible for him capturing my heart without warning. All I can think about is how lucky I am to have stumbled into his world, and I'm not ready to say goodbye. There are countless questions about how this could work or if it's even possible, but I want to take the chance. For once, I'm ready to prioritize myself and my own happiness—consequences be damned.

The trouble is, Shep has hinted at wanting me to stay after Christmas, but he hasn't come right out and said it. As much as it pains me to hold my feelings in, he needs to take the leap this time, without me coaxing him. Committing to being together is a big step, and he has to choose this—choose us—on his own terms. All I can do is hope that we want the same things, and that he's ready to step into the unknown with me.

CHAPTER 19

Dick The Halls

Shep

NOELLE IS NOTHING SHORT OF A MIRACLE WORKER.

It'd been years since I last stepped inside Cactus Bloom Café. I avoided the place because it held too many memories of my parents, especially during the holidays.

Still, as I considered which traditions to share with her, stopping there for Christmas Eve breakfast was a no-brainer. With her beside me, the dull ache turns into something peaceful. Even talking with Marge brought me comfort I never thought possible—a reminder of how loved my parents were, and that this town hasn't forgotten me, even after all the years I've spent keeping to myself. I would never have found the courage to walk back in there if it weren't for Noelle.

After our stop at the toy store, we dropped off a truckload of donations at the homeless shelter and spent the afternoon building a snowman in front of the cabin. For dinner, I made roast chicken, mashed potatoes, and garlic bread—another one of my mom's Christmas Eve traditions.

I left Noelle for what was supposed to be a quick check on the animals, but I ended up mucking out a few stalls and fixing a loose barn door latch, which kept me away for a couple of hours.

It's dark when I get back to the cabin, and I'm welcomed by the warmth of the fireplace. The tree's lights twinkle beside the flicker of candles on the mantel. Noelle's curled up on the floor, nestled in a pile of blankets and pillows, her e-reader in hand. She looks up, and that smile—bright and effortless—hits me so hard my knees damn near give out right there in the doorway.

"Took you long enough," she rasps, setting her e-reader down.

"Sorry, I had to muck out Blaze's stall—"

My apology dies on my tongue when she straightens up, stretching her arms overhead, the blankets falling away to reveal a sheer white bralette with red satin trim and matching panties.

Fuck me.

Noelle tilts her head, toying with her bra strap. "Something catch your attention, cowboy?"

I swallow hard, suddenly forgetting how to form a coherent thought. She's pure sin wrapped in white and red, the fabric hugging every curve like it was made to tempt me, and all I can think about is tracing every inch of her with my tongue.

With my control hanging by a thread, I scramble for a distraction, nodding to her e-reader. "What are you reading?"

A faint blush colors her cheeks. "A mafia romance."

"What's this one about?" I force my gaze to remain on her face.

After peeling my gloves off, I shove them into my coat pocket before hanging it on the rack by the door.

"A mafia boss falls for the woman sent by a rival to infiltrate his organization." Noelle wets her lips and sits back on her heels. "She's there to pay off her father's debt."

I have no clue what any of that means, but she obviously enjoys it, so I pay attention.

"Infiltrated by a rival?" I say, hanging up my hat. "Tell me more."

"When he finds out why she's there, he can't deny the attraction simmering between them."

I kick off my boots and move toward the fireplace. "What does he do about it?"

"I'm 75 percent in—and it's in the middle of a spicy scene where he's claiming her as his." Her voice drops to a whisper as she picks up her e-reader and holds it out to me. "Want a peek?"

I nod and bend down to take the device from her. I've never read a spicy novel before, but I'll be damned if I'm not curious about what's got her flushed, so I read aloud from where she left off.

I force my muscles to relax as Enzo pushes into me. The stretch is intense, causing a sharp burn and blurring the line between pleasure and pain.

"Oh god," I whimper.

"Your god isn't here, Carina. I'm the only one you'll be worshipping tonight," Enzo states.

Between his cock in my ass and the biting sting of the nipple clamps, I'm in shambles with tears streaking my face. He grips my hair, tilting my head back, and licks a stray tear from my cheek.

Out of the corner of my eye, I catch Noelle staring up at me, lips slightly parted, her gaze burning. Her unfiltered reaction keeps me reading.

As he pulls out and pushes back inside, the drag of his cock against my inner walls is unlike anything I've ever felt, unearthing sensations I never knew existed. When he adjusts his angle, I cry out as he hits a spot he found with his fingers earlier.

"Oh fuck, Enzo."

"That's right, scream my name, princess," he growls as he claims my ass.

This time when I look down, Noelle's hands are pressed to her thighs, squeezing them so tight her knuckles are white, and her breaths are shallow and uneven. Fuck, even I'm affected, causing my dick to strain against my jeans.

Enzo bands his arms around me, fingers toying with the chains attached to the nipple clamps. A shockwave of heat runs straight through every nerve as my eyes shutter closed.

"I might be taking your perfect ass now, but later, I'm going to fuck that perfect pink pussy, and fill you with my cum."

A low groan passes my lips at his wicked words.

I trail off and lift my gaze to Noelle, whose eyes are dark with want, a wet patch forming on her panties. Looks like we'll have to read mafia romances together again soon if this is the outcome.

"Is this your way of saying you want to try ass play?" I ask, my voice husky as I set her e-reader on the coffee table.

She did say a few days ago she wanted to try it, but I wasn't sure if she was ready.

Noelle draws in a shaky breath as she rests her hands on her thighs. "I want you to be my first, Shep."

I lean down and gently lift her jaw, making her eyes meet mine. "If we do this, I'll be your only."

Her expression lights up at the prospect. "I like the sound of that."

So do I.

More than anything. And once I finally get the chance to claim her in every way, I can't grasp the concept of being able to let her go.

I fold my arms across my chest, letting the silence stretch before speaking. "If you really want this, then get on all fours, baby."

Noelle scrambles to obey, spreading out one of the blankets and pushing the others aside. She ties her hair back then crawls to the middle, moving to her hands and knees, facing me. Her chest rises and falls in quick, shallow bursts as she peeks up through her eyelashes with a seductive smile, silently conveying it's my move.

"You're beautiful." I bend down to brush a stray piece of hair from her face. "I'll be right back. Don't move while I'm gone."

"Wouldn't dream of it," she sasses back.

"Careful, sweetheart. Don't forget who's in charge of your pleasure tonight."

I stand, leaving her with that warning as I stride to the bedroom where her suitcase is stashed on a chair in the corner.

I'm eager to further inspect her stash of toys, letting out a whistle when I see just how extensive it is. Good god, this company must have sent her every single piece from their holiday collection—but I'm not complaining. It gives me endless ways to play with Noelle. I take my sweet time sifting through the large pile. I want her dripping wet and aching by the time I get back.

My first pick is a silver butt plug with a star on the base. We've never played like this before, so I want to make sure I prime her well. Next, an emerald green blindfold with velvet trim catches my eye, so I grab that too. Then I choose a bullet vibrator in a glittery red. The last thing I take is a small bottle of peppermint-scented lube, chuckling when I see the bottle is in the shape of a candy cane.

Once I've gathered everything I need, I scan the room until my gaze settles on the bed. For what I have in mind, I think it'll be the most comfortable spot for Noelle. I set everything I've collected on the nightstand and head back to the living room to get her.

She's still on all fours, her ass angled in my direction and glances back over her shoulder. As predicted, her pupils are dilated, and she's trembling in anticipation. What I'm not expecting is to see that she's removed her panties, and I exhale sharply when

I spot the bejeweled butt plug in her ass. Looks like we won't need the plug I picked out after all.

God, the things I want to do to her.

My mouth goes dry as I move closer. "Someone's been busy."

Just imagining her preparing herself for me while I was at the barn makes my jaw tighten as I fight back a possessive growl.

She bats her lashes. "Are you surprised?"

I crouch beside her, my eyes glued to her heart-shaped ass as I run my palm down her spine. "As much as I love your enthusiasm, you disobeyed my instructions not to move."

"But I wanted you to see my new butt plug. Don't you like it, *Daddy?*" she purrs.

I groan at the nickname. "Hell yeah, I do."

My hands glide along her curves, tracking lines across her silky skin. I should have more self-control, but seeing her on display erases all thoughts of restraint. I trail my fingers down her lower back, taking hold of the base of the plug and slowly rock it back and forth.

Noelle drops her head back, groaning softly.

"That feel good, baby?" I ask, gently twisting the base in slow circles.

"Mmm."

"I'm glad because tonight is all about your pleasure. If anything feels uncomfortable, you tell me, alright?"

"I will," she promises.

Satisfied with her answer, I continue wiggling the butt plug, withdrawing it with deliberate care, inch by inch. Noelle shivers under my touch with each tug. Once the plug is out, I set it to the side, turning my attention immediately back to her.

I settle behind her, my chest flush against her back, pressing a path of kisses up her spine, one hand braced on the floor, the other moving to cup her breast. Noelle lets out a soft whimper when I pinch her nipples, and my lips follow the line of her shoulder blades. I'm all in for borrowing inspiration from a fictional mafia boss if it turns my woman on.

"Can I blindfold you?" I whisper into the nape of her neck.

I want to shut out the outside world so every brush of skin and sound is amplified for her.

"I trust you."

God, hearing those three words humbles me, a reminder of the faith she has in me.

"Is that a yes?" I ask, still toying with her nipples.

She looks back, beads of sweat glistening on her forehead. "Yes, blindfold me, Shep."

"All the toys I picked out are in the bedroom." I give her nipples a final tug before letting go, and she gasps sharply. "I thought you'd be more comfortable there."

"*Toys*. As in plural?" she questions, a spark of excitement in her voice.

"That's right."

I plant one last kiss on her shoulder before easing off and standing to my full height. Noelle pushes herself onto her knees, and I extend my hand, to help her to her feet. I lead her to the bedroom, and she goes straight to the bed, positioning herself on her hands and knees in the middle of the mattress. She lifts her eyes to mine, a smile playing on her lips as she waits for my instruction.

A quiet laugh rumbles through my chest. "Someone's eager to play."

"With you? Always."

I pull off my T-shirt and toss it to the ground, Noelle's gaze roaming hungrily from my chest down to my lower abdomen. Damn, when she looks at me like that, my blood runs hot, and the pull of wanting her takes over every corner of my mind. Next, I strip off my jeans and boxers, adding them to the pile of discarded clothes.

She presses her thighs together, letting out needy noises when my erection comes into view.

The sight of her in front of me, waiting for my command, has me in a frenzy. Unable to wait a second longer, I fist my cock, pre-cum dripping from the tip. I give my shaft a hard squeeze, grunting at the pressure. The relief is short-lived as every pulse reminds me of what I really want—to be buried deep inside Noelle's ass.

Her eyes grow wide when I grab the blindfold and the toys from the nightstand, moving it all to the edge of the bed.

"Close your eyes, beautiful," I order.

She immediately does as I ask, and I join her on the bed, hovering over her. "I'm going to put the blindfold on, alright?"

"Okay."

I place the soft material against her eyes and tie it behind her head. "I'm going to rub some lube on you now." I twist the lid off the bottle and pour a generous amount onto my fingers, massaging them together until it's warm.

Noelle hums softly as my fingers brush against her tight hole, coating it with lube. I add more to my fingers, spreading in another generous coat over her asshole. The sight of her glistening and prepped for me has me feral.

"Now I'm going to ease a finger inside. Push against me."

The butt plug was a good start, but it was much smaller than my cock. I want to start with more prep to make sure Noelle has time to adjust. She lets out a soft whimper, pushing her ass up as I slowly press the tip of my finger inside.

"Oh fuck," Noelle breathes, hanging her head.

"Too much?" I ask, holding perfectly still. "Want me to stop?"

She shakes her head, panting. "No. Keep going."

I ease my finger in deeper, mindful of every movement. I want this moment to be branded into her memory, a reminder of how deeply she craves my touch. Once my finger is fully seated, I carefully add in a second, scissoring my fingers to open her wider.

I must hit a particularly sensitive spot because she arches back, gasping audibly.

Fuck, she's so damn tight, and knowing my dick will be inside soon is enough to turn me into a primal beast.

"Feel that, Noelle? Those are my fingers fucking your ass, and soon, you'll be full of my cock," I murmur, leaning in to ghost my lips along her back.

"More," she begs.

When I'm able to slide my fingers in and out easily, I know she's ready for me.

"I'll start with the tip and slowly work myself in all the way. If at any point you want me to stop, tell me, and I will."

She nods, pushing her hips up to meet mine. I pour a generous amount of lube down the crease between her cheeks and rub my dick across it until we're both super slick.

I set the lube aside and grab the bullet from the edge of the mattress, placing it in Noelle's hand. Since she's blindfolded, I wait until her hand closes around it before releasing my hold.

"Is this what I think it is?" she asks, running her fingers along the smooth cylinder.

"If you guessed a vibrator, you're right. I want you to tease your clit while I play with your ass. Think you can do that?"

"Mm-hmm."

I lean down to press several kisses along her spine. "That's my good girl."

I want her to focus on making herself feel good while she takes me—that means toeing the line between pleasure and taking her to new heights.

A low hum fills the room, telling me she's turned on the device, and she shudders slightly when the tip touches her clit, arching into me. She holds herself up with her free forearm planted firmly on the mattress.

"Just like that."

I take hold of my cock and press the tip against her back entrance, easing my way past the initial resistance. She fits around me like a damn glove, and the world shrinks to her ragged breaths and the heat clawing through me.

"You're so big," Noelle moans.

"Breathe, sweetheart." I coach her as I caress the curve of her waist. "Breathe and let me in."

I inhale deeply, and it takes all my willpower to work inside her inch by inch, until my hips are pressed against hers. Noelle writhes beneath me as I stay still for several seconds, letting her feel the full stretch of me. Fuck, it drives me wild knowing I'm the only man who's ever claimed her here.

"You're doing great, baby," I praise. "Put more pressure on your clit."

She bobs her head as she does what she's told, the low hum of the device building to a steady purr, her free hand clutching the comforter as she groans.

Noelle lets out a pleading whimper. "Move, Shep. I need you to move."

Unable to deny her, I withdraw slightly, then slide forward in slow, measured strokes.

Desire hums between us, electric and unrelenting, the space dissolving into nothing but our bodies pressed together and our ragged breaths. I rub my other hand along her damp skin, keeping her in position.

Noelle's movements grow more insistent as she begins pushing back into me, soft gasps spilling from her lips. I can feel her muscles relax around me, and I pull out halfway before thrusting forward, burying myself to the hilt. I maintain a steady rhythm, gliding back and forth while she holds the vibrator in place.

"You're taking me so well. You love playing with yourself while I claim your ass, don't you, baby?"

"Yes. Oh my god, Shep," she stammers.

"Who owns this ass, Noelle? Say it," I demand, giving one of her cheeks a light smack.

"You do," she pants.

"Hell yes, I do. You're mine."

She nods frantically, every inhale sharp and uneven.

I'd meant to take my time, savoring the slow build of her climax before the inevitable fall, but seeing her like this has stripped me of all restraint. I'm desperate to have her quivering beneath my touch as she crashes over the edge with my cock in her ass.

Her throaty moans grow louder as she continues stimulating her clit with the bullet. With newfound determination, I adjust my angle, making sure to hit the sensitive spot I did with my fingers earlier. The effect of the dual sensations is immediate as her fingers claw at the comforter, arching her ass against my hips as she cries out my name.

"Come for me, darlin'," I command.

At my order, Noelle clenches around me. A series of grunts tears from her throat as her orgasm crashes over her.

I watch my woman unravel like a loose coil, collapsing into ecstasy as she mutters incoherently. When my name falls from her mouth between broken moans, nothing else exists. In her most vulnerable, unguarded moment, she calls for me—and the need to mark her, to claim her, to make her mine alone overwhelms all reason.

Noelle starts to relax, and she lets the vibrator fall to the mattress. I shove it out of our way and grip her hipbones, my fingers leaving marks as my thrusts become more erratic and I barrel toward my own release. The sensation of sliding through her slick ass has my brain short-circuiting. The rhythmic squeeze of her aftershocks is the last straw, and my orgasm surges into me.

At the last second I pull out, aiming my cock at her lower back, my orgasm coating her ass with streams of cum. My eyes darken as I watch it trickle down over her back entrance and along the swell of her hips.

As my lust-induced haze fades and I regain full awareness, I look down to admire my masterpiece, the gasping, trembling woman beneath me. We're nothing but a mess of sweaty limbs, the evidence of our carnal games dripping down the crack of her ass. She sighs heavily, dropping to her stomach, letting out a groan as she stretches out on the mattress.

As much as I loved playing, the desire to take care of Noelle has me leaning down to kiss her shoulder blade before drawing back.

"I'll be right back," I say softly.

She nods as I get off the bed and head to the bathroom to wash my hands and get a washcloth, wetting it under the tap till it's warm. When I return to the bedroom, I gently wipe Noelle's backside and toss the towel into the laundry basket before climbing onto the bed and gathering her in my arms.

I carefully remove the blindfold, and she blinks a few times, her gaze meeting mine. Her blue eyes sparkle like sunlight on water, and my chest tightens just looking at them. She pulls her hair from its disheveled bun, and it falls in messy waves around her face. Noelle is so damn beautiful, and I'm privileged to share this experience with her. I'd spend a lifetime cherishing her if she'd let me.

"You okay, sweetheart?" I ask, running my thumb in small circles along her upper arm.

She nods, absentmindedly playing with my chest hair. "Thanks for being so patient with me."

"Always." I press my nose into her hair, inhaling her sweet scent. "Why don't we get you cleaned up in the shower, and after we can watch a movie by the fire."

"Sounds like a dream," she murmurs into my chest.

As I carry her to the bathroom, I'm struck by the trust

Noelle's placed in me, a reflection of the bond that's grown between us. It's hard to grasp how people can form such a deep connection in a short time unless you've experienced it yourself. There's something special about discovering what makes a person tick—what their fears are and what their proudest accomplishments are. Despite our age difference, our contrasting lifestyles, and the fact that her time here is coming to an end, one thing is undeniable.

Noelle owns my heart, and I've fallen for her hook, line, and sinker.

That means letting her walk away isn't an option. Hell, I'd move to New York to be with her before I let that happen. I've kept my heart guarded under lock and key until a blonde-haired, blue-eyed whirlwind showed up on my doorstep, turning my world upside down. And I'll do whatever it takes to get the chance to prove just how much she means to me.

CHAPTER 20

All I Want For Christmas Is You

Noelle

WAKE TO SUNLIGHT POURING THROUGH THE WINDOWS, curled against Shep, my hand on his chest and his fingers intertwined with mine. He's heartbreakingly handsome like this, snoring softly. I let my fingers drift over the sharp planes of his face, gliding from his brow to the faint creases at the corners of his eyes. My exploration continues as I move over the slight crook of his nose, following its slope to his mustache. I trace the curve of his mouth, unable to resist leaning in to brush a kiss over his lips.

The scent of sweat and sex hangs in the air, and when he doesn't stir, a wicked idea comes to mind. I slowly push the covers off and move between his legs. My eyes land on his cock, fully erect—thick and rigid, even in sleep.

I reach my hand down to trace his dick with a featherlight touch. He lets out a sigh, but remains still, and I grin at the thought of having him at my mercy. I curl my fingers around his shaft, giving it a gentle squeeze. Precum leaks from the tip, and I bend down, flicking my tongue over the crown to lick it clean.

"Noelle?" Shep groans, his voice husky.

"Relax. Let me take care of you," I croon.

I trail my tongue along his slit, teasing him until each inhale grows short and ragged, which is when I finally take his cock in my mouth. Every muscle in his face is taut as he fights to keep himself in check. That won't do. He's held back parts of himself for far too long, and after last night, I want nothing more than to make him let go of control all over again.

My fingers curl around the base of his cock, rolling my wrist with measured pressure along his throbbing vein. His body tenses as I swirl my tongue around the crown, dragging it down the length of his shaft. I lick in long, teasing strokes, treating his cock like a peppermint stick.

"Please," he begs, his voice thick with arousal. "Suck me harder."

I hum around him, consumed with the need to make my rugged cowboy come. His desperate plea makes it that much hotter, leaving me quivering and soaked. His touch is my drug, and I'm addicted to making him ache for me the way I do for him.

I briefly pull him from my mouth to say, "Use me, Shep, and don't hold back."

I'm not going to risk him taking it easy on me because he's unsure if I really want this—I do.

"You like being my little fuck toy?" he taunts.

I nod as heat pools between my thighs, and I blush when he winds his fingers through my hair, urging me to take as much of him in my mouth as possible. He thrusts his hips upward, and I inhale sharply through my nose, tears prickling at the edges of my eyes.

He's so damn big, and though I'm fighting my gag reflex, my desire to please him has me determined to take every inch. I hollow my cheeks, swallowing hard as he slides deeper until the tip grazes the back of my throat. His grip takes over, fucking my mouth with unbridled urgency. He growls in approval as my swollen lips bob up and down around his shaft.

"Jesus Christ," he groans.

Shep's muscles tense as he nears release, and I cup his balls with my free hand, gently squeezing, pushing him to his limit. His cock jerks in my mouth as he comes, and I swallow eagerly. His eyes widen as I lap up every last drop that's trickled down his shaft. Once I'm satisfied with my work, I let his dick spring free from my mouth with a *pop*.

"You okay?" I ask with a silly grin.

Shep props up on his elbow, then reaches over to wipe my chin. "You're so damn pretty with my cum on your mouth." I catch his wrist and pull his finger between my lips, licking it clean. "That's my good girl," he croons.

Warmth blooms in my chest. I'm addicted to his praise and the way he treats me like I'm the most precious thing in the world.

He pulls me up the bed beside him, tugging the covers over us. I rest my head on his shoulder and meet his eyes as he smooths my hair with a tenderness that steals my breath.

"You set a dangerous precedent, woman," he says, nipping at my ear. "I could easily get used to waking up like that."

I drape my leg over his, dragging my nails across his chest. "That could be arranged."

"Keep talking like that and you'll never leave this bed again," he says.

I lift my head, unable to hide the smile spreading on my face. "You make it sound like a bad thing."

We avoid the unspoken reality that tomorrow night I'm supposed to be on a flight back to New York.

"There's just one small problem with keeping you here."

"What's that?" I whisper.

"Your Christmas present is in the living room."

I sit up fully, the sheets pooling around my waist. "You didn't have to get me anything."

He leans in and presses a kiss to my temple. "I wanted to, sweetheart. Get dressed and I'll show you."

Curious about what he has up his sleeve, I scramble out of bed, the taste of him still in my mouth. I put on one of his flannel shirts, buttoning it up before eagerly following him into the living room. He must have gotten up while I was asleep because the stockings we decorated a couple of days ago are now on the mantel, brimming with chocolate and oranges.

Under the tree, there's a single gift wrapped in crinkled brown paper, tied with a crooked red bow.

Shep picks it up, and exhales slowly as he hands it to me. "For you."

It doesn't matter what's inside. The fact that he took the time to wrap it himself makes it perfect.

I settle on the couch and peel off the paper, revealing a cardboard box. As I lift the lid to peek inside, my eyes widen, and my gaze snaps to Shep. He taps his fingers against his thigh, a faint crease between his brows as he studies me.

"Shep… I don't know what to say."

With trembling hands, I lift out the most beautiful wooden cottage. The door and shutters are painted in red and green and tiny snowflakes are carved into the roof. When I turn it over, I discover it's a music box. I wind the key on its underside, and it begins to play "Have Yourself a Merry Little Christmas."

Tears trickle down my cheeks as he sits beside me, drawing me close. His rigid posture loosens as I melt into his touch, relieved by my positive reaction. How could I not love the gift when it's obvious he poured his heart into every detail.

I trace the outline of the cottage with my fingertip. "This is the most thoughtful gift anyone's ever given me. When did you have time to make it?"

He's spent time in his shop every morning, but the detailing tells me he must have poured countless hours into it.

"I started the day you told me about the Christmas village your grandpa built for your grandma. It was clear it was special to you—and how sad you were when several of the cottages were damaged when you were moving." He pauses to reach out and wipe my tears with his thumb. "I know this one won't match the original set, but I worried that if I asked for a picture, you'd catch on and it wouldn't be a surprise."

I turn to fully face him, lifting his hand to my lips, placing a soft kiss on each knuckle. A silent thank you for bringing a masterpiece to life.

"It's perfect." Music drifts through the room, and I meet his gaze, conveying more with my eyes than I ever could with words. "Thank you, Shep."

Even when he insisted I'd have to leave after the snowstorm, he still went through the effort of making the cottage, even though there was no guarantee I'd ever receive it.

Shep has quickly become my confidant, and my safe place. He's been my anchor in moments of doubt and uncertainty, and if I thought I was falling for him before, this moment sealed the deal. I'm certain now more than ever that I don't want an expiration date on what we have. Whether we have another week, month or even years, it'll never feel like enough time with him.

Some of my happiest memories came from living in a small town as a kid and visiting that farm in Upstate New York. As I grew older, I brushed it off as a childish fantasy, convinced the real world demanded that I chase deadlines and achieve career goals.

Being with Shep has opened my eyes to the possibility that maybe I don't have to choose between pursuing my dream and living a peaceful existence with someone who adores me.

It's obvious he cares for me deeply, but is it enough for him to make room long-term for a whirlwind of a city girl eager to give small-town life a try?

Shep moves our hands to his lap and leans in until our noses brush. "We're going to make this your best Christmas yet."

"*Our* best Christmas," I murmur against his lips.

As promised, today has been nothing short of perfect. After breakfast, we visited Maple and the other animals, giving them extra carrots and apples for a Christmas treat.

In the afternoon, Casey and Amy dropped by with my gift for Shep. Amy and I had exchanged numbers at the diner, and I'd asked if she knew where to get a DVD player in town. I hadn't expected much luck, but they came through, finding one at the hardware store of all places, and even picked up some DVDs that the movie rental shop had for sale. I was blown away by their generosity and willingness to help me.

To make this Christmas even better, my parents managed to call from a port in Italy. They're loving their cruise, and I'm glad I talked them into going. They were relieved I wasn't spending the holidays alone, and they even chatted with Shep for a few minutes. His answers were short yet polite, and thankfully, he left out the part where I showed up on his porch after booking a fake rental.

By the end of the call, my mom was asking when she'd get to meet him in person but neither Shep nor I had an answer.

It's now late evening, and we're cuddled up on the couch, the fire crackling while we watch *The Holiday*. I'm nestled into his side, my head resting against his shoulder, his arm wrapped around me. His thumb idly traces patterns along my upper arm.

I couldn't resist roping my grumpy mountain man into watching a romcom, and after he begrudgingly agreed, he's now fully invested as we near the end. His lips twitch into a smile whenever Miles, played by Jack Black, cracks a joke or hums along to the film's score.

During the part where Arthur's in his study giving Iris advice, Shep comments, "That guy's sharp as a tack. 'You should be the leading lady of your own life' is pure gold."

I lift my head to look at him with a raised brow. "*You're* quoting Arthur now?"

"What can I say? Wisdom's universal, especially coming from another cranky old man," he says with a smirk.

I offer him a smile, but it falters after a few seconds.

Our playful banter is a bittersweet reminder that this could be our last full day together. He hasn't said anything about me driving to Phoenix tomorrow, and I can't bring myself to mention it, terrified he might not want the same thing I do. After all the memories we've made, especially the days leading up to Christmas, I'd like to think I know him well enough to trust that his feelings mirror mine, clinging to the hope that he doesn't want to part ways either.

Shep visibly stiffens beside me when we reach the scene where Amanda Woods says goodbye to Graham. His hand tightens around my shoulder as a subtle tremor ripples through him when he watches Graham linger at the cottage doorstep.

He's not the only one affected. Even after seeing this movie countless times, a knot still forms in my chest at the way Graham watches Amanda—eyes soft but desperate, like he's memorizing her face in case he never sees her again. And this time it hits harder, because the goodbye is shadowed by the one waiting for Shep and me.

I'm snapped from my melancholy thoughts when he pauses the movie.

I push myself off his chest into a sitting position and turn to face him. "Don't you want to finish it? I promise it has a happy ending."

"I don't want you to leave," he blurts out.

I freeze, my heart hammering. "What?"

Shep puts the remote down then takes my hands in his, his gaze searching mine. "I can't watch you drive away tomorrow and pretend I'm fine letting you go. You've turned my world upside down, and you're the first person who's made me feel something real in a long time."

My breath catches at his declaration, a swirl of relief and anticipation clouding my thoughts.

"You mean it?" I ask hesitantly.

He nods, his brown eyes earnest and unguarded. "More than anything. I don't think I could survive you leaving, knowing there's a chance I'll never see you again."

"I don't think I could either," I admit, my voice trembling slightly.

Until now, coaxing him to open up has been a delicate dance, and I was afraid that I'd scare him off. Yet now, he speaks freely, unafraid to express his true feelings. I'm unsure if his newfound courage came from watching the movie scene echoing our own situation, the looming goodbye pressing on him or both. Regardless, it leaves me with a renewed sense of hope, knowing that we're aligned.

"I don't know what my future looks like, but I want you in it," he states, his thumb moving in slow circles across my palm as he speaks. "I'd never ask you to give up your life in New York, though. All I want is to find a way for us to be together. Hell, if you decide that you want to go back tomorrow, I'll pack a bag and go with you if you'll have me. I'm sure I could rope in Jake or a ranch hand from town to look after the animals while I'm gone—for the right price."

I blink at Shep, unsure I heard him correctly. "*You'd* go with me to the city? The man who barely tolerates spending an evening in Pine Haven with a population of two thousand people?"

He nods. "There's nothing I wouldn't do for you, Sunshine." Butterflies swarm my stomach.

There's no question Shep would go to New York if I asked, but I can't imagine him in the big city with its endless noise and crowded streets. He thrives in the mountains, where life moves more slowly and it's quiet enough to think. I could never take that away from him. Honestly, I've come to love the peaceful pace, and this place holds a piece of my heart because it's where our story began.

I tuck my feet underneath my legs and scoot closer to Shep until my knees brush his. "I want us to have a real shot, and that means staying here with you. Everything leading up to this moment makes me believe our meeting was more than a coincidence. I'd like to think it was a touch of holiday magic that brought us together." I reach up to frame his face with my hands. "It'd be a shame to walk away from what's right in front of us. Don't you think?"

"Whether it was a little Christmas magic or fate intervening, I'm just glad you're mine." He leans in, brushing his mouth against my lips. "My main focus is making sure you're happy here, and that includes a seamless transition with your podcast."

I'm touched that he's already thinking ahead.

"You're right. There's plenty to plan, like finding a studio. It has to be big enough to fit all my equipment and also aesthetically pleasing for promotional content."

"What will you do with the one in New York?" Shep asks.

"Our lease ends in January, so I won't have to worry about it after that." I lower my hands, pulling back just enough so I can meet his gaze while I explain. "Most of my team works remotely, and Gemma mentioned she might move back to Vermont. If she does, I'd be the only one left in the city."

The only other reason to stay in New York is my parents, but now that they're retired, they've got travel plans lined up for most of next year. And I can easily plan my visits when they're home.

Shep runs his fingers through his mustache, swallowing hard. "There's an extra office at the back of High Noon. The place is closed Monday through Wednesday, so you could record there. Hell, we could even soundproof it so you could use it during events on other nights," he adds with a shrug.

I gape at him. "Really?"

My current studio is in an office building with walls so thin I can hear the janitor sneeze, so I record at night when it's quiet and I don't have to fight background noise. It would be nice to have a dedicated, soundproof space designed specifically for my podcast.

"Yeah. And I'll be close by if you need anything." He gives my thigh a reassuring squeeze. "Casey's gonna have his hands full once the baby comes, and it's about time I step up. After all he's done for me, I reckon it's only fair I return the favor."

It makes me happy to see him coming out of his comfort zone. He's recognized the sacrifices Casey has made, and is taking the initiative to show his gratitude, and I'm looking forward to making more memories with him at the honky-tonk.

"Think Casey will do the same for you one day?"

He quirks a brow. "What do you mean?"

"When you have kids, do you think he'll return the favor?" I repeat, anxiously waiting for Shep's response.

"Do you want a family someday?" he asks, his tone hesitant.

He's shared his desire to become a dad, but I've never told him how I feel about having children or that I've always wanted a big family too.

"I'd like three or four kids," I say.

He takes my hands in his, eyes lighting up. "Four sounds perfect."

There may not be any guarantees with Shep. The best-laid plans rarely go as intended, but I'd rather take the risk than spend my life wondering what might have been with the man I've fallen head over heels for.

CHAPTER 21

Meet Me Under The Mistletoe

Shep

’D BRACED MYSELF FOR THE DAY AFTER CHRISTMAS TO FEEL hollow—forced into another goodbye I wasn’t ready for. This time, though, I knew if I had to watch Noelle walk away, I wouldn’t survive it.

Thankfully, the worst-case scenario didn’t happen, and instead, I’m celebrating that she’s staying for the foreseeable future. Sure, we’ll go to New York in January so she can handle some business and pack her things, but we’ll be back on the mountain within a week. Until then, she’s all mine.

This morning, she was up earlier than usual, wanting to go on a walk by herself. I wasn’t thrilled with the prospect, but one look at those doe eyes and I was done for. Still, I made sure she was bundled up and told her I’d come looking if she wasn’t back within the hour.

She's got fifteen minutes left before I make good on my promise.

To keep myself preoccupied, I'm going through my closet, sorting through flannels, a handful of winter coats, and boots. Most of my clothes are decades old so it's about time I got rid of the things I never wear.

Noelle warned me that she has an extensive wardrobe, and I want her to have plenty of space to store it all once we bring it back from New York. The sooner she feels at home, the sooner she'll see a future for herself here—which is why I reached out to Casey and a local construction crew this morning about converting the empty office at High Noon into a soundproof podcast studio. They're fast-tracking the job and by the end of next week, it'll be ready for Noelle to use.

The bonus? With her office next to mine, it'll be added motivation to show up at the honky-tonk more often. I'm also looking forward to settling back into managing some of the day-to-day, like I used to. Casey's done a great job keeping things running smoothly, but it'll be nice to be part of the action again.

I've just started a donation pile when my phone rings. I'm not surprised to find that Birdie is video calling me; she tried yesterday, but I was a little preoccupied, so I sent her a text wishing her a Merry Christmas.

"Hello," I answer.

Birdie's smile fills the screen. "Glad to see your broody face. I was worried after getting that nice message yesterday that you'd had a personality transplant."

She has her phone propped up on the counter as she makes coffee.

"Sorry to disappoint," I say, attempting a scowl, but failing to keep a straight face.

She wipes her brow in exaggerated relief as she walks across the kitchen. "I was starting to wonder how I'd make it through the week without my regular dose of grump."

"A double shot of caffeine ought to do the trick."

"You're paying since you're the reason I need it to begin with," she tosses over her shoulder as she opens her fridge. "So, how's Noelle?" She slips the question in like it's the most natural thing to ask.

"What makes you think she's still here?" I reply with a half-smile as I try to fold a long-sleeved flannel with one hand.

It's obvious Birdie's itching for an update. Aside from her attempted call yesterday and a handful of texts, we haven't talked in a few days—and I can't deny I'm enjoying stretching out the suspense. She's merciless with her teasing, so it's only fair that I return the favor.

She stands near the fridge, hazelnut creamer in one hand, the other on her hip, looking at the camera with an eyebrow raised. "You might be the ancient one, but I wasn't born yesterday. Noelle had you the minute she set foot on your property, whether you realized it or not. And when you told me you were making her lunch, I knew you were a goner."

I don't bother setting her straight. Technically, I never admitted to making Noelle lunch. Birdie just assumed, and the last thing I want is her gloating about being right.

"I'm still not sure why you're invested in my dating life," I huff out with a sigh, tossing a pair of old jeans into the donation pile.

"Because you're my cousin and I want you to be happy." Birdie returns to the counter, splashing creamer into her coffee and taking a sip before adding, "So is Noelle still there or not?"

I rub the back of my neck. "Yeah, she is."

"Does that mean you spent Christmas together?" Birdie's voice is now three octaves higher.

"Yeah."

She straightens, and her eyes lighten up. "Does that mean the two of you are official?"

I press my lips together to hide my amusement. "Yeah, it does."

"Oh, for heaven's sake, Shep, you've got to give me more than that." Birdie huffs, setting down her coffee mug a little too hard, and it sloshes over the side.

A week ago, I'd probably have told her to mind her own damn business, but Noelle's sunny disposition must be contagious because Birdie's curiosity doesn't bother me as much as it used to. Hell, I admit I might even appreciate her meddling.

"Yeah, Noelle and I are together, and she's staying in Pine Haven indefinitely." I chuck a pair of old work boots into the growing giveaway pile. "Though we're headed to New York in a couple of weeks so she can handle some business."

I wince when Birdie lets out a high-pitched squeal. "Shut the front door! *My* cousin's going to the big city? Maybe I was wrong about the personality transplant. You must have been body-snatched."

I roll my eyes. "Do all women let their imaginations run wild?"

First, Noelle thinks I'm a serial killer. Now, Birdie's convinced aliens have taken me over. If they ever compared notes, they'd decide I was planning a zombie apocalypse by lunch.

"I call it staying alert to suspicious behavior. And you, cousin, have been acting odd. But it all makes sense now, considering you're head over heels." She grins as she wipes the coffee she spilled with a paper towel. "Can't wait to officially have a cousin-in-law!"

I nearly drop the phone. "Easy now. Noelle and I are taking things slow."

Truth is, I have no intention of taking it slow. Noelle's it for me. I can picture it now—my ring on her finger and her belly swollen with my kid. Some will say we're moving too fast, but I won't let anyone else dictate our timeline. Only Noelle's opinion matters when it comes to our future.

"Oh, please," Birdie scoffs. "You've always wanted a wife and kids. There's no way you'd let this opportunity pass you by." It's unnerving how easily she can read my mind. "Honestly, you deserve everything good coming your way, and I'm happy for you."

"Careful. If you get any sappier, I'll have to send you the bill."

"We'll call it even for the double shots of caffeine," she says, smiling over her mug.

All joking aside, I appreciate that Birdie cares and is invested in what happens with Noelle and me.

"Sounds like a…" I trail off when I hear a series of bumps mixed with mooing coming from the living room.

What the hell?

"Birdie, hold on a minute, will ya?"

I step over the pile of clothes on the floor, phone still in hand, as I leave the bedroom. I come to a sudden stop when I find Noelle crouched in front of Maple near the wide-open front door, holding out a handful of apple slices. The cow's tail is swishing as she eagerly munches on her snack.

"What's going on here?"

Noelle looks at me, her eyes sparkling. "Maple did it! She followed me to the cabin. I had to pretend I was on the phone, but I kept sneaking glances back, and she stayed right behind me the whole way here."

For the past couple of days, she's been going on about wanting to bring Maple to the cabin. I should've known she meant it when I found her with a lead rope. This is what I get for not putting my foot down early and telling her animals weren't allowed in the house. Though knowing Noelle, it wouldn't have made a difference.

I let out a deep sigh as I run a hand across my face. "What happened to taking a walk?"

She shrugs. "I did take one. To the barn. And of course, I had to check on the animals while I was there." She takes another slice of apple from her pocket. "Maple looked lonely, so I let her tag along back home."

I quirk a brow as I move closer to them. "Uh-huh."

I don't believe for a second that's how things went down. Still, as unamused as I am about having a literal cow in my living room, Noelle's beaming smile makes it impossible to stay mad.

"Aren't you going to introduce me to your lady friend?" Birdie pipes up, reminding me I didn't end our call.

Noelle tilts her head, curiously eyeing the phone in my hand. "Who are you talking to?"

"My cousin, Birdie."

Noelle ruffles the fur on Maple's head before standing. She sidles up next to me and takes my phone, holding it up to her face.

"Hi, Birdie. I'm Noelle. It's so nice to meet you," she says, giving the camera a cheerful wave.

Birdie's eyes light up, like she's just been given the best Christmas present. "Same here. I didn't think anyone could handle Shep's cranky streak. You're a brave soul."

"Don't let him fool you. Under all that grumbling, he's just a big ole teddy bear." Noelle reaches up to pinch my cheek.

"Am not," I grunt, nipping at her fingers.

Just because Noelle makes me smile and has me fussing over her doesn't mean I'm going soft.

"Oh please, you're—" Maple interrupts Birdie with a low moo as she wanders around the room and settles in front of the fireplace like she owns the damn place. "Maple sounds so grown up. How's she doing?"

"Just dandy. Apparently, she's an indoor cow today," I mutter.

"I promised her a movie marathon," Noelle reminds me, batting her lashes.

She flips the screen so Birdie can see Maple, sprawled out, resting her chin on her hooves, eyes half closed.

"Maple is so precious," Birdie coos. "And ignore Shep's complaints. He's totally smitten with her, too."

"Oh, I know. Just yesterday, I caught him in her stall, scratching behind her ear and calling her his favorite girl," Noelle says, smirking at me.

This is just perfect. I knew if these two ever talked, they'd conspire against me.

"Alright, I think that's enough for introductions for one day," I grumble, taking the phone from Noelle.

"Fine, but I'm coming to visit soon, and you won't be able to stop me from sharing all your embarrassing stories," Birdie taunts.

"Can't wait," Noelle says, leaning in to wave goodbye.

I hang up, close the front door, and when I turn around—Noelle is standing right behind me.

She fiddles with the bracelet on her wrist, giving me a cautious look. "Are you upset I brought Maple inside?"

I shake my head. "Not at all. Enjoy your movie marathon. I'll just have to wait to have you to myself until tonight."

Noelle steps closer, draping her arms around my neck. "Don't worry, I'll make it up to—" She stops short when she glances up, spotting the mistletoe above the doorframe. "How did that get there?"

I shrug, biting the inside of my cheek to keep from grinning. "No clue."

Truth is, I hung it up after she left for her walk. We'd spent the days leading up to Christmas celebrating both our families' traditions, but I want to start a few of our own. A kiss under the mistletoe felt like the perfect place to begin.

Casey gave me grief for asking him to bring some when they

stopped by yesterday. He's always bragged that Amy decorates every doorway with it, so I knew they'd have plenty to spare. I expect endless jokes at my expense, but this moment with Noelle is worth it.

She gives me a knowing look. "Must have been a belated gift from Santa."

"Must have." I capture her around the waist, pulling her against my chest. "It would be rude not to make the most of it."

She rises on her toes, pressing a hand on my chest. "We can't have that."

I trail kisses along her jawline, her breath hitching as she tips her head toward me. Our lips meet, urgent and demanding. I'm surrounded by the sweet scent of vanilla and sugar cookies, unable to think of anything but her warm mouth on mine. I lift her into my arms, and she instinctively locks her legs around my waist, her hands moving to grip my shoulders. I take two steps forward so her back is pressed against the wall.

"Thank you for staying," I murmur.

"Nowhere else I'd rather be."

Noelle nips my bottom lip, moaning as she delves her tongue inside my mouth. She tastes like sunshine and hot cocoa, and I look forward to showing her exactly what it means to belong to me.

A soft mooing sound makes me draw back, and I see Maple has wandered from the fireplace to stand beside us. She nudges my pant leg, and Noelle bursts into giggles.

I tilt my head, lifting a brow. "Still think bringing a cow into the house was a good idea?"

Noelle pats me on the chest. "Cheer up, cowboy. You said it yourself: Tonight, I'm all yours."

I tilt her chin, giving her another kiss. "Damn right."

CHAPTER 22

It's The Most Wonderful Time of Year

Noelle

New Year's Eve

IGH NOON IS PACKED WITH PEOPLE CELEBRATING. AT ten minutes to midnight, the party is at its peak, and the band shows no signs of slowing down.

"I really wish you'd let me bring out my office chair so you can sit," Casey grumbles to Amy.

"No way," she says, rubbing her baby bump, quickly shutting him down faster than a busted jukebox. "I'll wait my turn like everybody else."

We're standing at the end of the bar, waiting for a stool to open up for her. It's been half an hour, and no one's moved, all holding tight to their drinks, waiting to ring in the new year. Amy already shot down Casey's idea of kicking someone out of their seat.

"What's the point of being the boss if I can't do things like drag out an extra chair for my wife?"

"I'm totally telling Shep you called yourself the boss," I chime in with a wink.

Casey laughs. "Go right ahead. Maybe he'll actually fire me this time so I can finally catch up on season three of *Bridgerton*."

Amy scoffs. "Catch up? Like you haven't binged it twice already."

Casey shoots her a playful glare, and Amy and I both burst out laughing.

Over the past week, Shep and I have gone out with them several times. It's given them a much-needed break from her parents and a distraction from waiting for the baby to arrive. They've both welcomed me with open arms and were ecstatic to hear I'll be staying.

Casey helped Shep give me a tour of my new soundproof podcast studio tucked in the back of the honky-tonk. Gemma had all the equipment expedited and video-chatted with the guys to make sure they installed everything correctly.

"This Boot Scootin' Bubbly is amazing," I exclaim, taking a sip of my drink.

I passed the time waiting for a seat by ordering a cocktail from the hottest bartender in town. It turns out he can mix a drink after all.

I glance over to the other side of the bar, where Shep's behind the counter, sliding a tray of whiskey shots to a rowdy group of ranch hands hollering their appreciation. One of the bartenders was running late, and with the bar short-staffed, he jumped in as soon as he realized they needed an extra hand.

Casey and I were equally stunned that he offered to help out, but it warms my heart to see him taking small steps to be more social.

Amy frowns at her sparkling water. "I had a Boot Scootin'

Bubbly last New Year's Eve, and Jake nailed the peach schnapps to lime ratio. Wish I could have one tonight."

Casey drapes an arm around her shoulder and kisses her forehead. "Once the baby's here, I'll have Jake fix you one."

"Hope she decides to make her debut soon," Amy sighs, rubbing her belly. "There's no more room left in here."

"Our sweet pea will come when she's good and ready."

"I just wish she'd hurry it along so I can finally see her little face."

"She's stubborn, just like her mama," Casey replies, leaning in.

As they share a tender kiss, I look over at Shep again. This time, he catches my eye, a smile tugging at his lips. He goes over to Jake, who's handing out cocktails to a pair of women giggling like schoolgirls, and claps him on the shoulder, saying something in his ear. After Jake gives a quick nod, Shep turns around, striding toward me with purpose.

As he comes around the counter to join us, he draws me into his side, giving me a kiss of our own that leaves me weak at the knees.

"Howdy there, cowboy," I murmur.

"I missed you," he drawls.

"It's only been an hour, and I've just been a few feet away the whole time."

"Yeah, and within the first twenty minutes, I lost count of how many guys I had to stare down for getting too close. It was fucking torture when all I wanted was to make sure everyone knows you're mine," he growls, nuzzling his nose into my neck.

Casey clears his throat. "You two should get a room."

Amy shoots him a scolding look. "Leave them be. They're in that gushy, can't-keep-their-hands-off-each-other phase, and it's adorable."

Casey shakes his head. "I doubt Shep appreciates being called adorable."

"Oh, he doesn't mind. Do you, baby?" I give him a playful pat on the chest.

He winds his arm around me, drawing me close to whisper in my ear. "If it keeps a smile on your face, you can call me adorable anytime, darlin.'"

Shep waves down Jake, nodding toward a couple of rowdy guys lingering at the bar who haven't ordered anything. Jake nods back, and walks over, leaning across the counter to speak to them. One of the men complains loudly, but a sharp look from Jake shuts him up, and the two finally push off from their seats and head to the dance floor.

Shep taps Casey on the shoulder, pointing at the empty stools. "Better snag those before someone else does."

Casey claps him on the back. "Thanks, man. Really appreciate it."

He steers Amy toward the bar, helping her onto the stool, and she sighs in relief once she's settled.

"That was mighty kind of you," I tell Shep.

"Just doing my job, kicking freeloaders from the bar."

"Well then, you better order me another Boot Scootin' Bubbly so I don't end up on the chopping block too." I hold out my empty glass.

He leans in, nibbling my earlobe. "Brat."

I place my free hand on his chest, batting my lashes. "Someone's got to keep you on your toes, *Daddy*."

The fire in his eyes is unmistakable, making me wish we were alone so he could have his way with me.

The past week together has been absolute bliss. We've had breakfast with Casey and Amy at the diner, delivered fresh pastries from the local bakery to the homeless shelter, and checked on the animals twice a day. My favorite thing is when we're holed up in the cabin just the two of us, getting to know each other both in and out of the bedroom.

Shep's new fascination is watching me edit my podcast episodes, and he even went back to watch my old ones. He's still uncertain what a hype-girl is, but he's been supportive regardless. He had Casey help him create an account on the streaming platform so he could leave a comment on every episode he watches. I've read every one, and a few are cheeky, but it's endearing how supportive he is. It's a daily reminder of how lucky I am to have him.

In hindsight, losing CoreFuel Labs as a sponsor turned out to be a blessing in disguise. It taught me the importance of partnering with companies that value work-life balance and appreciate what I contribute. I'm learning to set clear boundaries and vet potential sponsors more carefully, and thanks to Shep, I'm learning to accept that it's okay to turn down opportunities that aren't in my best interest.

Gemma's technically still on vacation, but she's reached out to a few potential companies to fill the sponsor spot CoreFuel Labs left open. Twisted Temptations responded and said as long as the ad spots we have scheduled in the coming month perform well, they're committed to an ongoing partnership with us. Lucky for me, that means more toys for Shep and me to play with. Up next: red heart-shaped nipple clamps and fuzzy handcuffs for their Valentine's Day collection launching in February.

As the band launches into a slow country ballad, couples begin drifting to the floor.

"Let's dance," I tell Shep.

He shakes his head. "I'm too rusty."

"It's not the two-step. You just have to hold me close as we sway back and forth. But if you'd rather not, maybe I'll ask one of the ranch hands you were serving earlier," I tease, taking a step away from him.

He growls, tugging me back into his chest. "The only man you're dancing with is me, woman."

"I suppose you'll do." I wink, motioning to an open space near the stage. "Lead the way, cowboy."

Shep takes my empty glass and sets it on the bar counter before taking my hand in his and guiding me onto the dance floor. He slides his other hand around my waist, drawing me in until our bodies are flush. His breath is warm against my ear, sending a shiver down my spine. The man has captured my heart in a way no one else ever could, and there's nowhere I feel safer than in his arms.

"See, isn't this nice?" I muse.

"There's nothing better than holding you," Shep states.

I rest my head against his chest as the music drifts around us. "I was just thinking the same thing."

The room pulses with anticipation as the band announces it's almost midnight and counts down from ten to ring in the new year. My gaze meets Shep's, his hand grazing my cheek. There's no doubt this is where I'm meant to be, and I silently thank whoever scammed me into showing up at Shep's doorstep—the place where it all started.

As the countdown reaches zero, cheers erupt all around. Shep's lips find mine, giving me a kiss brimming with hope and the promise of a new beginning that we'll share together.

He draws back just enough to hold my gaze. "I love you, Noelle. I love you so damn much."

My breath catches, my eyes glistening with tears. "I love you too, Shep."

"You mean it?"

I hook my fingers in his collar, tugging him closer. "More than anything. You're mine just as much as I'm yours."

"Say it again," he demands.

"You're mine, cowboy, and I love you."

A spark of ownership flashes in his gaze. "I love you too, Sunshine. Always." I'll never grow tired of hearing those words.

I rise on my toes to kiss him again, smiling against his mouth.

Our path to love hasn't been conventional. It blossomed in a mountain cabin during a snowstorm, where I quickly fell for a grumpy cowboy almost twice my age. Some might call it reckless, others delusional—but for me, it's a holiday miracle. It's a gift to be with someone who will stand by me during the most difficult of times and make every moment together extraordinary. I'll never take it for granted, knowing what we share is rare, and no matter what our future brings, I'll always be dreaming of the next Christmas with the cowboy I love.

EPILOGUE

Holly Jolly Ever After

Noelle

One Year Later

WAKE UP TO SOMETHING WET AND WARM BRUSHING AGAINST my chin.

"Shep," I mumble with a sleepy smile.

It's not the first time I've woken up to him kissing me, his beard tickling my skin. But as the kisses come faster—sloppy and relentless—I furrow my brow. I crack an eye open, confused when I spot a tiny paw resting on my collarbone and a cold nose nuzzling my cheek.

That's definitely not Shep.

I blink against the morning light and scramble upright to get a better look at the culprit. A blur of black-and-white fur is on the mattress beside me, pouncing into my lap, tail whipping with enthusiasm. It's a border collie puppy, impossibly fluffy, with bright blue eyes full of mischief and a crooked red bow tied around a shiny silver collar. Its pink tongue darts out to lick my hand in greeting.

I giggle, cupping its face with my hands. "Hi there, little troublemaker. Where on earth did you come from?"

The puppy yips, nibbling at my shirtsleeve. Fully awake now, I realize I should figure out how this cutie ended up in my bed. Suspecting Shep had something to do with it, I glance over at his side of the mattress, frowning when I find it empty.

A clearing throat draws my gaze to the other side of the room, where he's standing in the doorframe, arms crossed. His Wranglers hang low on his hips, and without a shirt, the contours of his abs and the smattering of dark hair on his chest are on full display. If I had my way, he'd be shirtless around the house all the time.

"She likes you," he observes, nodding to the puppy.

"I like her too," I say, scratching behind her ear. "Any particular reason she's in our bed?"

It's not the first time we've had new animals around since we got together, but it's usually an injured horse or a small flock of hens in need of a new home. Not an adorable, tail-wagging puppy looking at me like I'm the center of her universe.

A grin tugs at Shep's lips. "She's your Christmas present. I know it's a day early, but I couldn't wait." He pushes off the doorframe and comes to sit on the edge of the bed beside me. "Birdie rescued her from a backyard breeder in Montana, and the moment I saw her photo, I knew she was meant to be yours."

Over the past year, I've lost count of how often I've dropped hints about getting a dog. I wasn't exactly subtle about it, and I started thinking Shep was avoiding the topic because he didn't want one. Turns out, that couldn't have been further from the truth. Even though I'd only brought up border collies specifically a handful of times, he took note and conspired with Birdie to bring home the perfect furry addition to our family.

I'm sure that as soon as Shep told Birdie, she diligently

searched for a rescue border collie until she found one. She has the biggest heart, and I'm lucky to call her a dear friend. We text almost daily, and it seems like every month she's sending another rescue our way. The energetic puppy in my lap is proof of her knack for finding animals she knows we'll instantly fall for and can't turn away.

I look at Shep, tugging my lip between my teeth. "Is she really mine?"

He pets the puppy, and she wriggles her butt, eagerly sniffing his hand. Looks like Maple isn't the only one charmed by the cowboy. Shep's joined us for several of our movie nights, and Maple always curls up at his feet like a giant fluffy dog. At the rate she's growing, though, we might have to move movie night out to the barn soon.

"The puppy is all yours," he assures me.

I lift her, showering her head with kisses, laughing when she enthusiastically licks my face. "Does she have a name?"

"Birdie called her Luna, but you can pick any name you want."

"Luna," I whisper with a smile, studying her soft little face. "It's perfect."

Shep scoots closer, resting his hand on my knee. "I promise you'll have more time to get acquainted in a few minutes, but I have another surprise, and she has to get off the bed for it."

"What's the matter, cowboy? If you wanted an excuse to get me alone, you should have said so." I adjust Luna into one arm, using my free hand to give Shep's thigh a playful squeeze.

A low laugh rumbles in his chest. "Trust me, I'd take you up on the offer on any other day, but this surprise requires you to be upright."

I raise a brow, holding Luna out to him. "Consider me intrigued."

Shep takes her from me, carrying her over to a crate in the corner that he must have put there before I woke up. There's a dog bed inside with several toys. He gives her a duck toy to play with and pats her on the head. He leaves the crate door open, but she's too preoccupied with playing to notice Shep returning to my side of the bed.

He takes his time, walking slowly. I notice his shoulders are tight, and he keeps rubbing his hands along his pant legs. Usually, he's calm as a clear sky—but right now, he's visibly on edge.

In the past year, a lot has changed for us both. He spends most weeknights at High Noon, and I often join him to record a podcast or to keep him company while he works. He even participates in a weekly poker game with Casey and some locals now. I usually spend those evenings with Amy and their baby, Cam. We order pizza and binge-watch the latest episode of *Love Island.* I'm glad for the friendships I've built in Pine Haven. The small town has quickly become my favorite place, and I'm proud to call it home.

I scoot to the edge of the bed, swinging my feet over the side.

"You alright?" I ask Shep, noticing a sheen of sweat on his forehead.

He nods, moving to stand in front of me. "Reckon I'm nervous. I have a very important question to ask you, and I don't want to mess this up." My stomach does a flip when he drops to one knee and takes my hands in his. "You've become my constant—the sunshine that chased away every bit of gray. I've wanted to make you mine since the day you showed up on my doorstep, and I can't think of a more perfect time to ask you to be my wife than on this Christmas Eve morning with just the two of us." He pauses, swallowing hard, and I give his hands a reassuring squeeze. "You're the person I want to wake up next to every day for the rest of my life, and nothing would make me happier than you agreeing to spend forever with me."

My heart is hammering so hard it feels like it could burst, and I realize this is the easiest decision I've ever made.

"Yes, of course. I'll spend forever with you." I throw my arms around him, burying my face in his neck.

This is what I've been hoping for since the day he asked me to stay in Pine Haven. I fall more in love with Shep with each passing day, and being with him has been nothing short of a dream. Together we've learned to cherish every moment—the mundane ones, the silly ones, and the life-changing ones like this. I've pictured him asking me to be his wife so many times, and now that he has, it feels surreal.

When I pull back, Shep fishes a ring from his pocket and slides it on my finger. The three-carat pear-shaped diamond glints in the morning rays.

I trace the intricate design with my fingertip. "It's beautiful."

"Only the best for my sunshine girl." He cups my cheek and kisses me, leaving me dizzy.

"I can't wait to tell Gemma and my parents," I exclaim.

In the past year, Shep has met everyone important in my life. My parents have spent most of their time on cruises and traveling through Europe, but fortunately, we were able to spend two weeks with them in New York this past summer. My mom was smitten with Shep the moment they met—though that might have something to do with the two dozen yellow roses he brought her.

My dad, on the other hand, was initially skeptical because of our age difference. However, after seeing how happy I am with Shep and how well he treats me, he gradually came around.

Shep chuckles. "You won't have to wait long to tell everyone."

I furrow a brow. "Are they expecting a call from us?"

He shakes his head. "Not exactly." Shep takes a seat next to me on the bed, his hand resting on my leg. "You're going to put on a pretty dress and the cowgirl boots we picked out last week because we're going to Cactus Bloom Café for Christmas Eve breakfast to celebrate."

One of the things I love most about Shep is that he always thinks of everything.

"You're just full of surprises this morning, aren't you?"

"Gemma, Birdie, and your parents all flew in to Pine Haven last night, and we're spending the next week with them." He lifts my left hand to his lips, pressing a kiss to my ring finger. "After I asked your dad for his blessing last month, I knew we'd want everyone here to celebrate our engagement and your favorite time of year."

My mouth falls open, tears prickling at the corners of my eyes. "Are you serious?"

"Sure am. They'll all be waiting at the diner in an hour."

"Thank you, Shep. Having them here will make it even more special."

"Anything for you, Sunshine," he vows.

God, this man is incredible. He knew how down I was about spending another Christmas without my parents and how much I've missed Gemma, too. We've seen her a few times when we've met in New York for business, but it's not the same after living in the same city for so long.

With her help, my podcast has been thriving. When I first told my audience I was dating Shep, he admitted he was intimidated by the thoughts of millions of people knowing we were together. I've kept most of his personal details private, but it was important to me to show that I was finally ready to live authentically—even if it meant facing scrutiny for our age gap or how we met. I wanted to show the world that age is just a number and that love deserves to always be celebrated, never judged.

It turns out people appreciated my transparency, and the episode where I shared the news about Shep and me became one of my most viewed. My audience was equally support-ive when I decided to cut back to three episodes a week. The change has given me the work-life balance I didn't realize I was missing and has allowed me time for all the things I love—in-cluding bingeing mafia romances on my e-reader, tending to our barn full of rescues, and soaking up lazy mornings with Shep.

"I have a surprise of my own," I say, barely able to contain my excitement. "I'll be right back."

Shep nods, leaning back on his hands, getting comfortable while he waits.

I hurry into the bathroom and crouch down to open the cupboard under the sink. Pushing past a stack of towels and a box of tampons, I grab the washcloth I tucked in the back. I carefully unfold it to reveal the white stick I tested yesterday while Shep was in his workshop. He's not the only one with life-changing news.

When I return to our room, Shep's right where I left him, sitting on the mattress. But the moment he notices what I'm holding in my hand, he scrambles to his feet.

"Is that what I think it is?" he murmurs, almost trembling with anticipation.

I close the distance between us and hold out the test so he can see the two blue lines. "Merry Christmas, Shep."

He stares at the object in my hand, his eyes glistening with unshed tears.

I stopped taking birth control this past summer, and after a few months, we decided not to let it dominate our thoughts, trusting that one day we'd get our chance to be parents.

His eyes widen, disbelief and joy on his face as the news sinks in. "I'm… really going to be a dad?"

"You are," I say, unable to stop smiling. "The best one there is."

Shep exhales a shaky laugh. "This is the best gift anyone's given me. Thank you for making my dream come true."

He winds his arms around my waist, lifts me, and twirls me around, laughing without restraint. I throw my arms around him, the pregnancy test still in my hand, loving to see him so genuinely happy. I'm overwhelmed with gratitude that he's finally getting the family he's always longed for, and that I'm the one he wants by his side through it all.

He slows down, gently setting me on the ground, but keeps me secure in his arms.

"I love you so damn much, Noelle."

"I love you too, Shep."

He leans in, capturing my mouth in a kiss—this one fierce and passionate. As he moves his hands along my curves, deepening the kiss, we're interrupted by a cheerful yip. I pull back to find Luna at our feet, chasing her tail.

"Looks like someone's eager to be part of all the action," I say.

Shep settles his hand on my belly. "We've got our work cut out for us this coming year, huh?"

I place my hand over his, grinning from ear to ear. "We sure do, *Daddy*, and I wouldn't have it any other way."

"Neither would I, Sunshine. Neither would I."

Our story is just beginning, and I can't wait to see all the memories we'll make as an engaged couple—and soon, as husband and wife. Shep's not one to drag his feet, so I have a feeling it won't be long before we tie the knot, especially now that we have a little one on the way. It's a good thing he's been set on wanting to build a bigger cabin near the barn come spring. I can already picture us there next Christmas Eve with our baby in my arms, living our own version of happily ever after.

Looking back, it's clear that fate stepped in during that spontaneous trip last year. One impulsive choice changed the trajectory of my life, and I wouldn't trade it for anything.

If you loved *Dreaming of a Cowboy Christmas*, be sure to keep reading for an excerpt from my small town, fake dating, age gap, spicy workplace holiday novella: *If You Give a Grump a Holiday Wishlist*.

CHAPTER 1

Presley

WHO THE HELL DOES JACK SINCLAIR THINK HE IS? I narrow my eyes at the email that just hit my inbox.

MS. STAFFORD,
THE WESCOTT ACQUISITION HAS BEEN FINALIZED. WE'RE MEETING WITH MR. WESCOTT AND HIS TEAM ON FRIDAY TO PLAN THE TRANSITION BEFORE THE NEW YEAR. HE AND HIS ASSOCIATES WILL BE CALLING IN REMOTELY. BLOCK OUT OUR CALENDAR FOR TOMORROW SO WE CAN PREPARE.

YOUR BOSS,
JACK SINCLAIR

It's official—I hate him. He knows damn well that today was meant to be my last day of work until after the holidays. He has no right to demand that I delay my well-earned time off. The deal is complete, and these meetings can wait until January. I guarantee I'm not the only one who thinks so. Just because Jack Sinclair doesn't have a life outside of work doesn't mean the rest of us don't.

For heaven's sake, I gave the man a year's notice.

I can't help but scoff when I see his signature. I'll never understand why he insists on signing every email with *your boss*.

How could I possibly forget that I work for a moody, high-strung asshole who has no regard for anyone but himself.

My phone chimes, letting me know my rideshare is waiting downstairs. I've already had to cancel my pickup twice because Jack is adamant that I be in the office when he is.

The handle of my suitcase peeks out from the side of my desk—another reminder that I was supposed to leave for the airport hours ago. Even if it wasn't rush hour, there's no way I'd catch my flight. I let out an exasperated sigh and cancel my ride for the third time today.

I wonder what the chances are my mother would let it slide if I couldn't make it home for Christmas. *Zero.* She'd drag the whole family to New York before she would let me skip out on spending the holidays with them in Aspen Grove. Plus it wouldn't be the same if they came here.

I frown down at the piece of paper on my desk. Every year since I was a kid, I've made a list of things to do during the holiday season. Some are long-standing traditions, and others are new things I want to try. Regardless of my mother's wishes, I can't help but wonder how many I could check off if I stayed in the city.

Presley's Holiday Wishlist

1. Go ice skating
2. Visit the local Christmas market
3. Try a roasted chestnut
4. Write a letter to Santa
5. Make a gingerbread house
6. Holiday movie marathon + hot chocolate
7. Decorate a real Christmas tree
8. ~~Kiss under the mistletoe~~

It would be a pain in the ass to haul a tree up to my fifth-floor apartment, and making a gingerbread house wouldn't be any fun without it being a competition with my brothers.

I crossed out "kiss under the mistletoe" because there's no chance of that happening, considering I haven't even been on a date in over two years. The last guy I dated, Brennan, broke up with me after a month because he said I was a workaholic. Apparently he needed to be with someone willing to put their relationship with him first.

It's not my fault Jack Sinclair doesn't understand the term "work-life balance." He's been the bane of my existence since I started working here. God, even his name is pretentious. It's like his parents wanted him to be a control freak with a stick shoved up his ass.

He might be a temperamental bastard, but I have to admit, his brilliance is undeniable. He's a thirty-two-year-old billionaire CEO of a global investment firm that he single-handedly built from the ground up. His credentials are impressive as hell, and working as his assistant for the past three years has taught me more than a decade of climbing the corporate ladder ever could. And the generous salary doesn't hurt either.

At six-two, Jack commands every room he walks into, and I admit that he's sexy as hell. He has honey-colored eyes, black hair that's always perfectly styled in a crew cut, and a rugged jawline that accentuates his features. Did I mention he looks utterly irresistible in a three-piece charcoal-gray suit? I always assumed that the stereotypical hot billionaire type was only reserved for romance novels, but Jack is proof that's not true.

If only he had a personality to match his appearance.

"Ms. Stafford," he calls from his office, as if he has a sixth sense that I'm ignoring his email.

He's never embraced the concept of sending me a chat or calling me on the phone like every other executive does at the company. No, he prefers to call me into his office to talk face to face.

I fold up my wishlist and tuck it into my pocket before marching into his office.

"You shouted, Mr. Sinclair?" I deadpan.

"Why haven't you responded to my email?"

"You mean the one you sent two minutes ago?"

"Yes." He doesn't bother looking up from his computer. "Block out my calendar for tomorrow so we can prepare for our meetings with Mr. Wescott's team."

"Unfortunately, I'm not available." I square my shoulders, bracing for his imminent outburst.

He stops typing in favor of glaring across at me. "Why the hell not?"

I'm glad I finally have his undivided attention.

"Because I'll be out of town. It's been on your calendar since January, and I've sent you monthly reminders so you wouldn't forget that I'd be out of the office during the last two weeks of the year."

His jaw tightens. "Reschedule."

God, the nerve of this man. I clench my fists, trying to suppress my anger before I say something that'll get me fired. You'd think after three years of hard work and dedication I would have earned an ounce of his respect, but apparently not.

"Let me get this straight: you're asking me to change my holiday plans with my family?" There's a hint of disdain in my tone. "Mr. Sinclair, I'm not canceling my vacation."

"This is the biggest acquisition in the company's history. I need you here," he states.

I shrug. "Well, I'm unavailable. As of yesterday, Wescott International is officially a subsidiary of Sinclair Group. Whatever you need my help with can wait until the new year. I'm sorry my personal life is getting in the way of you doing business, but I haven't taken a single day off since last December, all so that I could go home for Christmas, and you're not taking that away from me." I stand firm, refusing to give in. "I've already missed my flight, and my poor mother will be in a frenzy when she finds out."

He taps his chin thoughtfully, his gaze fixed on me. "Where does your family live?"

"Aspen Grove, Maine?" I say it like a question, not sure why he cares.

I expect him to call me insubordinate and tell me to pack my things and never come back. Instead, Jack picks up his phone and begins furiously typing away, ignoring me again.

Just as I'm ready to walk out of his office, he glances up. "Finish whatever you're working on. We're leaving in ten minutes," he instructs. "I'm assuming you have your suitcase here if you were planning to go straight to the airport?"

I tilt my head, frowning. "Um…yes. I'm confused. Where are we going?"

"Aspen Grove. Clearly you weren't taught how to compromise, so I'll just have to come with you. We'll work from the hotel."

I burst into laughter, not able to stop myself. Just when I think Jack might have finally grown a sense of humor, the scowl on his face tells me that's not the case.

He's not kidding.

I run a hand across my face and begin pacing his office. "You can't be serious."

He lets out an exasperated sigh. "I don't waste my time with jokes, Ms. Stafford. We're at an impasse, and I've provided a viable solution. I fail to see the problem."

"You can't just invite yourself to come home with me."

"Why not?" He shrugs. "I'll stay at a hotel, and you can help me during the days and spend the evenings with your family. Once I head back to the city, you can have until the new year to yourself."

I guess that might work.

Wait… Why am I entertaining this idea? The last thing I want to do is to bring my overbearing boss back to Aspen Grove.

"What if I set up a conference call for us tomorrow? That way you can stay here."

"No."

"Why not?" I practically screech.

"You know how I feel about you working remotely. It's not nearly as efficient as being in the same room together, and it's far too distracting."

He's right. I do know how he feels about remote work, but I hoped he'd cave because of the circumstances. If I can't get out of this, I'm damn well going to make it work in my favor.

I come to a stop in front of his desk, turning to face him. "I have conditions."

Jack laces his hands behind his head, leaning back in his chair. "I'd expect nothing less. What are they?"

I place my hands on my hips. "I want a thirty percent raise, effective immediately. I've met every target you set for me and the company had record profits this year. I think we can both agree that I'm an asset to this organization and have more than earned it." I state with more confidence than I feel. "Oh, and I don't want my family to know you're my boss; it'll only complicate things."

My family knows how hard-pressed Jack can be when it comes to business, and the last thing I need is for my mother to go postal on the man who makes my work life harder than it should be.

"You drive a hard bargain, Ms. Stafford. I accept your terms. Anything else?"

I'm about to say no when a harebrained idea pops into my head, and the words tumble out before I can think better of it. "Yes. I want you to help me with my holiday wishlist."

I blink, instantly questioning my own sanity. My holiday plans weren't meant to include Jack coming home with me or asking him to help me with my wishlist, which involves some of my favorite winter activities. He'll probably hate every second of it, which is more satisfying than it should be. Who knows? Maybe some Christmas cheer will help melt that icy exterior of his. One can only hope. If nothing else, if he agrees, I'll get the sheer entertainment of seeing Jack Sinclair ice skate and make gingerbread cookies.

I'm definitely going to regret this.

No, scratch that. I already do.

"I'm sorry, your *what*?" he asks, confusion written all over his face.

I pull the folded piece of paper from my pocket and place it on Jack's desk.

"Every year, I make a list of things I want to do while I'm visiting home that help me get in the holiday spirit."

He hesitantly unfolds the paper, his eyes widening with every line he reads.

"A letter to Santa Claus. Really, Ms. Stafford? Do you also leave out milk and cookies on Christmas Eve?" he says, his tone teasing.

"It's a tradition." I shrug. "I've written him a letter every year since I was a kid."

His impassive expression makes me think he's not impressed with my answer, and his lips form a thin line when he gets to the end of the list.

"It looks like you already have someone to help you this year," he says flatly.

"What are you talking about?"

He slides the letter in my direction, pointing to *kiss under the mistletoe.*

"It's been crossed off, and I know for a fact *that* particular activity requires two people to participate," he states.

Oh my god.

My cheeks flush. How could I have forgotten that was on there?

"I crossed that item off because it's not something I can do this year." I keep my voice steady.

He tilts his head, and narrows his eyes. "And why is that?"

"If you haven't noticed, Mr. Sinclair, I don't exactly have a lot of free time to date," I say in a snarky tone. "And I'm not the kind of person who goes around kissing strangers."

A brief glimpse of relief crosses his face, but it's quickly replaced with a stoic expression. His eyes dart between me and the list as he contemplates his next move.

"I'm sorry, but you'll have to find someone else to help you." Jack pushes the list back to me.

"Then I guess you'll have to find someone else to help *you* prepare for the meetings with the Wescott team." I fold the sheet and slip it back into my pocket.

"You're being unreasonable," he gripes.

"And you're being a grinch," I counter. "I suggested a fair solution, and you shut me down. You have no right to get upset, considering you're not willing to give as much as you take. Now, if that's all, I need to leave for the airport to see if I can get on standby for the next flight to Maine."

When Jack doesn't reply, I turn to leave. I'm done letting him take advantage of me, consequences be damned. He'll have to find someone else to order around until January because it won't be me.

I'm nearly out the door when a hand wraps around my wrist, gently tugging me back. I look over my shoulder to find Jack standing behind me, his mouth set in a tight line and his pensive gaze locked on me.

"Ms. Stafford, please don't go. I apologize for overreacting." He says the words slowly, like they're painful to get out. "I don't usually celebrate the holidays, but I'm willing to make a concession and help you with your wishlist as long as I'm back in New York by the day after Christmas. I accept your conditions; do we have a deal?"

He extends his hand, and as much as I'm tempted to turn

him down and give him a taste of his own medicine, I can't do it. This feels like the perfect opportunity to finally unravel the mystery that is Jack Sinclair.

A smirk tugs at my lips. "It's a deal." I shake his hand to solidify our agreement.

My eyes flit to Jack's face when his hand closes around mine, the warmth of his skin a stark contrast to my own. He wears an unreadable expression, conflicting with the tenderness of his grip. I'm caught off guard when his thumb brushes across my knuckles, but when I look down, he's already released my hand, leaving me to wonder if it was just my imagination.

Why do I have the feeling this arrangement is going to be far more complicated than either of us bargained for?

Read the rest of Jack & Presley's Holiday Novella HERE!
https://geni.us/AEGrump

Want more Shep & Noelle? Grab the extended epilogue of *Dreaming of a Cowboy Christmas* to catch up with them a year later as they celebrate their first Christmas as parents, surrounded by family and friends. Type this link into the browser to read it: https://dl.bookfunnel.com/3ibn5buz90

Thanks again for reading *Dreaming of a Cowboy Christmas*. If you enjoyed it, please consider leaving a review on your preferred platform(s) of choice. It's the best compliment I can receive as an author, and it makes it easier for other readers to find my books.

OTHER BOOKS BY
ANN EINERSON

All Books Available in Kindle Unlimited

<u>HOLIDAY NOVELLAS</u>

If You Give a Grump a Holiday Wishlist (Presley & Jack)
*A small town, fake dating, one bed, spicy
workplace holiday romance.*

The Holiday Claus (Brooks & Lila)
*A holiday romance where a grumpy billionaire falls for his best
friend's sunshine sister, wrapped in an age gap,
only one bed spicy novella.*

<u>SILVER SADDLE RANCH SERIES</u>

Wrangled Love (Jensen & Briar)
*Tension quickly turns to temptation in Bluebell, Montana, between
a single dad and his nanny in this steamy age gap, best friend's
brother, small-town cowboy romance.*

<u>ASPEN GROVE SERIES</u>

If You Give a Single Dad a Nanny (Dylan & Marlow)
*A swoon worthy, single dad/nanny, age gap, he's grumpy, she's
sunshine, banter-filled spicy small-town romance*

If You Give a Billionaire a Bride (Cash & Everly)
*A marriage of convenience that starts with a Vegas wedding
between a reformed playboy and his best friend's sister in a banter-
filled spicy billionaire romance.*

If You Give a CEO a Chance (Harrison & Fallon)
*An enemies-to-lovers, second-chance love story between a retired
hockey player and his new live-in private chef,
in a banter-filled spicy romance.*

STANDALONES

When You Give a Lawyer a Kiss (Dawson & Reese)
*A workplace romance between a grumpy billionaire and his new
assistant in an age gap, banter-filled, spicy love story.*

The Spotlight (Conway & Sienna)
*A best friend's brother, opposites attract, dating in secret,
spicy rockstar romance.*

ACKNOWLEDGMENTS

So many people made this book possible, and I can't thank you all enough for your love, kindness, and support. *Dreaming of a Cowboy Christmas* wouldn't have been possible without each and every one of you.

To Bryanna—For being my ride-or-die through this wild publishing journey. Part dev editor, part therapist, and full-time work-wife—you've stuck with me through every plot twist, late-night call, and looming deadline. This book exists because you never let me quit and believe in me, even when I didn't always believe in myself.

To Becca & KP—Your feedback is invaluable, and I can't thank you enough for cheering me on from the sidelines.

To Jess—For being my creative partner from the start. Your talent for bringing each story to life with stunning graphics and videos never fails to inspire me. I'm incredibly lucky to have you in my corner.

To Tab and Kaity—I can't thank you enough for the time, care, and heart you poured into helping bring these characters to life. I'm so grateful for your patience with all my DMs, questions, and concerns. Forever grateful for you both!

To Britt, Emily, Jenny, and Sarah—I couldn't have asked for a better editing team. I'm grateful for your expertise and for pushing me to write a story worth reading.

To Wren, Caroline, Kat, Ceilidh, Charley, Sarah, Cori, Hunter, Page, and Jenna Lynn—Thanks for reading *Dreaming of a Cowboy Christmas* early and providing the honest critique that challenged me to raise the bar and deliver my best work.

To Sam—For designing the most perfect holiday cover. It was love at first sight, and it makes my heart so happy that my readers love it as much as I do.

To my ARC/Content teams—Thank you for all your thoughtful messages, posts, stories, reviews, and comments. Your endless love and support never cease to amaze me.

Most importantly, thank **YOU**. There are so many incredible books to choose from and I'm honored you took a chance on Shep & Noelle's story. None of this would be possible without you! Every single tag, share, and DM means the world and motivates me to keep writing on the days I think this might be for nothing. I hope you enjoyed your time in Pine Haven, Arizona!

ABOUT THE AUTHOR

Ann Einerson is the author of enchanting contemporary romance novels that will keep you hooked until the very last page, complete with heroes who fall hard and the heroines who keep them on their toes. She believes sometimes the best family is the one we find, curiosity is good for the soul, and a good book isn't complete without banter.

You can find Ann surrounded by her ample supply of sticky notes ready for inspiration and ideas. When she's not writing, Ann enjoys spoiling her chatty pet chickens, listening to her dysfunctional playlists, and going for late-night treadmill runs. She lives in Michigan with her husband.

Keep in Touch with Ann Einerson

Website: www.anneinerson.com

Newsletter: www.anneinerson.com/newsletter-signup

Instagram: www.instagram.com/authoranneinerson

TikTok: www.tiktok.com/@authoranneinerson

Amazon: www.amazon.com/author/anneinerson

Goodreads: www.goodreads.com/author/show/29752171.
Ann_Einerson

9 781960 325136